OTHERS AVAILABLE BY DK HOLMBERG

The Cloud Warrior Saga

Chased by Fire
Bound by Fire
Changed by Fire
Fortress of Fire
Forged in Fire
Serpent of Fire
Servant of Fire

The Dark Ability

The Dark Ability
The Heartstone Blade
The Tower of Venass

The Painter Mage

Shifted Agony
Arcane Mark
Painter for Hire
Stolen Compass

The Lost Garden

Keeper of the Forest
The Desolate Bond
Keeper of Light

SERVANT OF FIRE

THE CLOUD WARRIOR SAGA
BOOK 7

ASH Publishing
dkholmberg.com

Servant of Fire

ISBN-13: 978-1518887642
ISBN-10: 1518887643

ASH Publishing
dkholmberg.com

SERVANT
OF FIRE

THE CLOUD WARRIOR SAGA
BOOK 7

CHAPTER 1

A Summons

THE VAST EXPANSE OF INCENDIN spread all around Tannen Minden as he stood on a ridge overlooking the waste, ignoring the draw of the Fire Fortress for now. Hard, cracked earth split beneath him to form canyons where the rock dropped off to nothing but blackness. The plants growing throughout Incendin were equally dangerous, from the spiked shrubs scattered across the hard rock to the spindly trees that almost seemed to twist toward him as he neared. Even the thorny cacti that grew with flashes of green seemed out of place in the rest of the barren Incendin landscape. With every step, plants seemed to move with him; some even sprayed poisoned needles. Tan had learned to place a barrier of wind around him, but he feared the moment the wind would fail him.

Everything about this land seemed designed to torment, but more than that, to prevent access to its people. Without his ability to shape, he wouldn't be able to safely make his way through.

In the distance, Incendin stretched toward the rocky shores of the sea. For a place as dry and hot as this one, massive waves crashed along its eastern shores, each wave powerful, as if the ocean attempted to reclaim these lands—or maybe the waves were Par-shon's way of attacking, using water to slowly wear away at their enemy.

There was beauty here as well. Tan had seen it, not only from the strange, rare trees with long needles for leaves that flowered when the conditions were right, but also from some of the people he'd now fought beside. Once, he would have considered them enemies. Now, they were allies.

They had to be, or everyone on the continent would suffer.

His eyes were drawn back to the Fire Fortress, which rose toward the wisps of clouds that filtered the hot sun. He tried to ignore it, but it called to him, demanding attention. Spouts of flame shot from the top of the fortress, both stronger and different than the last time he'd seen it. The black walls that made up the fortress reminded him of a similar tower in Par-shon. Tan sensed no runes upon the Fire Fortress, nothing that would place him in the same danger that he'd experienced in Par-shon. The only danger was the fortress itself and the people within.

"Are you certain you wish to do this?" Cianna asked.

The fire shaper stood next to him, the bright midday sunlight catching off her flaming orange hair, making it glow. Heat radiated off her skin, billowing like a furnace through the silky maroon shirt that matched the tight leather breeches she preferred. A playful smile danced on her lips, and her eyes darted from Tan to the Fire Fortress, and then back to the massive draasin Sashari that was crouched a dozen paces behind them.

The draasin remained in place, wings folded up against her body, and her long, barbed tail flicking at the ground, as if sweeping back the attacking plants. Through the fire bond, a connection he shared with the elementals of fire and none other, Tan felt her wariness, but also the sense of respect she carried for Cianna. He no longer had to strain to reach the other draasin through the fire bond. Now it came easily to him, the only shaper he knew who was able to reach the elemental connection.

"They summoned me," he answered. When the summons had come, a strange call from the elemental kaas through the fire bond itself, Tan had known he needed to answer. That kaas—an ancient experimental joining of fire and earth—would call to him through the bond told Tan how urgent the need was.

"And Theondar?"

"He has more to worry about than this," Tan said.

Cianna placed her hands on her sides and laughed. The sound carried over Incendin before catching the hot wind and disappearing, almost as if ashi, the wind elemental of these lands, stole the laughter. "You think that Theondar cares so little about his Athan that he wants you running off to the Fire Fortress alone?"

Tan twisted his ring, the marker of his office, on his finger. He'd accepted the role of Athan, but it still didn't feel like it fit him completely—not after the sacrifices he'd made. Perhaps it would in time. Roine claimed that Tan had done as an Athan should, making the hard choices of one meant to lead. Those choices were the reason shapers had died. Elementals had died. Asboel had been injured. Those choices had been his fault. Could he make them again?

Could he afford not to?

"Serving him, I do for the kingdoms," Tan said. "In that role, I speak with his voice. But in this, I think I come to Incendin to represent the elementals."

"They cannot be trusted," Cianna said.

By *they*, she meant the lisincend. It was a typical argument, especially for Cianna, who had grown up in Nara, which lay along the border with Incendin. How many times had those she loved been attacked by Incendin? More often than even Tan, and he had lost his father, his village, and almost everyone he'd ever known to Incendin.

"They fought with us," Tan reminded her. "They fight Par-shon. And the lisincend have been brought back to fire."

Cianna sniffed. "You claim this, but you'll have a hard time convincing others of that. Too much has been lost."

"Sashari has told you."

The hard edge to Cianna's face softened as she looked over at her bonded draasin. "She claims the fire bond has changed, that you work closely within it now. She's said nothing about Twisted Fire."

"Because the lisincend are no longer twisted. Not as they once were."

Tan took a step toward the rock, feeling the heat of Incendin all around him. Another step would lead him off the ridge, forcing him to use a shaping to lower himself to the valley below. A low howl echoed off the rock, a hound's distant cry no longer as terrifying as it once had been. They might have his scent, but they would not be able to injure him.

Incendin had changed, not only for him. Like all change, it would take time for others to understand what it meant. Tan wasn't even certain that he fully understood the consequences of what he'd done by bringing the lisincend into the fire bond and healing them so that they were no longer twisted. All he knew was that it needed doing.

And then there was the bond that he'd forced, an action he had never thought to take, one that in some ways made him no different than the Utu Tonah.

Tan pushed away the thought. That was *not* the reason kaas called to him.

4

"You will have me wait?" Cianna asked.

"I would have you with me," Tan said. He would rather have Amia, but as First Mother to the Aeta, she served in a different role. The people of the Aeta needed her, and he wouldn't risk her coming to the Fire Fortress. Besides, like many, Amia still hadn't fully moved past what Incendin had done to her family. Tan had stood witness when the lisincend had attacked her mother and others of her caravan, and had seen how Incendin had thought to sacrifice her in the name of creating another lisincend.

Cianna laughed darkly. "Do you know how long I've dreamed of visiting the Fire Fortress and destroying it?" she asked. "Nara has fought Incendin for generations. My people have struggled with Incendin stealing our people, the same as they steal Doma's shapers." Fire surged from her, and Tan doubted that she shaped it intentionally. "Worse are those of Nara who make the crossing willingly."

"You would take away their choice?"

"No," Cianna said, jaw clenching as she glared at the Fire Fortress. "I would take away Incendin's seducing them. How many fire shapers have the kingdoms lost to them? How much stronger would we be if they had not taken our shapers?"

The question was different than simple concern for the kingdoms. Fire shapers were not revered within the kingdoms, not as they were within Incendin. Other shapers viewed them as lower than those able to manipulate the other elements, and many feared an Incendin influence even when there was none. In the short time that Tan had actually experienced the university, he had faced the same fears in the way that the masters sought to understand where each student came from. He remembered all too well Master Ferran's disbelief when Tan described what he'd gone through with the lisincend. Now Ferran was one of Tan's most ardent supporters.

5

"And how much worse off would we all be had Incendin not managed to withstand Par-shon all these years?" Tan asked.

Cianna pinched her eyes closed and let out a frustrated breath. "Why do you wish for me to enter the Fire Fortress with you?"

"The others will fear that my loyalties are in question."

"No one questions you, Tan—"

He raised a hand, silencing her. "They question whether I am more concerned about the elementals. And they should question. I don't deny that I serve the elementals, or that I think the Great Mother gifted me with the ability to speak to them for me to offer my protection. But few will question *your* motives when it comes to Incendin."

"I'm of fire. I will *always* be questioned."

"You should look through my eyes, Cianna. You have more respect among the shapers than you realize."

She fell silent a moment. Then she sighed. "What is your plan? You think you can simply shape your way in? They'll view that as an attack, you know."

"This was never about shaping our way in," he said. "This was an invitation, and one I have to answer."

Reaching for fire and spirit, connecting to the fire bond, Tan listened for kaas. The great serpent of fire had been like the lisincend, twisted and sitting outside of the bond, but Tan had managed to heal it. At least, he thought he had. Part of that healing had required him to forcibly bond kaas to another. It had been necessary, but Tan still struggled with how that made him any different than Par-shon. He could tell himself that he'd done it to help the elemental, but hadn't he done it to save others? Wasn't that the same thing that Par-shon did?

Tan's connection to fire told him how Sashari waited, warily listening to everything around her, using the fire bond and her senses to monitor both Tan and Cianna. Distantly, he sensed Asboel, though the draasin remained motionless, still reeling from the battle with kaas that had left him wounded and weakened.

Healing hadn't managed to bring Asboel back to what he'd once been. The nymid had tried, but healing elemental powers, especially one of fire, was difficult. The nymid had managed to restore Tan when he'd embraced fire too closely and nearly transformed into one of the lisincend, but healing Asboel was beyond them. His wings no longer caught the air as they once had, and his injuries persisted. Tan tried not to think of whether Asboel would ever manage to heal.

Then there was Tan's connection to Honl. The attack with kaas had left Honl changed and different as well. Not damaged, at least not in the same way that Asboel had been damaged, but not quite like the rest of the ashi elementals. Where before he'd always been somewhat indistinct, nothing more than translucent air, now he had shape and form. Tan saw him less often than before, though he could call on him if needed. Honl was there, distantly at the back of his mind, but not as present as he had once been.

The distant sense of kaas burned beneath the ground. The great serpent was unlike any of the other fire elementals. He was powerful and strange, a twisting of fire and earth, an experiment done by the earliest kingdoms' shapers, and for reasons Tan still didn't understand. What would make those shapers think they could twist the elementals? What would make them think that they had the right to experiment?

Asboel chuckled distantly in his mind. Since his injury, he was more prominent in Tan's mind, as if experiencing the world through Tan since he could no longer safely fly. If they survived the Par-shon attack, he thought there might be a way for Tan to use his shaping to help Asboel fly once more. For now, he remained safe, dependent upon Tan to keep him that way.

You think differently than those of that time, Maelen. And the threats of this era are different than what they knew.

Sashari perked up as Asboel communicated with Tan. Had she heard? Asboel was bonded to Tan differently, the connection changed by necessity when Par-shon had nearly stolen the bond. Now, spirit and fire wove together, tying them in ways that the initial bond had never managed.

And you think differently than the draasin of that time, Asboel.

It was not always the case.

Both had changed much since the bond, and Tan didn't think that either of them would undo those changes, but he would undo the damage. In time, he *would* find a way to heal his friend.

You will observe? Tan asked.

A surge of annoyance came through the bond. *That is all I have remaining, Maelen. Were you not so interesting, I might have begged the Mother to return.*

The response saddened him, but he understood. Without his wings, Asboel couldn't hunt. Without the hunt, he did not feel like the draasin.

But Asboel was still fire. He was still his friend. Tan would find a way to restore him.

But not today. Today was about the summons.

Tan embraced the fire bond, pulling on it tightly, welcoming the sensation of fire all around him. With the fire bond, Tan called to kaas, knowing that the great serpent of fire would hear.

"Be ready," he said to Ciara. Shifting his attention to kaas, he sent a different message. *Tell Fur I come.*

CHAPTER 2

The Fire Fortress

THE FIRE FORTRESS LOOMED OVERHEAD, and this close, there was more than a sense of the heat coming from it. More than the flames simply raging, there was a distinct power that radiated, pushing outward like a warning. The fortress seemed like a collection of jagged rocks, each set together and fused with a shaping to hold it in place. Massive peaks rose from the top, stretching impossibly high into the air. The heat from the flames shooting off them could be felt from the ground, and the energy from them pulsed out and away, stretching beyond Incendin. It was this power that kept Par-shon at bay.

Curving out and around the fortress was a massive city unlike anything Tan had ever seen. Huge walls arched away from the fortress like long, slender arms that cradled the city itself. Through the wide gate leading into the fortress itself, Tan noted homes of stacked stone leaned against each other, with canopies of cloth stretching between the buildings and casting shade onto the street below. Further into the city, the buildings rose higher and higher, shaped into place. The fortress stood above everything, casting a long shadow.

"Are you certain this is wise?" Cianna asked as Tan's shaping lowered them to the ground outside.

Tan sensed, but couldn't see, shapers all around him. Coming here, to the heart of the Incendin power, was a risk. During the last attack, he'd seen how Incendin had the ability to separate him from his shapings, but so far, they had not. With enough shapers and lisincend, they might be able to overpower anything that Tan or Cianna could do. The hope that he clung to was that they would not, that his healing of the lisincend had changed enough of them to allow him a safe passage.

"Fur called me through the bond," he told Cianna, watching to see how she'd react. Fur had once led the lisincend—he might still, for all that Tan knew—and had Asboel not responded to Tan's call before he ever learned how to shape or control his connection to the elementals, Fur might have destroyed Tan and Amia. The shaping that had helped the other lisincend had been used on Fur, pulling him back into the fire bond, healing him enough that he was no longer twisted. Still transformed, he served fire differently and managed a level of control that had not been there before. There was enough control that Tan had risked securing kaas's bond to him.

"You can't trust him."

"Probably not," Tan agreed.

Cianna bit her lower lip. Heat surged off her, more than she once would have managed; the connection to Sashari gave her a greater access to fire than she once had. "You haven't asked for Cora. Is she here?"

"Cora's connection to the fire bond is indirect," Tan answered slowly. "I can sense *her*," he said, not willing to speak aloud Enya's name, knowing how names carried power for the elementals, "but not where she might be."

Enya and Cora still struggled with the bond between them. How much came from the fact that Enya had once had a shaping twisted onto her, and how much came from the fact that Cora still mourned the loss of her bond? Those were answers his connection to fire couldn't provide.

Four men stood on either side of the gate leading into the city and into the fortress within. They wore thick leather helms twisted into the shape of a wide jaw lined with jagged teeth. Each held a long sword, which was planted into the hard earth, and wore a shield strapped to his back. They watched Tan and Cianna but said nothing.

Tan couldn't tell if they were shapers. If they were fire shapers, he had no way of knowing, not without reaching for spirit and pushing that shaping down onto them, something he was unwilling to do unless it was necessary. For all he knew, they might be able to withstand a spirit shaping.

When he stepped forward, the men moved aside, almost as one, parting and revealing an open doorway inside the arch that led through the tower and into the city. Cianna eyed it and glanced up at Tan, mouth pursed into a thin line.

Tan held onto a shaping of each of the elements, ready to unleash it to explode away from Incendin if needed, but he sensed nothing that made him fear that he'd need to use the shaping.

"Are we to wait?" Tan asked.

None of the soldiers answered.

Through his prepared shaping, he felt the drawing of kaas and the strange connection to Fur through the fire bond, and felt pulled. Once inside the Fortress, Tan had no idea whether he would ever manage to escape.

This was the reason he'd come. Finding a way to work *with* Incendin was worth risking an entry to the Fire Fortress.

As he stepped beneath the arch, the air shimmered slightly, reminding him somewhat of how Honl once had shimmered when taking his translucent form. Tan took reassurance in that. "If Lacertin could do this," he said to himself, softly enough that only Cianna could hear.

Her back straightened slightly, and he heard her take a soft breath.

They stepped into the fortress. All around him, the air was hot and blew across his skin with a familiar caress. Ashi blew through here, not afraid of the fortress or those living within it. It eased Tan's mind to recognize that a familiar elemental was found here.

The door led into a wide entryway. Smooth tile of flat black echoed beneath his feet. Tan paused long enough to look around him, stretching out with a sensing of earth and fire, probing to learn what his eyes might miss. Next to him, Cianna's eyes were wide as she peered at everything.

The fortress held hundreds of people. Awareness of them pressed in on Tan through earth and spirit. He could almost point out every single person, from servants making their way through hidden halls to the lisincend stationed around Fur on a level far above him.

The walls glowed with an intrinsic light. The air within the fortress smelled of the bitter scent of char. There was something about it that was soothing, yet it set him on edge. He found it a strange dichotomy.

"Up," Tan said quietly.

The stairs were much like the floor, made of a dark slate that felt slick and warm beneath his booted feet. The stair was wide near the main floor and curved around to the next level. Once there, it narrowed the higher they climbed. There were no windows and no other light. Still, they were not in complete darkness. The walls of the Fire Fortress glowed all the way up.

There was a part of Tan that wanted to shape himself through the Fire Fortress, but he recognized the opportunity he and Cianna had to see something that few outside of Incendin had ever seen. Other than Cora and Lacertin, Tan had never spoken to anyone who had been to the Fire Fortress and returned.

Their feet echoed off the walls as they walked, the sound carrying away from them. The air had a strange heated odor, almost bitter, that filled his nostrils as they climbed. The pull on the fire bond drew him ever higher. Strangely, no one stopped them as they made their way up. If not for his sensing ability, Tan might have thought that the Fire Fortress was empty.

They reached a wide landing. There were no more stairs up, and the sense of Fur or kaas drawing him came from along the hall. Tan inhaled deeply, steeling himself before stepping forward. Cianna stayed a step behind him, her quick breaths the only sign of her anxiety.

"I can get us free from here if needed." Tan said it more to reassure Cianna, but some of the tension left his shoulders, almost as if the reminder had given him permission to shape if he might need to get them free.

"You've said the Fire Fortress reminds you of Par-shon," Cianna said quietly.

"Maybe once it did," Tan agreed. They reached a tall, arching door, rising nearly twice Tan's height, made of a deeply lacquered wood. Like the rest of the Fire Fortress, it appeared to glow softly, as if imbued with heat and fire of its own.

"What's different?" Cianna asked, stepping forward to run her hand just over the surface of the door.

"In Par-shon, I wasn't scared, but I should have been," he answered. Had Tan known then what he'd learned of Par-shon, he would have been too terrified to act when it was needed. Maybe he wouldn't have found a way free from the room of separation and had his bonds stolen like Vel and Cora. "I didn't know that I should fear the Utu Tonah, or that I couldn't break the runes holding me within the room of separation. Had I thought it impossible, I might have failed. Sometimes ignorance is helpful," he continued.

She sniffed. "And sometimes, knowledge is dangerous."

Tan touched the door. "All knowledge is dangerous when used the wrong way," he said.

As if waiting for him, the door pulled open on a shaping of fire.

Another shaping built as soon as the door opened. Not from Tan or Cianna, though they both held shapings ready, but from the three lisincend standing along a wall of blackened windows that overlooked the city. They were each winged lisincend, of the kind that had required a sacrifice of Aeta in order to complete the transformation, making them appear like some grotesque blend of man and draasin. The shaping stretched up and out of the tower and, Tan noted, also *through* the fortress itself, leaving the walls glowing and warm. This was the reason the Fire Fortress seemed to burn.

"You understand the purpose of their shaping?"

Tan's breath caught at Fur's voice. It was gravely and powerful, much like the lisincend towering to Tan's left. He made a point of turning slowly, knowing that if Fur attacked, the other lisincend would likely follow. He and Cianna would be able to hold it off, but only for a while. Bolstered by kaas, Fur would be able to draw more fire through him than Cianna could, and perhaps more shaping power than even Tan. That had been the gamble Tan had taken when he shifted the bond to Fur.

"I understand how fire washes over the city. I feel the way it burns through the fortress," Tan answered.

Fur chuckled. One of the winged lisincend flicked her gaze toward Fur and ran a long tongue over leathery lips before returning her focus outward, toward the city.

Tan blinked. Not only to the city, but beyond, to the sea as it roiled toward them on dark and angry swells. The shaping didn't simply let fire wash over the people of the city. This was the shaping that held back Par-shon.

Fur's thick laugh came again. When he approached, heat practically sizzled off him. The veil that once obscured the lisincend to Tan was no more, another gift of the draasin, or perhaps simply the fire bond.

"You understand now. You sense the power of the shaping, yes?" he asked.

"I sense Par-shon," Tan answered.

Fur leaned toward him, his flat nostrils flaring slightly as he sniffed. "Yes? Well, I *smell* them." He leaned back. "Much as I once smelled you." A dark smile split his mouth, drawing his lips tight. "You think that I would forget our chase? Or how you sent the draasin after me?"

Cianna tensed. A shaping built within her.

Tan considered soothing her with spirit. He couldn't risk Cianna acting and risking what needed to happen. They *would* find a way to forge an alliance, however uneasy.

"And do you think *I* will forget how the lisincend destroyed my village?" Tan asked softly.

Fur's eyes narrowed a moment, and then he laughed again. "You have changed much since that time. I think you would be a fitting challenge now. Perhaps you would not even require the draasin to aid you."

"I didn't answer your summons to fight, Fur."

Fur slithered toward the window, placing his hands against the glass. "And I did not summon you to fight." His head leaned forward so that his smooth, sloped forehead touched the glass. In the reflection, Tan saw how his nostrils flared, leaving a hint of steam. "I have been warned that might not go well for me, servant of fire. I cannot help but wonder, though." Fur admitted.

15

The other lisincend continued their shaping. Great waves of it swept from them, building with incredible strength. Through the fire bond, Tan was able to detect what they did. The skill with shaping was more than Tan possessed. Perhaps not the strength, not now that he was bolstered by the elementals, able to draw not only from Asboel, but from all of the fire elementals around him, but the control impressed him and reminded of watching Amia learn spirit shaping with the First Mother. There was a drawing sense from the shaping, an appeal to fire. Tan had to resist the urge to join in.

Cianna continued to hold her shaping, wrapping herself in it so tightly that heat shimmered from her, layering over her like a blanket.

Fur pushed away from the window and sniffed, the thin smile parting his lips. "You should have made the crossing, little one. You would have learned much in the Sunlands."

Tan stepped forward before Cianna could react. He'd seen Cianna's sensitivities to Incendin thinking that shapers from Nara—shapers like herself—should have crossed Incendin to learn. "This is why you called me here?" he asked. Kaas had summoned, but the elemental had done so on Fur's behalf.

"You did not wish to see the fortress?"

Tan watched the lisincend, felt their shaping as it pulled on him. Fur didn't call him here to exchange barbs, but why *had* he called to Tan? "You would like me to help," Tan realized.

Fur's neck creaked as he shifted his attention to Tan. "And if I did? Would you help, Warrior?"

Tan crossed his arms over his chest. Fur tested him, but why? Through kaas, Fur would know what Tan had done for the elementals. Through the fire bond, Tan could sense Fur, even if he could not communicate with him quite like he could with the elementals. There was a hesitancy within the bond which contrasted with his confident posturing and comments.

"I will help," Tan said. "As I did with the other lisincend."

Fur glanced at the winged lisincend, who were shaping. "Yes. The transformation. It is different now. That was you."

It was less of a question than a statement, though Tan sensed a curiosity within Fur. The lisincend would understand how Tan had managed to keep them from being twisted by fire when he hadn't managed to. "I have been changed by fire, Fur. I know how it burns, how it can control."

Fur blinked and his lips twitched. Heat radiated off him, more powerfully than what Cianna shaped, probably more powerfully than what Tan could draw. "You were transformed and returned?"

Tan wondered if there was a part of Fur that longed to be restored. "By water. The elementals restored me."

"If you have known the strength of fire and lived, why help the lisincend? Why help *me*?"

Could this be why Fur had used kaas to summon? Did he only want answers?

Even in that, the summons was valuable. If Tan could convince Fur that he was needed, that all of Incendin and the lisincend were needed, then they might have a chance of surviving Par-shon.

"You destroyed my village. You killed an entire family of Aeta, people who did nothing but travel through your lands," Tan began slowly. The winged lisincends' shaping faltered slightly, as if they listened. Tan suspected that they could shift the focus of the shaping to him. He might be able to withstand fire, but would it matter with the power they drew? He might live, but would Cianna? "In spite of all that, I know the power that surges within the lisincend. Corasha Saladan shared with me the reasons your shapers embraced fire," he continued, making a point of using the same descriptions that Cora had used when they had once spoken of it. "If we are to find a way to work together to stop

17

Par-shon, the lisincend will be needed. Your shapings might hold Par-shon at bay for now, but for how much longer? They have shown how they can reach Doma, how they can attack the Sunlands, and how they are willing to trap the elementals."

Fur's mouth twisted as Tan said the last. "What they do is an abomination," he spat.

Tan took a slight step back. Had the bond with kaas made Fur feel that way, or did all of Incendin feel the same about the elementals? The lisincend had not hesitated to attack the draasin, but had that been them, or was that because of the way that fire twisted them?

"You would see the elementals protected?" Tan asked carefully.

Fur breathed heavily as he stared out the window, eyes locked on the dark clouds swirling in the distance. The Par-shon storm was held back, but for how much longer? The Utu Tonah could force the elementals to bond. With enough numbers, Par-shon would be able to overpower even the strength of the Fire Fortress.

"They should exalt power that they abuse."

"The lisincend did not always feel that way," Tan reminded him.

Fur pulled his back straight. "No. Trust that I now understand the mistake."

Tan didn't have to simply trust Fur. Through the fire bond, the strength of his conviction flowed, an overpowering respect for fire that burned within him. "Kaas has taught you much." This time, Tan hesitated, needing to ask the question that had plagued him since the attack. "Does he mind the bond?"

Fur flashed teeth at Tan, his long tongue sliding out and running across his lips. "It was not of his choosing at the time."

"And now?"

Fur sniffed. "Now it is different."

Tan waited for Fur to explain further, but he did not. Kaas didn't share anything more through the fire bond, other than to share that he no longer resented it. Since Tan had healed the elemental, drawing on the strength of the other elementals to do so, kaas had been able to re-join the fire bond. That healing was the reason Tan held out hope that he could see Asboel healed.

Asboel crawled toward the front of Tan's mind, reminding him that he had always been there. *It is different, Maelen.*

It doesn't have to be, Tan said.

You do not have the power of the Mother. It was a gentle admonishment.

Tan pulled his attention back to Fur. "You haven't answered me, Fur. I admit that I was curious to see the Fire Fortress for myself, but why have you summoned me here?"

"No. This is not why I have asked you to come. There is something else that I need." Fur strode past him and reached the tall, arching doorway that led into the room. He paused at the door. "Come."

CHAPTER 3

Beneath the Fortress

TAN FOLLOWED FUR through a long hall and then to a narrow stair that they took to the bottom of the Fire Fortress. The lisincend was so tall that his head brushed the ceiling as he walked, forcing him to bend slightly at the neck. Heat radiated from his thick skin, and a shimmery cloud swirled around him as they made their way down the stairs. All around, the walls glowed with a soft, orange light, making the lanterns stationed every dozen steps unnecessary.

Cianna remained behind Tan, but she placed a hand on his shoulder as they trailed after Fur. At each landing they passed, Cianna's hand gripped more tightly for a moment before easing. Her breathing came in short gasps behind him and caught at times, particularly when a stronger shaping surged through the fortress walls.

Tan felt much of the same anxiety. Fur hadn't said anything since they left the room overlooking Incendin, but he still felt the shaping that the lisincend worked. It filled the fire fortress, flowing through it and then out and away. There was a part of Tan that was drawn to the shaping, a part that wanted to join in what the lisincend did and add his ability to it. The shaping itself was complex. There was a pattern to it, but it hadn't repeated for as long as Tan had been in the Fortress. So far, he hadn't worked out how it kept Par-shon away, or even how to replicate it. In many ways, it reminded him of the shaping the First Mother had used to heal Cora.

When they reached another landing, Fur paused at a wide door made of blackened metal that seemed impervious to the heat glowing all around. He twisted a long nail into the lock and pried it open, using a shaping as he did so. He cast a glance over his shoulder before stepping into the darkness on the other side.

"Tan," Cianna whispered. "He's leading us *below* the city."

Tan peered into the darkness, but Fur had already disappeared. The walls glowed along the stairs, but without the same intensity as those higher up. The deeper they went, the more difficult a time Tan would have in getting them free if Fur were to do something to trap them. At least near the top of the tower, he had the promise that he might be able to shape them free. They could explode through the glass and depart on a shaping of lightning. Down beneath the city, escape would be much more difficult.

Still, Tan wanted to know where Fur was taking them. Kaas wouldn't have called to him if Fur intended him harm, would he? No, the fire bond would have warned him. Asboel would have warned him, and he sensed nothing but interest from the draasin. "I don't think he intends to harm us," he said.

"This is Fur you're talking about."

"Yes. And he's different. Ask the draasin if you don't believe."

Sashari would be able to tell Cianna how much had changed within Fur. The draasin could reach the fire bond and could share with Cianna how Twisted Fire no longer burned in him. Asboel had remarked on it, though Tan knew the draasin still held a grudge against the lisincend for what he had done, and how he'd stolen the hatchlings. At least the painful sense against the fire bond was no longer there.

"I'll keep us safe," he promised her.

She let out a pent-up breath and nodded.

Tan followed Fur, and Cianna held onto his shoulder as they went.

They continued downward. The stairs were even narrower here than they had been on the upper levels, and the heavy stone pressing up against him made Tan all too aware of the weight of the fortress overhead. Now Cianna gripped both his shoulders as she followed him down, and she pressed close enough that he felt the warmth of her minty breath on the back of his neck.

Fur waited for them at the bottom of the stairs. "You would help?" He pointed to a series of doors carved out of stone and marked with iron in the shapes of runes for earth. "Then help us here."

"What is this?" Cianna asked. It was the first time she'd spoken aloud to Fur.

Tan reached out with a sensing of earth and recognized that elementals were woven into the stone. Mixing spirit with it, he listened through the stone and sensed what Fur wanted him to do.

Behind each of the doors was a lisincend. Most were like Fur, lisincend made before the secret to the winged lisincend had been learned, though there were a few winged lisincend held behind the doors. All raged against their capture. Their fury beat on the walls but was subdued by earth, the cells bolstered by a surprising source: kaas.

"You want them all healed," Tan said slowly.

Fur touched the nearest door, tracing a glowing pattern over the stone, and then withdrew his hand. "The lisincend have been powerful since the first of us embraced fire, but you are right, Warrior, that we have no control. It has long been our shapers who keep the flames atop the fortress burning. The lisincend could not focus on the shaping long enough. It is why our greatest shapers were exalted but trapped within the fortress, required to hold the shaping. Now, with what you have done, the lisincend are able join the shaping and bind fire in ways that have withstood Par-shon."

"How many are there?" Tan asked.

Fur touched the next cell, tracing a long nail around the iron. His mouth tightened as he did. "More than your kingdoms would believe," he said. "Once, I would never have thought to hold my lisincend behind stone. But they remain different than those you have altered. Controlled by fire as they are, they are weaker than those healed and brought back to fire. Weaker, but they have numbers. When they attacked, I realized they needed confinement." Fur faced Tan, long fingers clenching and unclenching as he did. "You will fix this, Warrior."

Cianna made her way around the dozens of doors. "Each of these holds one of the lisincend?" she asked.

Fur growled softly, making a sound that reminded Tan of the draasin. "There should be more, but many have died."

"Good," Cianna said. Anger seethed from her as she studied each of the cells. Tan wondered if she might find a way to attack the lisincend, even buried behind the stone as they were.

Fur started toward her, but Tan stepped between him, blocking him. "You called us here, Fur," Tan said. "And you want our help."

Fur breathed out a low grunt.

"If I am to do this, will you work with us?" Tan asked.

Fur focused on the nearest cell. "You will do this so that we can attack Par-shon."

That was almost reason enough for Tan. He wasn't certain that he could help this many of the lisincend. When he'd done it before, it had taken the help of the elementals, the power of Asboel, and the drawing of enormous amounts of spirit. What Fur asked of him amounted to weakening him, possibly leaving him helpless. At the least, he would need to bind each of the elements together to make the shaping work. At worst, he wouldn't have the strength needed to save even one. Tan wasn't even certain that he could do it here, buried beneath Incendin like this, without other elementals for assistance.

In spite of that, he had to try. The lisincend had been powerful fire shapers before they transformed. Now that they had embraced fire—and survived the transformation—they were even more powerful. This was exactly the kind of strength Tan would need for them to face Par-shon.

Once, he had sought allies to face Incendin. It was then that he'd learned of Par-shon. He didn't miss the irony that he now went to Incendin seeking allies against Par-shon.

Cianna stopped at his shoulder and leaned toward him. "Think about this, Tan. How many lisincend are here?" she whispered. "How many will attack the kingdoms if they're released?"

Tan couldn't take his eyes off the runes that locked the doors closed. Earth holding fire. He would not have believed that the lisincend— particularly Fur—would confine the lisincend. There had been no remorse when the lisincend attacked before, no sorrow when his home had been destroyed. If Fur was willing to confine dangerous lisincend, wasn't this exactly the change that he'd intended?

If only Cora could be here to help him understand what Fur intended. What purpose did he have for the nearly three dozen lisincend, fire shapers with enough strength to overpower the kingdoms?

"Where is Corasha Saladan?" Tan asked.

Fur let out a low rumble. "She has alternative commitments."

"What does that mean?" Tan asked.

"The Sunlands are a place of fire. It is drawn here, to the fortress. That is why we are able to withstand Par-shon when others fail. Warriors serve a different role."

"I will not help you until I know where she is."

"You *will* do this, Warrior."

Tan pulled on a shaping, wrapping Fur in air and earth, squeezing tightly enough for the lisincend to feel the effects. Ashi blew through even this lower level, augmenting Tan's shaping.

At the back of Tan's mind, Asboel roared a soft warning.

Then Tan released Fur. "You do not command me. I am Athan to King Regent Theondar."

Fur faced Tan, drawing himself to his full height so that his head brushed the stone overhead. He loomed over Tan and stepped forward. "And I am Fur, First of the lisincend."

Tan didn't move, but neither did he pull on a shaping. He refused to let Fur see him scared or nervous, but he would not antagonize him. "Where is Corasha Saladan?" Tan asked again.

Fur chuckled. "Yes, you *have* grown fierce, Warrior. I remember how you cowered before me the first time we met. Heal them, then you will see the Saladan."

There was something Fur was keeping from him, something more than needing the lisincend healed. Maybe he knew how Tan needed to see Cora, how Tan intended to bring the warriors together as they once had been. Or maybe it was nothing like that, and Fur simply wanted the lisincend healed for the reason he claimed, hoping to use them in the shaping of fire that kept Par-shon from their shores.

Tan made his way down the hall, letting his hand trail over the stone. Fur walked next to him, keeping pace and sniffing at the air, leaving a haze of heat around him. There was elemental strength here, but different than in the kingdoms. How much of it was because of

25

what kaas did, and how much from the rune? He couldn't tell. There was no sense other than the wild rage from the lisincend on the other side, more than Tan had ever suspected.

"How many risk fire?" he asked Fur.

"Any may choose to embrace fire."

"How many shapers have you lost to this?"

"The Sunlands once were home to the most powerful shapers of fire. Like your kingdoms, our shapers have grown weak. We reclaimed some of that lost power by embracing fire, but there was a price. With any shaping, there is always a price."

A different concern occurred to Tan. "You will not use spirit shapers to create more lisincend."

"You do not command Fur."

"If these are healed, there will be no others."

Fur's thin eyes pulled into narrow slits. "And if they come willingly?"

Tan couldn't imagine what it would take for a spirit shaper to willingly offer themselves for the creation of the lisincend. The transformation that he'd witnessed had been horrible. It seemed unlikely that any would sacrifice themselves for such a purpose. "There will be no others," Tan said again.

Fur tipped his head. Then he nodded. "No others, unless they choose willingly."

That would have to do. "If I do this, it will not be done here. I will need access to elementals not found beneath the earth."

"Tell me, Warrior, what do you require?"

Tan thought for a moment. "What I need is a place—"

"You will not remove the lisincend from the Sunlands."

Tan shook his head, thinking of what he knew of Incendin. With Asboel, he had traveled extensively over the land. He had seen much, but what he needed required the right place.

Asboel helped, pushing an image into Tan's mind, reminding him of a place they had seen together. Tan opened his eyes and pulled his back straight. "There is a place within the Sunlands that should work well."

CHAPTER 4

Restored

"THIS IS RIDICULOUS, Tan."

Tan grimaced at Cianna, resisting the urge to shield his face from the wind and sand blowing around him. It whipped through the stilted trees with long, slender needles that grew along the side of the stream. One of the trees actually flowered, producing a simple bloom of milky white that sent its fragrance into the air, only to be assaulted by the sand and dust, almost as if Incendin did not want anything of beauty to survive.

"What's ridiculous?" he asked. "That I had Fur bring the lisincend here, or that I've offered to help?"

Cianna laughed and immediately covered her mouth to keep the sand from blowing in. "Both, actually." She cupped her hand over her brow and frowned, her face going slack. "Sashari says they're coming."

Tan gripped his sword and unsheathed it, readying for what he'd agreed to do for Fur. Here, in this part of Incendin, standing near the border between the kingdoms, but still far enough into the dangerous waste that no rescue could reach them, he could draw upon each of the elementals. That connection would let him draw on more power than he could shape alone, and the warrior sword would help him augment it, binding the elements as he required to craft the shaping needed to heal the lisincend. If only he could remember what it was he'd done the last time. Then, it had been about trying to stay alive. With kaas attacking, Tan had used the only shaping he could think of to survive, and that shaping had demanded that he pull the lisincend back toward the fire bond. It was the same shaping that he'd needed to use on kaas.

Of all the elements, fire would be easy—not only because he could draw from the draasin, but because there were other elementals of fire within Incendin. Saa and saldam were found here. Inferin was here, but rare. There might even be other elementals of fire that he had no name for, elementals that could be called to his aid. More than anything else, the ability to borrow from the elementals might be the greatest gift the Great Mother had given him.

Beyond fire, Tan's connection to ashi and the wind allowed for a strong connection. Other elementals of wind blew through Incendin, though none quite as strong as ashi. Ara preferred the cool and damp of the kingdoms. Wyln seemed more common in Doma, searching for the sea spray as it blew in from the ocean. The only wind elemental that he rarely saw in the kingdoms was ilaz, but even ilaz could be found in Ethea, drawn by the place of convergence.

The heavy sense of earth pushed against his senses as well. Nothing like golud, the elemental that preferred the heaving mountains or the deep underground far beneath Ethea, but there was elemental power here nonetheless. Tan didn't know if it was nodn or another elemental of earth, one that he had yet to learn its name. In Incendin, his sense of earth was different, and it pulled on him like sand blowing through the wind and the hot rock teetering, just on the verge of falling, or even the massive cracks that split the land. Much like water had been different in Doma, earth in Incendin was very different.

The challenge within the Sunlands was water.

Water was rare in Incendin. Tan might have bonded the nymid, but he needed to be able to reach a source of water to use the bond. Incendin had no real rivers to speak of. The border with the sea was like much of the rest of the land, brutal and harsh. Only a few small streams snaked through the Sunlands, providing meager access to water. This was what he'd sought before leading Fur here. Without a source of water, Tan wasn't certain that he'd be of much help to the lisincend. Even with water, he wasn't certain that he could do what he needed to do.

With a shaping of lightning, Cora crashed to the ground, carrying Fur with her. She wore the dark red leathers of Incendin, and her chestnut hair was cut shorter than the last time he'd seen her, more angular and giving her face an even more youthful appearance. A slender warrior's sword hung from her waist—another change to her—and one hand gripped the hilt. Her sharp jaw clenched as her gaze landed on Tan. A question lingered in her eyes, though she remained silent, stepping back and behind Fur, deferring to the lisincend.

Tan wondered again what it must have been like for her before Fur's healing. The mindless lisincend held much power in Incendin, and yet they chased objectives that perhaps only Fur really understood. Fur ruled the others, at least until Asboel had hunted him, leaving him injured and creating a void within the lisincend that Alisz had attempted to fill. That had been the extent of Tan's understanding of the lisincend.

Fur carried another of the lisincend, now bound within fire, wrapped with tight ropes of flame looping around wrists and ankles and spiraling around the lisincend's stomach and neck, pulling tightly so that the creature could not escape. The lisincend looked much like Fur, with a sloped forehead and narrow, slanted eyes that took in everything as they landed. Heat steamed from both, but only Fur appeared at ease. The other lisincend surged against the bindings, straining to get free.

Tan studied the bonds, wondering if he could shape something that required the same level of tight control, and thought that he could. The shaping reminded him in some ways of the tight shaping Lacertin had used the first time Tan had seen him. Had Lacertin learned from Fur, or had it been the other way around?

"This was your doing, then?" Cora asked, stepping toward Tan once the other lisincend was settled.

Tan glanced at Fur. "He didn't tell you?"

Cora's brow furrowed and her expression darkened. "The First thinks he must no longer answer to any. Once, he was accountable to the king, but now even that has changed. I blame you, Tan."

"I blame him for many things, but it does me little good," Cianna said.

Cora's mouth twitched, as if she almost smiled. "The First claims we were needed here. He would not explain why."

"Fur wouldn't tell me where you were. The bond didn't either," Tan explained. He needed time alone with Cora before he spoke to her about the other part of his plan.

"Did you fear that I'd disappeared, Tan?" Cora asked. "You know that there are other ways of reaching me."

"There are other ways," Tan agreed, "but I didn't want to impose upon the draasin." And he hadn't known whether Enya would respond the same way that Sashari did. She still had a certain reservation about the bond, in spite of the fact that she had willingly accepted it, though her options had been to bond or risk the Utu Tonah forcing a bond.

31

Cora's eyes narrowed at the same time that Cianna laughed.

At the sound, the bound lisincend surged against the shapings wrapped around him. A loud, hissing bellow that mixed with a shaping erupted from him. In response, a series of low, steady howls rolled toward them, slowly echoing closer.

Tan turned toward the sound. His reaction to the hounds changed each time he heard them. This time, with Fur and Cora with him, would it matter if hounds approached?

"The hounds will answer the call," Cianna said. "You might heal these lisincend, but can you heal the hounds?"

"I don't know if it will be necessary," Tan said, looking at Cora.

"I don't control the hounds," Cora said. "They are ancient animals, older than the lisincend. The First earned their trust and can lead them."

Tan hadn't known that. He knew they were different, though not quite why. Could they be healed the way the lisincend had been healed? The fire bond told him the hounds were twisted by fire, much like the lisincend. If they were, couldn't he find some way to help them as well? Only, he didn't know what would happen to him if he healed the hounds.

He had experience with the lisincend. The shaping required to pull them back to the fire bond was difficult, but Tan had managed it with both the winged lisincend and with Fur. He could repeat it. But the hounds? A part of him wondered if he would have to destroy them. Whoever created them might be too twisted to save.

"Let's get moving," Tan said. "Fur, will you keep the hounds from disturbing me?"

Fur grunted softly, making a point of avoiding the bound lisincend as he answered, "The hounds no longer respond to my command."

Tan blinked.

Cora jerked her head around. "You no longer command them?"

Fur flared his nostrils and started to answer, but Tan waved him off. There wasn't time for discussion, not if the hounds approached. "Cianna, you will need to keep the hounds at bay while we heal the lisincend. Try not to harm them." She arched a brow at the comment. "But destroy them if you need to." Cianna nodded once. Tan turned to Fur. "What do you intend when they're healed?"

"There is a period of disorientation," Fur said. "It takes time to understand the change."

"Maybe it would have been better to remain in the Fire Fortress," Cianna said as she lifted to the air with a shaping of fire. She'd learned how to twist fire to hold herself aloft, a trick that Sashari had taught her.

"You visited the Fire Fortress?" Cora asked.

"Kaas summoned on behalf of Fur."

"And you came? After everything that happened, you answered the summons of kaas?" Cora's eyes widened with the question.

"I've told you that we'll need to work together," Tan answered.

"You know what that creature did," Cora said.

Tan hadn't expected Cora to object to his working with kaas, but then, she'd seen what happened to Asboel and how kaas had attacked other elementals. "And I know how kaas has been changed. Ask the draasin if you need, Cora, but don't doubt that change can be real. All of us will need to change if we're to survive what Par-shon intends."

Cora breathed out slowly. "You know the last man of the kingdoms to visit the Fire Fortress?"

"Lacertin," Tan said. "I know."

Cora's shoulders sagged slightly with the mention of Lacertin. They had been close, though Tan still didn't know or understand the depths of the relationship between them. It was close enough that

Cora mourned his passing, but not close enough that she knew he had worked on behalf of the kingdoms the entire time he'd been in Incendin. And not enough for Incendin to have asked for his help with Parshon.

Tan stepped over to the bound lisincend. It surged against the bindings of fire wrapped around it. Tan reached over the fire, unmindful of the heat radiating from it. The lisincend hissed, sending steam and a sputtering flame from its mouth which did not harm Tan. Tan wasn't certain what shapings of fire *would* harm him. Not the draasin's. And not lisincend. Would something like kaas harm him, or had the fact that he'd begun to fully understand fire, had embraced his connection to the fire bond, given him the ability to withstand shapings like that?

Would he ever be able to manage something similar with the other elements? Would Tan find himself immune to shapings of water, air, and earth? His connection to fire was deeper than the others, but Tan still didn't understand *why*.

"Your fire will not hurt me," Tan began, intentionally leaning into the draasin. "And it will not twist you any longer," he said.

Tan reached for the connection to fire, using spirit to help him join the fire bond more fully. Awareness of it burned all around him. Fur practically glowed. Cianna was out there, connected indirectly by Sashari. Tan could reach the draasin, were he to try. Cora, tied through Enya, pulled on the fire bond as well.

The connection showed him more than just those around him, but it was what was outside the fire bond that he reached for. The lisincend was there, just beyond the bond, twisted by the shaping that had turned him into the lisincend. That shaping had given him much power, but had taken away the control required to truly serve fire. Without that control, what was left was nothing more than anger and rage that burned, augmented by fire.

Could he repeat what he'd done with Fur and the other lisincend? There were so many that needed to be restored that Tan didn't know if he could do it alone. Amia had helped when he had brought the lisincend back into the bond, but his sense of her was distant this time, her focus elsewhere. Vaguely, he sensed her shaping and knew that he couldn't risk distracting her, not as she worked with spirit with strength enough for him to recognize the shaping.

Could he do this without her help? He didn't necessarily *want* to; Amia had always provided the support and guidance that Tan needed. She had the experience with shaping spirit, but didn't Tan now have the knowledge that he needed to nudge the lisincend, to undo the damage the twisting had done to them?

Fur waited. The bound lisincend surged again, straining to attack Tan. Heat began to build within him.

Tan had failed when he tried to heal one of the lisincend on his own before, but then he'd thought to heal the lisincend back to the shaper it was before. What he planned now was different. He couldn't afford to fail this time, not if they were to work together with Incendin as they faced Par-shon.

He pulled on power through his sword, the runes along the blade glowing with a soft light. The lisincend's attention was drawn to it, as if the sword was what he should fear.

"You will allow this shaper to destroy me, Fur?" he hissed.

Fur said nothing. For that, Tan was thankful.

Tan pulled on more power, reaching for all of the elemental energy around him. Once, he would have thought that Incendin had a dearth of elementals, but he'd learned that wasn't the case. The elementals were found everywhere, both within the kingdoms and outside. The elementals might be different, and the ways to reach them might be different, but they were there.

Elemental powers answered Tan's silent summons, as if they understood what he prepared to attempt.

The fire bond told Tan what needed to be done. With a twisting of fire and spirit, he found the way fire worked through the lisincend, the way it twisted outside of the bond, the shaping that had transformed the fire shaper and turned him into something both more and less than what he had been. This shaping had stolen his control, had taken away his ability to suppress the fire raging through him.

A shaping of spirit mixed with fire helped pull the lisincend back toward the bond. Tan drew strength through the warrior sword. Without it, Tan didn't think that he would be able to complete the shaping. He felt resistance, more than he remembered from shaping the other lisincend, and then fire unraveled, drawn back toward the fire bond and the source of Fire.

There was a surge of spirit as the shaping took hold.

The lisincend gasped and his head sagged forward. Tan waited, but he felt nothing else. With a sigh, he released the shaping and realized with a start that he felt nothing from the lisincend.

CHAPTER 5

The Depth of the Bond

IS IT DONE?" Fur asked.

"It's done," Tan said, drawing as much strength back to himself as he could, using the nameless elementals all around him, as well as those he knew. Ashi restored him, the nymid flowing through the stream helped, and even Asboel distantly helped from within Ethea. With each breath, he pulled his back straighter, letting the power of the elementals fill him. Tan took a step toward the lisincend, his boots crunching on the hard earth of Incendin, and the hot sun, barely at midday, burning in his eyes. "Can't you sense it?"

Fur tipped his chin to the side and sniffed at the air. He remained like that for a moment, then dropped the bands of fire, slowly easing the lisincend to the ground.

The lisincend recovered slowly, but when it did, it lunged, diving toward Fur with a powerful jump. "You would do this to me, Fur?" he hissed. Flames shot from the lisincend, lancing and twisting together, attempting to bind Fur with the same shaping that had been used to hold him in place.

Fur pushed back, and the other lisincend tumbled to the hard rock and struck at Fur's head. Fur caught it and bent his arm away.

Tan readied a shaping and stepped toward them, but Cora caught him with a hand on his shoulder and drew him back. "This is for them to settle, Tan," she said.

"What if Fur is hurt?" He needed Fur to lead the lisincend, but more than that, he needed Fur to hold the bond with kaas, at least until they knew whether the serpent of fire would attempt to destroy elementals again. Kaas might have been returned to fire, but Tan didn't trust it as a free elemental, not without knowing what might happen. Because of that, he needed Fur.

Cora's mouth parted in a tight smile. "The First has battled for his position for many years. I do not think even his brother can wrest it from him."

"Brother?"

Tan considered the other elemental as Fur battled him. There were similarities to the shape of the jaw and the smooth, leathery features of their faces, but with the lisincend, it was difficult to tell. They had much the same build, both powerful and muscular, and Tan would have once been terrified to see either.

"You didn't know?" Cora asked.

"I agreed to heal the lisincend. He didn't share who they were."

The intensity of their fight sagged, and Fur simply held him off, not attempting to hurt him. The other lisincend circled around Fur, steam rising as he worked to create a heat veil. Ashi blew through, sending sand and dirt to distort the veil, blowing away the effects of the lisincend's shaping.

"There are many powerful shapers who embraced fire," Cora said softly. Sadness and longing mixed together in her voice. "Many think of Fur as the first, but our shapers have embraced fire for centuries. Fur serves as the First, but there were others before him, as there will be after. His brother has always been envious of Fur. Many were, wishing to lead the lisincend and to control the pack."

"I'm sorry Alisz couldn't be here."

"My sister would not have been so easy for you to pull back into fire," Cora said. "She was always interested in power, in whatever form that would take. In that, she rivaled Fur. I think he saw in her many of his own traits. That might be why he resisted allowing her the transformation for so long."

The lisincend had stopped fighting, and Fur stood over his brother, tightly gripping his neck. Fur's breaths came heavily and he lifted his brother, throwing him toward Tan. "You said he was returned."

Tan felt for the fire bond, pulling on spirit to help guide him. The lisincend was no longer twisted, not as he had been. "He *is* healed, Fur."

"Then why does Issan attack?"

Issan growled softly and jumped to his feet, pushing up with a shaping. He didn't attempt to attack, but he held a shaping. "You defer to the kingdoms now? Have you fallen so far, Fur?"

Fur leapt and landed in front of Issan. Tan noted that one cheek was bloodied and his left eye had already started to swell. "I am the First of the lisincend. You will not speak to me with such contempt!"

Issan tilted his chin forward. "No? You do not deserve anything *but* my contempt. Under your rule, you allowed others to distort the shaping. And now this." Issan surged with heat, creating a veil around him that cleared with a gust of ashi. Issan snorted again and shifted his attention to Cora. "And you," he said. "I know you. You should serve the throne better than this."

Cora stared at him defiantly, one hand clenching the hilt of her sword, before looking away. The lisincend smiled.

Tan debated shaping spirit over the lisincend, soothing him the way he'd seen the First Mother of the Aeta soothe her people, but would that only encourage Issan to think that Fur served him? Something had to be said, but Tan didn't know what it should be.

"How long have you abandoned your people, Fur?" Issan went on. "Was it the defeat that changed you? You allowed the others to challenge you? After your defeat, you should have stayed hidden. The Sunlands would have been better for it. Stronger."

Fur's back stiffened. A shaping built, one of power that he drew through the elemental he was now bonded to, with strength enough to incinerate a city. Not for the first time, Tan wondered if he'd made a mistake in pushing kaas's bond onto Fur. If he attacked, if he chose to fight the kingdoms rather than Par-shon, it would take considerable strength to stop him. That was strength they didn't have to spare, not with as few shapers as the kingdoms now had, and not with how easily Par-shon managed to force bonds upon the elementals.

"There was no defeat," Fur said.

"No? Then this scar was of your choosing?" Issan pointed toward the long scar running down Fur's cheek. There was a matching scar along his back, equally deep and ugly.

Asboel crawled to the forefront of Tan's mind, intrigued by the lisincend fight, watching through Tan's eyes much like Tan had once used his. *No, Maelen, they were of my choosing.*

Then you let him escape, Tan teased.

Careful, Maelen, or you will see how sharp my teeth and talons remain.

Tan suppressed a grin.

"Enough, Issan. Do you no longer feel the urgency of fire? Can't you feel the control return?" Fur asked. He circled around his brother.

"How long has it been since *you* controlled fire, rather than having it burn within you, demanding your anger and rage? How long has it been since you were able to push away those urges?"

Tan was pulled forward as Fur spoke. Cora tried holding him back, but he shook her hand off his shoulder. He had known the urgency that Fur described. Fire had consumed him once before. Had Amia not been there, he would have completed the transformation, letting fire twist him completely. Once changed like that, there was no control. Only fire.

"What makes you think I *wanted* control?" Issan asked softly.

Fur raised his arm as if to strike and then caught himself, lowering it again. "Had I no control, you would already be dead," Fur said.

"Had you still listened to fire, you would have killed this shaper long ago," Issan answered.

Fur growled.

Tan stopped in front of Issan, looking up at the lisincend. Fur stood next to him, and Tan made an effort to ignore him. He couldn't let Fur see the remaining nerves he felt standing next to him—not if he intended to partner with Fur—or the hint of anger that remained whenever he thought of what the lisincend had done to his home, and to Amia. Issan could see his anger, though.

"Try," Tan said to Issan.

The lisincend tilted his head. "Without Fur standing by your side, a shaper of the kingdoms would not be quite so arrogant."

Tan glared at Issan. Let the lisincend see that Fur did not work with him for no reason. If he had to prove the same to each of the lisincend, then he would. "Do not interfere," Tan said to Fur, sheathing his sword. Let Issan see that he would not need to use his weapon.

"You think to order me?" Fur asked.

"Let him attack. Let him see why we must work together."

"You are strong, Warrior, but Issan is powerful in ways you cannot—"

Issan lunged toward Tan.

"Tan!" Cora yelled.

He had been ready, earth's shaping telling him to expect it. Tan jumped, drawing on air and sliding only a few steps to the side. Issan spun, sending a shaping toward Tan that missed as Tan jumped over his head and landed behind him. Tan didn't shape anything—he waited.

Issan slithered toward him with a dark gleam to his eyes. Heat built within him, swirling in a shimmery veil. Tan could see through it, could see Issan as he burned with fire, almost as if looking with Asboel's eyes.

Drawing on ashi, he pulled away the veil. "Try," Tan said, urging the lisincend.

Issan lunged again, this time swinging his fist as he jumped, mixing a fire shaping with it.

Tan stood fixed in place. With a shaping of earth to strengthen him, he caught Issan's fist and threw him back. The lisincend spun, but as he did, he lashed out with thin streamers of flame that he wrapped around Tan, binding his arms and neck. Tan chose not to move.

Issan came to his feet, a dark smile on his face. "Is there anything you would say to him before I destroy him?" he asked Fur.

A fleeting eagerness crossed Fur's face. "Release him," Fur commanded.

"You would enable a shaper of the kingdoms after how Lacertin betrayed us?" Issan pulled on the flames, drawing Tan toward him.

"Release him!" Fur said again.

Issan roared, and heat surged off him as he pulled on Tan.

Tan allowed himself to be pulled forward. When he reached Issan, he waved away the shaping and stepped free.

Issan bellowed.

"Do you think Fur so weak that he would work with just any shaper?" Tan asked. "Do you think me so stupid that I would come to the Sunlands if I couldn't defend myself?"

A flash of darkness caught Tan's attention.

Almost too late, he realized that Issan had called hounds to him. Where was Cianna? She should have been watching for the hounds, keeping track of them so that he didn't need to fear a surprise attack like this.

Tan called on the wind and hovered above the ground, just out of reach of the three hounds converging toward Issan. The lisincend sneered at Tan, a shaping of fire streaming from him. Not toward Tan, but at Cora.

Tan jumped to block it, but he would be too late. The shaping would hit her.

Pulling on earth, he sent her tumbling as a chunk of rock flung her to the left. Tan landed where she'd been standing, and the fire shaping struck him. It didn't harm him, melting away.

Tan smoothed the earth again.

The hounds snarled. They were nearly as tall as the mountain wolves of his homeland. Long fangs hung down from their jaws, curling toward their lower lips. They had short, black fur that jutted from thick hides. Stubby tails pointed up as they attacked.

They were creatures of fire, though Tan had never really understood them. Much like the lisincend, they could draw on fire itself, but they were twisted. And from what Cora had said, they had existed before the lisincend.

The three hounds converged as one. Issan roared triumphantly, leaping toward Tan on a shaping of fire. Tan might be able to shape his way free, but he risked injuring not only the hounds, but also

Issan. If he was to convince them to work together, he would need them unified.

With a calming breath, he reached through his sword, pulling on each of the elements. Tired from his previous shaping, he didn't take the time to slowly craft the shaping, combining it with the strength he could summon from the elementals around him, borrowing even from Amia and using her connection to spirit. There was a flash of power, and then everything stopped.

In that moment, Tan reached for the hounds, sensing where they were within the fire bond. It was a nebulous sort of thing, and he didn't detect them within it—he hadn't expected to—but they were even further outside it than the lisincend, possibly even further than kaas had been. He expected them to be mindless creatures that would need nudging back into the bond, but there was something about them that was familiar.

Using a shaping of spirit mixed with fire, he pulled the hounds back toward true fire. Unlike with the lisincend, that wasn't enough. The lisincend were shapers of fire, twisted by the way they had embraced it too closely. Restoring them to fire required Tan to use only the combination of fire and spirit.

The hounds were different. At first, he didn't know why. Fire would not be enough to restore them. Tan tried each of the elements, moving on to wind, and then water, before realizing that earth was needed.

Why should the hounds be similar to kaas?

Tan added earth to the shaping, binding it to the hounds. With the added element, he was able to draw them into the fire bond. They came slowly, and Tan had to strain, forcing him to draw upon ever more elemental power around him—not more strength of fire, but of earth.

He reached deep within the earth, drawing from the elemental that he sensed there. Something stirred, leaving the ground shaking, the only other movement around him. It would not be enough. Tan strained, stretching out with earth sense, reaching for Ethea and golud that would be found there. The earth elemental sent a rumbling answer and added to what the earth elementals of the Sunlands could offer.

Then he felt something change.

It came slowly, with terrific effort. Earth mixed with the fire burning within the hounds, both slowly fusing, as the twisted fire that raged through them eased, replaced by a simmering flame of true fire.

The fire bond shifted, welcoming them.

Tan sagged, dropping to his knees. Everything surged forward again.

A dark shadow swept toward him, lifting him into the air. The shaping had drained him, leaving him too weak to resist. If he were attacked, he would not be able to fight back.

Rest, Tan.

Honl?

You drew too much; you risked too much.

What did I do?

Listen to your bond and you will understand.

Tan focused on the fire bond as Honl held him in the air. Issan lurched forward, stumbling toward where Tan had been. Fur stood off to the side and craned his neck until he found Tan wrapped in the shade of Honl. Cora crouched on hands and knees, staring at the hounds with rage in her eyes.

A dark shadow drifted across the ground. Tan didn't need to look up to realize that Cianna and Sashari flew, rejoining them.

All of this he saw as well as sensed within the fire bond. There was something else, something burning differently than he would have expected: three hounds, burning with a controlled heat of elemental fire, but fire tempered by the strength of earth. The combination reminded

45

Tan of kaas, but the hounds were less of fire than they were of earth, and more than simply hounds.

They are elementals? he asked Honl. *Did you know?* This last he sent to Asboel.

The draasin crawled toward the front of Tan's mind. Tan sensed a hesitance from him before he answered. *Not before you restored them. I did not think they'd survived.*

Asboel had known.

This was another experiment? Tan asked.

Asboel breathed out heavily. He reached through the fire bond, touching the hounds. As one, they turned their eyes to the west and north, toward Ethea, where Asboel remained hidden within the den buried beneath the city.

Not the same as kaas, Asboel said.

The elementals gradually restored Tan's energy. He assumed control of the shaping and lowered himself, reaching the hard-packed earth and avoiding the sharp needles from a cluster of brush. The hounds sat, watching Tan. Bright intelligence shone in their eyes, but the dark malevolence was gone. More than that, he *heard* them in his mind, the heavy, rolling sound more like earth than the hot breath of the fire elementals.

Issan stared at the hounds and then at Fur before finally turning his attention to Tan. "What did you do to them?"

Tan inhaled deeply and reached to pull Cora to her feet. Cianna had Sashari land behind them. Tan registered Sashari's surprise at the sudden connection of the hounds to the fire bond, a connection that was more solid than what the lisincend managed.

"The same as I did with you," he answered. "They are restored."

Issan stretched out a hand, and one of the hounds sniffed at it before briefly baring its fangs. Issan took a step back.

Fur approached warily. "I think that I am pleased I did not attack you," he said.

Tan braced his hands on his thighs and chuckled.

"You will heal the rest?" Fur asked.

Tan looked from Issan to the hounds. The process would take significant strength on his part and would keep him in Incendin longer than he intended, but how could he refuse, especially now that he understood what the hounds were? If they were the result of the kingdoms' experiments, he had no choice but to do all that he could to heal them. And with the lisincend, they might have enough strength to truly oppose Par-shon.

"I will heal the rest," Tan said.

CHAPTER 6

He Who Leads

WHEN TAN FINISHED HEALING the last of the lisincend, he sat along the bank of the stream, letting the cool water run over his hand. The nymid swam within the stream, working up his arm and around his neck, bolstering his fading strength. Warm wind gusted around him, and Tan allowed the elementals to help restore him. Even the distant sense of earth elementals aided him. He had called upon them more than expected.

Cora crouched near him, eyes fixed on the sky. The sun had shifted, now nearly reaching the horizon as day changed over to night. Within Incendin, the fading sun didn't mean the air would cool. The ground radiated nearly as much retained heat as the sun. Cora breathed slowly, but Tan sensed the tension within her.

Cianna remained atop Sashari, circling above the Incendin waste, watching over him as she had during the day-long shaping.

"I cannot believe the strength you display," Cora said after a while.

Tan breathed out shakily. The effort of healing the lisincend—most were like Fur, the traditional lisincend that the kingdoms had known and feared for years, though a few winged lisincend remained—had taken significant strength. Drawing from the elementals around him had helped, but it still left him weakened. Physical tiredness mixed with mental fatigue, and his head felt like it was in a fog. He could easily shape fire now, but the lisincend had required shaping fire and spirit, and with strength that he rarely used.

The other shapings had gone better than with Issan. Most reacted to the shaping with a stunned confusion, but they recognized that fire pulled on them differently within moments. Only one other lisincend had the same anger at being taken from the call of fire that Issan had displayed. Fur had some history with that lisincend as well.

"It's not all mine," Tan said. He stretched out his hand, letting water pool there. The nymid collected in the water, leaving it tinted with a faint, shimmery green. He felt the sense of them at the edge of his mind but didn't call to them. The connection to them was different than what he shared with Asboel, or even what he shared with Honl.

The wind elemental remained. Honl swirled around the nearby trees, fluttering at branches and pulling on the long needles. How had he known when to come? Where had he been in the time since Tan had last seen him?

He still didn't know what it meant that Honl had changed, but there was no doubting the change that had taken place. Once, Honl had been like all the other ashi elementals, little more than a translucent, warm wind that blew around him, able to take on a more meaningful shape, but barely anything that he could see. Over time, Tan had managed to see Honl more easily, but now it was something different. Ever since Tan had saved him from kaas's attack, Honl had transformed, as if the

49

act of combining spirit and wind had turned the elemental into a new type of creature altogether. He feared what it meant for his bond pair.

"The nymid?" Cora asked. She put her face close to the water in his cupped hand and then, surprisingly, dipped her face down until she could take a drink. The nymid receded from her and allowed her the water.

Tan let the water dribble back into the stream. "The nymid. The draasin. Ashi," he said, glancing toward Honl, who still swirled. There was a slight tug on the connection between them, but little more than that. "Even the earth elementals of these lands."

"The Sunlands do not have elementals of earth," Cora said.

Tan tapped the ground. Deep within the earth, he felt the rumbling sense of whatever elemental called these lands home. Kaas slithered through as well, but he did so where the earth elementals here allowed. Before the bonding to Fur, kaas wouldn't have asked permission to pass, simply devouring elementals as it came through. The bond had changed that much, at least. And now the hounds. They were fire and earth, like kaas, but in a different proportion.

"The elementals live everywhere. Most simply don't know how to reach them."

"When I first spoke to saldam, I thought I'd imagined it," Cora said. "There were stories of shapers able to speak to the elementals, but none had done so in centuries. Most thought the ability lost."

"I spoke to the nymid first," Tan said. "They saved me when Fur hit me with a shaping."

Cora stiffened. "And still you work with him?"

"Fire consumed him then," Tan said. That was what he had to tell himself; otherwise, he wouldn't be able to find it within him to work with Fur, and the kingdoms—and all the elementals—needed Tan to be able to work together with Fur to withstand Par-shon.

"I thought you spoke to the draasin first."

Tan smiled, thinking back to when he'd first met the draasin. "When I spoke to the draasin, I was trying to reach for the nymid," he explained. "I still didn't understand the connection, only that I had spoken to them and that they had helped. Without the nymid, I would have died. There was something else in the lake, frozen deep beneath the surface. When I reached it..."

You were strong even then, Maelen.

You nearly destroyed my mind.

Asboel laughed.

"That was when you discovered the draasin?" Cora asked.

"They were kept there, held by the nymid and golud and possibly ara. The others had agreed to their task, but not the draasin."

Tan wondered now if the others had been forced as well, but differently than the draasin. The shapers of that time had harnessed the elementals, and they could have used that harnessing to require their assistance. Otherwise, why would they have agreed to serve?

"She remembers," Cora said.

"So does he."

"I can't imagine what they experienced. What must it have been like to remain trapped as they were?"

"It should not have happened," Tan said.

And yet, had it not, the draasin might well have been hunted to extinction by the shapers of that time. If they had, the world would have lost out on the great elementals of fire, leaving it somewhat lessened.

He hesitated, the reason that he'd come looking for Cora returning to him. "You know that I answered the summons to reach you, Corasha Saladan. I could reach through the fire bond, but that would place the burden of my request upon the draasin, and that should not be the reason for me to come." He sighed, thinking that Roine might not appreciate what he said next. Theondar would have understood once, but he had changed and become the man known as Roine, much as they had all changed. "There are so few of us remaining."

Cora frowned. "So few of who?"

"Warriors. The kingdoms have two. The Sunlands?"

"Only me," she said softly.

Tan had suspected as much, but he hadn't known for sure. "There is much that the warriors can do if we worked together," he suggested. "In the archives of Ethea, there are many ancient texts. There are some that speak of a time when the warriors worked together, regardless of nation. They served a different purpose."

Cora's eyes closed. "They were known as the Order of Warriors," she said. "Your archives are not the only places with writings of the past. But much has changed since then. Our peoples are too different. The Order became something else, and the kingdoms claimed their Cloud Warriors."

When Tan had been a child, he had never thought to even meet one of the fabled Cloud Warriors. They had last served the kingdom the generation before him, back when his parents would have been at the university. To most, the last of the kingdoms' warriors had died when Tan was young. Theondar and Lacertin had remained, and now there was Tan. None had known that Incendin had warriors of its own.

"Must they be changed so much? We have worked together before, even if we didn't know that's what we were doing at the time."

Cora traced a finger along the ground. Earth responded to her shaping, cascading into a mound of dust around her. She swirled this, turning it into a funnel, and then released it away from her. "I wish that he could have lived to see what you've accomplished," Cora said.

With the mention of Lacertin, Tan touched the sword sheathed at his side. He'd originally carried Lacertin's, but it had been lost in

Par-shon. "It's because of him that all of this is possible," Tan said. "Without Lacertin, we wouldn't have secured the artifact, and we would not have uncovered Althem's plan."

Red rimmed Cora's eyes and she squeezed them shut. "He didn't know about Par-shon. The First would not allow him to be involved in the shaping."

Tan had wondered if Lacertin had known. If he had, he might have encouraged a different tactic with Althem. Perhaps then he might have recognized the need for what Althem planned, or at least part of it. Maybe Althem had intended to realign the lisincend with fire. With the artifact, it might even have been possible.

"I wish I could have known him better," Tan said. "How much would he have been able to teach me?"

"Now? Not as much as you might think, Tan," Cora said.

Earth sensing told Tan that Fur approached. The lisincend towered over Cora, his long shadow stretching across the land. "He betrayed the Sunlands as he betrayed the kingdoms. A man such as him deserves no mourning," Fur said to Cora.

Her face remained neutral at Fur's comment, but her fingers reached for her sword and squeezed. Tan didn't think Fur noticed.

"You have done what was asked of you," Fur said to Tan.

Tan stretched and sat up, leaning toward Fur. The work had been difficult. The complex shaping required to pull the lisincend back into the fire bond had not grown any easier, but he became aware of a deep power each time he succeeded. It was as if fire itself appreciated the shaping. "And now will you do what was requested of you?"

Fur lowered himself to his knees. The heat that usually radiated from him had eased, lessening the soft glow to his skin, making the scaled surface of his black hide seem more like the draasin. "The Sunlands will stand before Par-shon, Warrior. We do not need the kingdoms' request to keep the Sunlands safe."

Tan took a deep breath, drawing in the warm air of Incendin. Sitting by the water had left him feeling strengthened; some of the weariness had washed away, as if the nymid had bolstered him even more. "Tell me, Fur, how is it that the Sunlands withstand Par-shon?"

Fur crossed his arms over his chest. For that moment, heat flared, leaving his skin flashing orange with heat. It surged against the fire bond as well. "There is a shaping of fire that we mastered long ago. For many years, it has served to hold Par-shon away from our shores."

Tan thought about Doma and wondered if they could be taught a similar shaping. If Doma managed to use water in the way that Incendin used fire, could they keep Par-shon from attacking, or was it already too late? Maybe there was nothing that could be done to keep Doma truly safe.

"What is this shaping?" Tan had sensed part of it while in the Fire Fortress, but not enough to truly understand. Not enough to be able to recreate it.

Fur sniffed. "Only those who truly serve fire can use this shaping."

Tan smiled at the lisincend. "You think that I don't serve fire?"

"I no longer question you, Warrior. It is the rest of the kingdoms I question." He leaned back, resting his thighs on his heels. "I never thought a time would come when I would consider a Warrior of the kingdoms worthy of fire."

Behind him, Cora laughed. "You have him wrong, Fur. Tan is not of the kingdoms."

Tan glanced at her and frowned.

Cora only shrugged. "Deny it if you wish, but you serve more than the kingdoms. If all you cared about were the kingdoms, you would have abandoned Doma."

"My cousin was there," Tan reminded her.

"And you would not have aided the Sunlands. You claim you do so to unite us against Par-shon, but you serve a different master than King Theondar."

Fur's mouth tightened, and heat flared from him briefly.

"Theondar might dispute the idea that he's a king," Tan said. "But I've never denied the fact that I do what I can to help the elementals. That's what the Great Mother called me to do. That's why I've been given the gifts that she's granted."

"You think to rule all over us all then, Warrior?"

"I'm not meant to rule," Tan said. "Much like the elementals were not meant to be forced to serve."

Cora snorted. "See, Fur? I have told you that he is a strange one. He has the power to rule, but thinks that he should not. Imagine what would have become of the Sunlands had you—"

Fur cut her off with a soft snarl. Cora fell silent, but a hint of a smile played across her lips.

"What else would you have of me, Warrior?"

"You know what I have asked, Fur. There is nothing more."

"Nothing? You asked only that we oppose Par-shon."

"Which means that you no longer attack the kingdoms. You will leave Doma and her shapers alone. You will not cross into Chenir. Par-shon is the enemy. Meet with Theondar and convince him of your intentions."

Fur looked at Cora. "You are wrong, Corasha Saladan. *Now* he seeks to lead."

"Attacking each other only weakens us all, and most of us have been weakened enough the way it is. We need our shapers and the elementals to stop Par-shon. I will see the forced bonds removed and the harnessed elementals freed. I will see an end to the rule of the Utu Tonah."

55

Fur chuckled and rose to his feet. "Bold words, Warrior, but when he is gone, another will take his place. Such is the way of power. Someone must hold it. It is the same even within your kingdoms. When the king fell, Theondar took his place." He motioned to Cora. "Come. We will return. The others will need to learn the shaping. Do not worry about Par-shon, Warrior. The Sunlands will keep the shores free of them."

Cora hesitated, raising a hand in farewell, before going with Fur. She shaped lightning, and they disappeared.

As they departed, Cianna and Sashari landed. Cianna tapped Sashari on her side and the draasin took to the air, circling for a moment before disappearing.

"You are tired," Cianna said, throwing herself to the ground next to Tan.

He was struck by how much these lands suited her. Maybe not the people—though Cianna had once told him about those who'd once lived in the nation of Rens and how they had gone to found Nara and Incendin—but the arid earth and the bright, hot sun overhead suited her nearly as much as it did the draasin.

"It was necessary work," Tan said.

"The lisincend and how many hounds?"

Tan let his eyes fall closed. The hounds had been the hardest. Like Issan, many of the lisincend had called hounds to them. The connection didn't require a shaping, at least not one that he saw. He hadn't discovered how they had managed to reach the hounds, but they had come, much like the three that had attacked when Issan summoned them. Each time, Tan had paused and healed them. Each time, he'd been forced to reach deep into the earth and call upon the earth elementals that were buried deeply, summoning the power of Incendin elementals, but also of golud deep within the kingdoms.

56

With each healing of the hounds, he sensed a new addition to the fire bond. Now they were out there, hunting through Incendin, but no longer the mindless creatures they had been. If he reached for the fire bond, he could find them and maybe call to them as he did with the other elementals.

"They're like kaas: elementals that had been twisted together," Tan said.

"So Sashari said." Cianna inhaled deeply. "She is pleased with what you've done. She tells me that Fire is pleased."

Tan hadn't needed Asboel or Sashari to tell him that. Each time he'd pushed one of the hounds toward the fire bond, there had been something of a surge in power, almost as if Fire welcomed them, more so than even the lisincend. As they were mixed with earth, he hadn't expected Fire to embrace them, but then again, Tan knew so little about the source of the elemental power.

"She returns to the den?" Tan asked.

"Asboel needs to eat," Cianna answered.

Tan twisted the dark ring which marked him as Athan on his finger. It was marked with the rune for each of the elements. It was difficult to balance the needs of the kingdoms with those that he felt compelled to follow for the Great Mother. Could he really do both, or would one suffer because he was unable to give the required attention?

As part of that attention, he felt the need to heal his friend, to restore Asboel so that he could once more soar within the clouds, riding on the winds, and look down upon the world. The draasin deserved that freedom. After all that Asboel had done, he deserved that.

"What will you do now?" Cianna asked.

Tan looked up and sighed. If the lisincend and Incendin held out against Par-shon, they had more time than he thought, but how much more? "I'm not sure," he answered.

Cianna clapped him on the shoulder. "You should rest. Even shapers such as yourself need to sleep. You've stopped Par-shon from attacking and you've saved rogue elementals. Maybe it's time to find your woman and take a day for yourself."

Tan wished there was the time. "Par-shon won't rest simply because I'm tired."

"And the world will not end simply because you took a day to yourself." Cianna stood and shaped fire, spiraling it in such a way that she lifted into the air, flying in a way that reminded Tan of the Par-shon shapers. "I will tell Theondar that you still work with Incendin," she said. "You will find time of your own and return when you are refreshed." Then she soared away, moving quickly toward the kingdoms, leaving Tan wondering if he would ever find time of his own.

CHAPTER 7

A New Elemental

TAN LET HIS FINGERS RUN through the water for another moment. Then he stood, glancing toward the sky where Cianna had disappeared. He sensed the fire shaping that she used and could track her. He should return, using a shaping of lightning to reach Ethea, and find what Roine needed of him as Athan . . . but he didn't want to, at least not yet.

Honl, he called.

The wind elemental separated from the tree and swirled toward him on a thick, inky dark cloud. As he landed before Tan, a figure materialized out of the cloud, more distinct than ever before. "You're troubled, Tan."

Tan shook his head. He'd actually *heard* Honl. His voice was breathy and soft, but it had not come through the bond between them. That was still there, and Tan could reach for it if needed, but could Honl have changed so much that he no longer needed the bond to speak? "You can talk."

Honl laughed, and it sounded as airy and light as his voice, drifting quickly away on the warm Incendin wind. "I've always been able to speak."

"Not like this."

"No," Honl agreed. "Not like this."

Tan wondered what this change meant. Whatever he had done had allowed this change in Honl. Was this what the Great Mother wanted from him? Was this how he was meant to use his gifts?

The change hadn't been intentional, though. Tan had only done what was needed to prevent kaas from destroying the wind elemental, but doing so had required mixing spirit with the wind.

Did Honl resent what had happened to him? Seeing the cloud that was now Honl, Tan couldn't tell. The bond didn't share the answers, either.

"Walk with me?" Tan asked.

"Of course."

Tan started north, toward the kingdoms, walking with a mixture of wind and earth, moving dozens of steps with each one that he took. He could simply shape his return, but he would listen to Cianna and take this moment for himself. Probably no more than that, but he needed time to recover and consider what he'd experienced with both the lis-incend and the hounds, and what it might mean for both.

"What does it mean that the hounds are elementals?" Tan asked as they walked.

The Incendin landscape changed quickly with each step. All of Incendin was rocky and wild, with great valleys set into massive cracks of open earth, but parts of it sloped differently. Large, jagged fingers of rock forced Tan and Honl to take to the air to make their way up before descending again. Plants changed as well, and Tan passed them too rapidly to trigger the deadly needles some of the plants could shoot. Tan made a point of staying above most of the plants, coming down only in open areas where the ground was hard and clear of the poisonous life around him. He sensed no other life, not even the hounds that he'd healed. Incendin—at least this part of Incendin—was barren.

"There are many elementals," Honl answered.

Tan sniffed, thinking of the elementals that he sensed all around him, elementals that he had no name for but were nonetheless present all around. There was no doubting that there were many. He thought back to when he'd first discovered his connection to the elementals, when he realized that he was able to reach the nymid and the draasin. Even then, he hadn't realized how commonly the elementals were found.

Time had changed much about his understanding. They weren't just drawn to places of convergences, though there was something about those places that was unique. They were found throughout the land, a part of the land in ways that Tan still didn't fully understand.

"But elementals created by forcing together opposites? Fire and earth, much like kaas. Why would the ancients have attempted such things?" he asked.

They paused atop a tower of rock. Spread out to the south beneath them was all of Incendin. Distantly, Tan could make out the flames spewing from the top of the Fire Fortress as it burned with an intensity unlike anything he'd ever seen. Power radiated from that shaping. Even from here, part of him was drawn to it, itching to join in the shaping.

To the north, Incendin slowly blended into Nara and the kingdoms, eventually rolling into the plains of Ter before reaching Ethea. Tan couldn't see the capital, but the bonds between Asboel and Amia pulled on him, guiding him even if his eyes failed.

To the east, the great Gholund Mountains separated Incendin from Galen, but also from Chenir. Tan had never visited Chenir, at least no longer than it took to stop kaas from attacking and to save Honl. There were shapers there with a different understanding of the elements and a different way of reaching the elementals. They would need to work with Chenir as well if they hoped to stop Par-shon.

"You ask why your ancestors would force the elementals to change when you have done much the same."

"I'm sorry for what's happened to you," Tan said. Honl stood off the rock, the shape of a man made of black shadows and darkness. Warmth radiated from him, much like it did from the draasin.

Honl faced him. "That was not my point, Tan. You serve as the Mother has directed, and I do not think it was my time to return to her. This," he said, sweeping a hand over himself, "is a form of my choosing. I can be any other form should I wish it."

With the words, he shifted, becoming the shape of the lisincend, the hounds, the draasin, before resuming the shape of a man.

"This feels the most fitting," Honl said.

"What does it mean that you can speak?"

"I think that I could always speak. I am of wind, and wind is the elemental of life, of voice and music. When you saved me, you fused spirit to me, giving me language and understanding."

Tan still didn't fully understand how. What did it mean that Honl had been fused to spirit? What would it mean for Honl to have the understanding that spirit offered, or to be the only one of his kind?

"You're no longer ashi, are you?"

Honl shimmered for a moment, the dark cloud that created his form drifting apart for a moment. "Ashi is wind. I am wind, but now I am something more. Perhaps ashi," Honl said.

Even Honl didn't know what he was. How was Tan to know?

"Thank you for helping when Issan attacked," Tan said.

"You do not need to thank me, Tan. The bond still connects us."

"That didn't change?"

"Did the bond change with the draasin when you reforged your connection with spirit?"

Tan knew that it had. Before nearly losing the bond with Asboel, he had been able to understand the draasin and had been able to speak with him, but when Tan had saved the bond, it had required the addition of spirit. They had both chosen the connection, but the choosing had granted both Tan and Asboel a deeper understanding of one another. Maybe that was why Tan had been able to reach the fire bond. Maybe it was not his ability at all, but something borrowed from Asboel.

Honl started away, drifting on another step and making his way forward. Tan followed him, reaching the ground with a shaping of earth and wind so that he landed atop a massive boulder. Another dozen steps, and they reached the border of Nara and the kingdoms.

Tan paused, letting the sense of the barrier wash over him. It vibrated against him, but not as strongly as he thought it should. Something about the barrier had changed.

Honl passed over, blowing through, briefly becoming a dark cloud again as he passed over the barrier. He lingered, looking toward Incendin, before facing Tan once more.

Earth sensing told Tan that something else watched him from deep within Incendin. He reached out with earth, trying to understand what he sensed, but he realized that was the wrong element to choose. Using fire and spirit, he reached for the fire bond.

There, he glimpsed a massive hound watching him. Tan didn't remember healing one quite so large, but he didn't sense twisted fire within her. She aligned with fire, drawing strongly on the fire bond, burning within it, but she also held strongly onto earth, using it to obscure herself. Without the fire bond, Tan wondered if he would have even known she was there.

She bounded toward Tan and landed almost at the border, as if sensing the barrier, and then lowered herself to sit. Eyes of deep orange stared at him, watching him with an intelligence he didn't remember from the other hounds.

Honl drifted toward him in cloud form and then shifted into the shape of a man. He stood next to Tan, his insubstantial form allowing shafts of sunlight to filter through. "She waits for you, Tan."

Tan glanced at Honl. "You speak to her?"

Honl tipped his head to the side, farther than would be possible for a person not made of smoke and wind. "I hear the way she calls to you," he said.

"I hear nothing."

Honl shifted into a shape that resembled the hound and then back into the shape of a man. "Only because you are not listening."

Tan focused on the fire bond, letting himself feel the way fire called. This bond was the reason he could speak to Sashari and Enya, the reason he was able to reach the hatchlings and name Asgur, allowing him to live. With the fire bond, he could reach kaas where it slithered far beneath the earth—now near the Fire Fortress—serving Fur and the bond that had formed between them. In time, Tan hoped to reach saa, perhaps saldam and inferin. Why couldn't he reach the hounds?

He sighed out a shaping of fire mixed with spirit, combining them together as he reached for the hound. As Honl suggested, he sensed her waiting.

The call was distant. No . . . not distant, but deep, a heavy rumbling that reminded him of earth. Not of golud, but of another elemental, one that he'd heard speak to him. Nodn was an elemental of earth, different than the vast golud, and one that Tan had managed to hear.

The hound called through fire, but also through earth.

Tan added earth to his shaping, mixing fire and spirit with it, letting them all join. As he did, the rumbling sound of the hound came to him, a deep, echoing call that suddenly filled his mind with nearly the same power that Asboel had initially managed.

He grabbed his head and pushed the awareness to the back of his mind, fighting for control. The hound sat on her haunches, her deep orange eyes simply staring, as if oblivious to the pain she had nearly caused him.

Who are you?

That was the first question the hound asked, the call that she sent like a deep, fiery rumble through the earth. She had asked the question over and over, waiting for the time when Tan would hear her and answer. Since he had not, she had continued with the question, sending it with increasing strength until he would eventually have no choice but to hear and answer.

I am Tan, he sent.

The hound's ears perked and she stood. She paced in front of the barrier, long snout sniffing at it for a moment before stepping across. Her short tail twitched as she did, as if what she sensed of the barrier had given her some discomfort.

Tan reached through his ability with earth, sensing the hound. As he did, a familiarity clicked within. He remembered the healing of this hound, one of the first that he had brought back to fire. Like all the other hounds that he'd healed, there was strength to her, and a sense of massive and deep power that rivaled any of the elementals that Tan had ever encountered.

You are different, he said.

She circled around him, sniffing as she did. Tan had not been this close to one of the hounds before—at least not one that lived—and there was something very disconcerting about the way she circled him. She briefly bared her teeth to Honl, and sunlight flashed off her long fangs.

Changed. This form is different than before. It is more fitting.

Changed. Had she changed like Honl had changed, or was there a different way that the hounds had been created?

You should no longer have to fight against fire, Tan suggested.

Fire is there, but there is more.

Earth.

Her head swiveled toward the north. Toward Ethea, he noted. *Earth and fire should not mingle.*

And yet they do, Tan said.

You have brought me to fire. How?

The question seemed to have another layer beyond what she asked, though Tan had a difficult time trying to determine what that might be. *How have you changed?*

She stood, circling Tan and giving Honl a wide berth. Somehow, she seemed even larger than she had before. *I know little before my birth.*

Tan paused. *When were you born?*

The hound drew her eyes to the sun and sniffed at the air. *When I first saw you.*

Tan turned to Honl. "Did you know?" he asked.

"Know?"

Could he have been wrong? Had the hounds *not* been elementals when they roamed free? Or maybe they were elementals the same way that kaas had been one—powerful and wild, but without a true connection to the element. Now that Tan had drawn them into fire, solidifying the connection, they had become something more.

How had he managed to do something like that? He shouldn't have the ability to *create* an elemental. And he hadn't, he didn't think. All that he'd done was to take the power that already existed and bring it into the proper alignment. Fire had allowed what he'd done. Had Tan attempted something Fire opposed, he doubted he would have succeeded.

"The hounds were not elementals before?" Tan asked.

Honl ran a hand over the hound, passing through her before standing again. "She is fire and earth. You said so yourself."

"That's not what I mean," Tan said. "Were they not elementals before I healed them? Was kaas?"

Honl shifted into a thin cloud and then back into his manlike shape again. "Does it matter what was? All that matters is what is."

Tan had no answer for that, but it *did* matter to him. How many others were there like kaas and the hounds? How many other experiments existed from that time so long ago? Was that part of the secret that the Utu Tonah knew? He'd alluded to a knowledge that few within the kingdoms possessed, knowing that the elementals had once been harnessed, and he'd known about kaas. What else might there be?

The hound stopped circling and sat in front of Tan. She was massive, her head nearly coming to the height of his shoulders, and she looked something like a small horse. Jagged claws jutted out of enormous paws, and her dark brown fur had streaks of black running through it, making her look as if she'd streaked herself with soot.

Do you have a name? Tan asked.

She sniffed at him, turning her head from side to side. *Name?*

What can I call you?

Honl solidified, becoming more distinct, and stepped between Tan and the hound. "You know the power of names," Honl warned. "If she is new to the world, then she is too young to take a name, Tan."

The hound flashed her teeth at Honl and nipped at him, her jaw passing harmlessly through where his arm should be. Honl patted her head, as if she were nothing more than a dog.

Tan thought about the meaning of names and what he knew of the draasin. Asboel hadn't wanted the draasin named before they were ready. Honl, too, had made mention of how ashi had not come to know names until they had existed for longer. In some ways, the nymid still didn't have a specific name. They were more like a community, all interconnected. If the hound truly was new to the world, he couldn't force a name upon her.

I will call you hound until you choose a name, Tan said.

When will I choose?

Surprisingly, it was Asboel who answered, reaching through the fire bond, using Tan as something of an intermediary to reach the hound. *You will know. Fire will guide you.*

The hound sniffed at the air, turning toward Ethea. *What if Fire is not meant to name?*

Asboel remained silent, leaving the question for Tan, but Tan didn't know what would happen if fire wasn't meant to name. Would earth?

Tan didn't have a strong enough connection to earth to know the answer. *Where will you go now?* Tan asked instead of answering her question.

Asboel answered again. *Hunt. You are fire and earth. Let them burn through you. And prepare.*

The hound stood and circled Tan a few times, then she barked once and bounded off, streaking along the border of Nara and Incendin before finally fading from view.

Tan faced Honl, but the wind elemental didn't seem to notice. He hovered a few feet off the ground, staring after the hound.

"What will happen with her?" Tan asked.

Honl let out a warm breath that left wind swirling all around them. "It is different for each," he said. Honl turned toward Tan. "Fire burns within her, but there is earth. They must find the balance and understand what it means."

"Like you?"

Honl seemed to smile, though in his current form, it was difficult to really tell. "I know what it means when wind and spirit have joined." He drifted away from Tan, moving on a shaping of air before facing Tan. "There are many whom you've healed. Only a few of the twisted remain. It will be better when you heal them too."

Tan took to the air and stood next to Honl, staring out into the distance much like the wind elemental. He let his focus wander, sensing along the earth until he found the hound. She was out there, not far away, almost as if she were still watching him. He couldn't shake the sense that something momentous had changed, or a nagging sense of worry that he might have done something he should not have, much like what had happened with Honl.

Tan wasn't the Great Mother. He wasn't meant to have the power to create elementals, but Honl was something different than he had been before: no longer ashi, but not completely foreign, either. There was much about Honl that was the same as the elemental that he'd always known.

Was that what it was like for the hounds? They were fire, but they were earth as well. Tan had done nothing more than restore them to fire, hadn't he?

Yet the sense of effort required for the healing nagged at him. He had needed the strength of earth, found only in the power he'd borrowed from golud and the Incendin earth elemental. What if Tan was responsible for the hounds?

Honl remained next to him, occasionally becoming more indistinct, before returning to a more solid form. Tan waited for the wind elemental to say something more, but he did not. Eventually, they made their way toward Ethea.

CHAPTER 8

Return of the Athan

THE PALACE WAS A WELCOME change after the dry heat of Incendin. Tan's boots echoed across the tile as he marched along the hall, searching for Roine. The king regent would be here somewhere, though Tan had no idea where.

A group of small children scurried across the hall, forcing Tan to stop as they ran through wide double doors that led to a room that had once been designed as a ballroom. Now it was used as a place of study, where master shapers worked with the children of Althem, guiding them through lessons meant to strengthen their ability to shape. A few already managed faltering shapings, attempting them as they ran. Tan smiled when he saw them.

"There are a few who will be skilled in time," Roine said.

Tan's earth sense had told him that he approached. "Any with the ability to shape more than one element?" They would need more warrior shapers to rebuild what had been lost.

"It's much too early to know," Roine answered. He wore a simple navy jacket and dark green pants. A warrior sword hung from his waist, the only remnant of the time before he'd assumed the title of King Regent. As with Tan, much had changed for Roine. It suited him. After decades spent hiding from his name, he now embraced it. "You went to Incendin?" he asked.

"Fur summoned me."

"So you didn't go as Athan." Roine raised a hand before Tan could object. "I know that you serve more than one role, Tannen. You might be Athan to the kingdoms, but that responsibility pales before what the Great Mother has asked of you." Roine started down the hall, motioning for Tan to follow. "You know, meeting you has made me a man of faith," he said with a smile. "Once, I would not have felt that the Great Mother asked anyone to serve, but once I'd never seen the draasin, never known the strength of the nymid, or heard of ashi. Or met you." Roine opened a door leading to an unadorned hall and sighed as he continued onward, finally stopping at a small door that opened into Roine's private study.

Tan took a seat and waited for Roine to do the same. "Fur wanted me to heal the lisincend."

Roine leaned on his elbows across the desk. "And you agreed?" Roine's eyes narrowed slightly as he took in what Tan imagined to be his weary expression and the way his shoulders slumped forward. He was too tired to put on a better face in front of his old mentor.

"They would be a threat otherwise. I would have you meet with Fur. Discuss how we can work together—"

Roine shook his head. "No, Tan. Some things do not change simply because you want them to. I know what Fur is. I have for far longer than you."

Tan sighed. "We will need them if we want to stop Par-shon." He thought about the shaping that he'd seen the lisincend working, and the way that they held back the oncoming Par-shon attack. "Without the lisincend, Par-shon would already be on our shores."

The corners of Roine's eyes twitched, pulling tight. "I've been waiting for your return to tell you this," he started, "but I think they will soon reach Chenir."

Tan's breath caught. Would he have known had he not spent his time healing the lisincend? "And their shapers?"

"They fear Par-shon, and they are outnumbered."

"How do you know?"

"Zephra sends word." Roine's eyes tightened again when he mentioned Tan's mother. Roine and Zephra had grown close over the last few months in a relationship they thought to hide from him, as if Tan would mind.

"I will go," he said. He was still weary and hadn't taken nearly the time that he needed to recover. He should visit Amia first, but now that he was in Ethea, he sensed her easily and knew that she was occupied elsewhere. He would go to her soon, but Roine needed to know what he'd seen. They had their own responsibilities now, and that sometimes kept them apart.

Roine shook his head. "Not on this. You are valuable here."

"Roine," Tan started, "if Par-shon manages to build much strength in Chenir, it won't be long before they reach the kingdoms. It won't matter what Incendin does."

Roine set his hands down onto the desk. "You know that I've asked that the barrier be abandoned?"

The barrier had once been designed to keep Incendin from crossing into the kingdoms, giving the people and shapers of the kingdoms a measure of safety, but it had done something else that Tan did not think was expected: the barrier had also prevented the elementals from passing through.

Not all. The draasin were able to cross, but they were different in some ways than the other elementals. Wind would blow across, but it weakened as it passed through. Tan hadn't learned what happened to golud. And now the hounds. She had managed to cross without much difficulty, but if the barrier were lowered, it would no longer block the elementals from traversing the border.

"If the barrier is gone, I need assurances that my warrior remains. The people need to know that you will be here. That the elementals will answer a call for help." Roine grabbed a roll of parchment and flattened it across his desk. It was a map depicting the entire continent, with the kingdoms in the middle. Chenir jutted off to the north and Roine pointed toward it, making a motion toward the mountains that separated the kingdoms from Chenir. "Others can help in Chenir, Tan," he said.

Tan leaned back in the chair and stared straight ahead. His mother would let him know if he were needed, wouldn't she? And Chenir had shapers as well, so they weren't helpless. "There's another thing," Tan began. Roine tilted his head to the side to listen without raising his head from the map. "I discovered a new elemental."

At that, Roine lifted his gaze from the page to meet Tan's eyes. "While you were in Incendin?"

"While I was healing the lisincend. Other creatures were separated from fire that I managed to bring back to the fire bond." Tan didn't know if he'd spoken to Roine about the fire bond before, but he needed to know *why* Tan felt compelled to help the lisincend and the hounds.

Roine blinked and slowly sat up, letting out a slow breath. "The hounds?"

Tan nodded. "As I healed the lisincend, some called the hounds."

"The same hounds that have been hunting and killing everything that they can? The same hounds that the lisincend used to hunt with? Those hounds?"

Tan sighed. After everything that he'd learned, there still seemed to be so much that he didn't know. The hounds were like kaas, created by the ancient shapers as an experiment, determined to fuse together fire and earth, elements that should not have gone together. Would he ever know what elementals were used to create kaas or the hounds? The archives might have records, but would he even *want* to know?

"The same hounds created by our ancient shapers," Tan said. "The same shapers who created an elemental that very nearly destroyed the kingdoms."

Roine worked his tongue over his lips. His hands splayed across the top of his table. "The hounds were created by kingdoms' shapers?" he asked softly.

"As far as I can understand."

Roine leaned back, letting out a whistle of air as he did. "Why? How could they have thought that such a creation could—"

"I think I'm the wrong person to ask why the ancient shapers abused the elementals. We thought they understood them, that they worked with them, learning together. But those shapers simply *used* the elementals. They didn't work with them at all. They wanted their power, no differently than the Utu Tonah."

"They couldn't have all been like that, Tan," Roine said. "Were they all like that, then we would still have harnessed elementals."

"Don't we?"

The corners of Roine's eyes tightened, drawing them to narrow slits. "Not in the kingdoms, we don't."

Tan nodded slowly. "The hounds are different now."

"If you brought them back to fire, I would hope they aren't nearly as deadly."

Tan thought about the hound and her massive form. She could still be deadly, though whether she would be was a different matter. "They're larger—at least the last one I saw was," he said.

Roine chuckled and ran a hand through his hair. "Weren't the hounds bad enough when they were the size of a wolf?"

"I'm not sure they're really even hounds anymore." He didn't know what they were, but calling them *hounds* felt wrong somehow. If they were truly different, if he'd really pulled them back toward fire, then maybe he should find a new name for all of them.

"Get some rest, Tan. We have much work to do to keep the kingdoms safe, and I fear you will be critical in making certain we succeed."

Tan paused at the door as Roine continued staring at the map. He watched his friend and the way that he frowned while poring over the map of the kingdoms and everything around it. Worry pinched his eyes, an expression that had been there for as long as Tan had known him. Only when Roine was with Tan's mother did the lines at the corners of his eyes fade. After everything they had been through, both of them deserved that measure of peace.

CHAPTER 9

Reunion

TAN FOUND AMIA IN THE HOUSE that they shared. It was small compared to some within the city, but cozy and comfortable. They'd claimed it after the attack that had left much of this part of the city destroyed. This house had been one of several untouched by the flames that had leveled more than Tan could fathom, even now. After the months that they'd been here, it was as much his home as anyplace.

Amia waited for him near the window overlooking the street. She'd left it open, probably to watch for him as he made his way back to the house, and it let a cool breeze into the room. Once, Honl had blown everywhere Tan had been, and the ashi elemental had left a warm breeze trailing after him, but since his healing, he no longer did. Ara sent gusts throughout the city, bringing the scents of the street—those of bread baking, the fragrant scent of the florist along the street, or the smoked scent of meats—and even the joyous sounds of life throughout the city, sounds that had faded for a time after the attacks that Ethea had faced.

"I didn't think to find you here," Tan said, closing the door behind him.

Amia hurried over to him and threw her arms around his neck. Her long, golden hair was braided and hung down her back. Ribbons of different colors had been twisted into the braid. She wore a bright dress, striped with orange, red, and green, and she smelled of lilacs.

He hugged her tightly, not wanting to let her go. The bond formed between them, the long ago shaping that had connected them, told Tan that she felt much the same way.

"You didn't come to the wagons," Amia said. She stayed close to him, sliding her arm behind his back.

"Roine needed to know what happened." Tan explained to her the lisincend and the hounds. "I'm not sure what it means that the hounds are elementals," he finished. "Or if it was something I did, or whether I only healed what had already been done."

She closed her eyes and her fingers went to her neck, running along the gold band she wore there. Once, it had been a silver band that marked her as Daughter of the People, but Amia had discarded that when she felt as if the People had abandoned her. Roine had given her the gold band as a way of thanking her for the service to the kingdoms. She still wore it, even though she now served as First Mother.

"The hounds?" she said.

"I need to go to the archives and see if I can learn anything there," he said. "I thought the hounds a creation of Incendin, that the lisincend had somehow used their shaping to twist them into what they were, but if they were never Incendin . . . "

Tan didn't know how to finish. If they were never Incendin, then it meant that the kingdoms were responsible for the hounds, much as they were responsible for kaas. Even the binding of elementals that Par-shon forced upon them was reminiscent of the harnessing the ancients once did to the elementals. Could it all be their fault? Was this war nothing more than repairing the mistakes that had been made long ago?

"And the lisincend?" Amia asked.

"As far as I know, they have all returned to the Fire Fortress. The shaping that makes the fortress burn keeps Par-shon away. It used to be their shapers responsible for it, but now the lisincend can join. Their shaping is even more powerful than what those shapers were able to manage."

Tan went to the window and looked out. The street below had been fully restored. Buildings that had once been built of wood were now made of brick and stone, as if the shaped fire that had attacked the city would not be able to tear through the brick just as easily as it had the wood. No part of the city was ever permanent. The university, once a place that had stood for centuries, had fallen during the attack. It had been rebuilt by the master shapers to again house and teach those of the kingdoms with the potential to become the next warriors, but it was different than it had once been.

"There was a hound that came to me as I crossed into Nara," Tan said. "She was different from the others." He squeezed the windowsill, thinking of the intelligence in the hound's eyes. "Or maybe she was the same. I don't really know what happened to the hounds after they were healed. They are fire and earth, like kaas, but different, more attuned to earth. She followed me through Incendin, and probably through the kingdoms."

"There's a hound in the kingdoms?" Amia asked. There was an edge of fear in her voice.

Tan turned away from the window. "If the hounds are healed, does it matter?"

Amia touched his cheek. "Tan, how quickly you forget what the rest of the kingdoms have gone through because of the lisincend and the hounds. You know they're different because you healed them, but others—even other shapers—won't understand. I hope you warned her to remain out of sight."

"Actually, Asboel suggested that she hunt."

Amia's eyes widened. "Are you certain that was a good idea?"

"I'm not going to confine the elementals."

"You confined the draasin."

Tan had confined the draasin, but it had been necessary at first. The draasin hadn't been seen in this world for the thousand years that they'd been frozen at the bottom of the lake at the place of convergence. Without Amia's shaping preventing them from hunting people, Tan had no idea what would have happened.

Even without the shaping, he thought it unlikely that they would have attacked. The draasin enjoyed the hunt, but everything that Tan had seen told him that the draasin would have avoided hunting people. They would have stayed away from shapers, fearing capture and the risk of harnessing.

"And that was a mistake," Tan said. If the hound had followed him into the kingdoms, he would have to find her—not to restrict where she hunted, but to warn her that others might be afraid. "When the elementals were restricted, it was about the same time that we stopped reaching them. It was about the same time that shapers became less powerful. I wonder if the creation of the barrier had anything to do with the fact that we haven't seen a warrior shaper in a generation."

"The barrier remained when you discovered your abilities," Amia reminded him.

"But would I have ever learned what I can do if not for us going to the place of convergence? Would I ever have learned to speak to the nymid, and then the draasin . . . " And then the others. Was it that place that had allowed him to learn to speak to all of the elementals, or was it something about him?

She pulled him against her, hugging him tightly. "Why do we keep coming back to what happened there?" she asked.

"Because it seems that everything started in that place. The elementals. The artifact. Whatever the ancients had intended, it's all about what they did then."

"And the artifact?"

Tan thought about it. The artifact was a device of significant power, one that Althem had once intended to use to practically change the world to the way that he wanted. When Tan had held it, he'd felt as if he could shape anything that he wanted, that he could have brought his father back, that he could have destroyed the lisincend with a thought. And if he had . . . he would never have learned that they could be healed, or that the hounds could be restored. Fire would have lost another elemental.

"I still haven't learned why they created the artifact, what they intended to use it for, or even why they hid it once they had created it. Now that it's gone . . . " Had he told her that the artifact was damaged?

"And if it wasn't, don't you think that the threat Par-shon poses is enough to think about using it?" Amia asked.

Tan had considered it, but had abandoned that thought. What would using the artifact make him? What would he become? He'd already felt the temptation of the artifact; what else would he do if given the chance? "I'm glad that it's gone. I could never use it, because I don't want to be like him," he said softly.

Amia's brow furrowed as she studied him. "The Utu Tonah? You are nothing like him."

"If I begin to think that I know what is best, then I start down that path."

Amia's frown softened and she touched his cheek again. Tan leaned into her soft touch. "If you didn't think that you know what's best, you would have never done any of the amazing things you've managed."

"And what makes what I think is right actually right?"

"Your heart. Your connection to the elementals, and through them, to the Great Mother. There are certain things that are simply the way they should be, and then there are other things that must be taught. Not everyone can reach the elementals the same way that you can. Only a few people have ever touched true spirit. These are what give you credibility. These are the reasons you know in your heart what you must do," she said.

Tan sighed, thinking of everything that had happened to him since he first left Nor. So many had died because of what he'd done. So many more had been hurt, but how many more would have suffered had he not acted?

"You think I should have used the artifact?" he asked.

"I don't know the answer to that. I can't shape the elements the same way that you can. I've never drawn through the artifact to know what it feels like to hold that much power. I remember what I felt through the bond when you did so, and I remember the power that surged, but only you can answer that question." She pressed her palms on his chest and smiled. "There was a time when you could go to your mother, and then to Roine for advice on what needed to be done, but those days are past you. You must lead now."

"I'm the Athan, Amia. I think that Roine has already asked me to lead."

"No," she said. "There will come a time as you fight Par-shon when you must decide. And it might be different than what Roine would want, or your mother, or even Fur as leader of the lisincend. There is no one else who has been given the gifts that the Great Mother gave to you, and she did so for a reason. I know that you don't always want the responsibility that's been placed upon you, but you have it." She stepped back and crossed her arms over her chest, surveying him. "Now, what will you do with it, Tannen?"

What would he do? Tan didn't even know the answer, but he suspected the time would come—and likely soon—when he would have to make a choice.

CHAPTER 10

Along the Fire Bond

THE TUNNELS BENEATH THE CITY were ancient, older even than Ethea itself. Walls of solid stone rose on either side of Tan, pressing against him with a weight than seemed like it came from more than simply the stone itself, but from the centuries that these tunnels had existed. Within Ethea, only a few knew of them. Once, only the archivists had known, using their ability to shape spirit to reach the tunnels and to travel beneath the city as they chose. Tan suspected this was how they spread their spirit shapings, controlling the university's shapers and ultimately attempting to control the king.

The sense of golud filled the stone, a rumbling sort of awareness that Tan had felt in such strength in only one other place: the place of convergence within the mountains of Galen. Even there, golud had not been nearly as potent as what he sensed here. The nymid mingled with golud, earth and water always complimentary, and left the stone with a damp green sheen that glowed along the walls.

He trailed his hand along the stone, letting the sense of the nymid wash over his fingers before stopping at a pool glistening with nymid. Since bonding with the water elemental, Tan had an increased awareness of not only water, but of all the elementals. Through that connection, he recognized that there were several other elementals of water that mingled within the pool, elementals that he had once not even known about. Knowing that they existed did nothing to help him understand what they were, or even what they could do, but he was surprised nonetheless. Even within the stone, there were other elementals.

Not simply golud infused these walls, but other elementals of earth, deep and distant and otherwise silent to him. Tan had not bonded earth and wondered if he would. He might have known earth sensing first, but the shaping of earth had come the hardest, and his connection to golud and the other earth elementals was the weakest. They responded, but not in the same way as wind or water. And nothing was quite like his control with fire.

Tan continued through the tunnels and stopped at the door that led to the draasin den. The single rune for fire was there, and Tan had added one for spirit so that he was the only one able to open the door. He pressed through the rune and it opened with a soft hiss.

The air on the other side of the door was hot, and steam drifted out from the draasin den. Tan shaped a ball of flame for light, and as he stepped inside, he caught a flash of blue scales scurrying along one of the walls that quickly disappeared through a hole in the wall made by golud.

A pile of bones along one wall gleamed with the soft light of his shaped flame. The fallen rock, the remnants of the hole leading to the other part of the den, was stacked off to the side. Asboel sat with his tail curled around him in front of the rock, his long snout angled off to the side and resting atop his forelegs.

Maelen, Asboel said with a snuff of steam. He swiveled his head toward the back of the den and peered in the direction the hatchlings had disappeared.

Through the fire bond, Tan could tell that Sashari was with them. Asgar grew big and was allowed out to hunt all by himself more frequently. The other young draasin had not taken to hunting alone again since they'd recovered her.

Tan made his way toward the injured wing and ran his fingers over the thick rope of scarred muscle. The leathery wing itself had been damaged as well, the patchwork of scars a new part of Asboel. The draasin had survived a thousand years in the ice only to suffer a nearly fatal attack from a wild elemental.

Are you well? he asked.

Asboel snorted. *You ask questions you know the answer to, Maelen. You need not be foolish, or feel too badly for me. I still breathe. I enjoy the touch of fire. The hatchlings grow bold. There is much to experience.*

Tan sensed the twisted way the muscles had come together in the wing and the damage to the skin overtop. He had done what he could to heal the draasin, but there were limits to his ability, and limits to what the elemental would allow. Not that Asboel didn't want healing, only that healing elementals was different than healing people. Tan didn't have the knowledge or the skill or the strength. It was possible that he had none of what he needed to help his friend.

I wish there was more that I could do for this, he said. *With the hunt that comes, I will need you, my friend.*

And I should be there, Maelen.

It was the first time he'd sensed sadness from Asboel about the injury. Usually, Tan sensed nothing but frustration that the wing no longer worked as it should. There was occasional anger—the draasin was accustomed to being the most terrifying creature, and this left him uncertain of his place and position—but never sadness, and never the sense of longing that he detected now.

Asboel breathed out a streamer of steam that left Tan unharmed. *You didn't come here simply to check on my recovery, Maelen. Your conversation with the Daughter has troubled you.*

Why have you always called her that?

The Daughter? She has the hand of the Mother upon her. Much like you, Maelen.

Tan didn't feel like he had the hand of the Mother on him, but Asboel wouldn't understand the concern that Tan felt over what he would need to do. Somehow, he had to get all of the nations together. They had worked together only a few times, and only when Tan had summoned, demanding that they help. Could he get them to see the need on their own, without having to be forced into helping?

Tan lowered himself to his knees and looked at Asboel. His golden eyes still held much of the strength Tan had first been struck by, that cunning intelligence that shone bright behind them, but there was a weariness to them now. The draasin had lived countless centuries. He was the eldest, the elemental that the other great elementals all revered. And because of Tan's bond with him, he'd come to harm that he should not have.

You still think that you can control the draasin? Asboel asked. *You sense the fire bond; you understand how it burns. Do you think that you can control Fire?*

I can control fire, Tan said. *Otherwise, I would be no better than those twisted by it.*

No, Maelen. You have never controlled Fire. You can use it, borrow of its power, but controlling Fire is not possible. The draasin are Fire, and even we do not control it.

87

Then how do I use it?

You serve fire, perhaps more than any other I have known. That is the reason you've been granted access to the fire bond, the reason you have done what your ancestors could not.

What exactly did my ancestors attempt?

Asboel crawled forward, placing his wide nostrils so close to Tan that he could hear the air whistling in and out of his lungs. This close, Tan smelled an odor that had been masked before—that of decay. He reached out with his earth sensing but couldn't discover what he smelled.

Your ancestors thought they could recreate the work of the Mother, but unlike you, they did not have her blessing.

You mean the experiments with the elementals? Asboel hadn't shared much about what he knew of that time, almost as if he feared Tan's learning. Why would he share now? Kaas had been healed. Many of the hounds were restored, though he suspected some still remained. What purpose would it serve to share with him now when he'd withheld it from him before?

Asboel let out another breath. The scent of rot came from deep within him. Tan had never noted it before.

Experiments. There was another term at that time, though few know of it, Asboel said. The sharpness to his eyes faded a little and he blinked. *I have much time to think, Maelen, and to remember. I have forgotten much over the years, but now? Now I do nothing but sit.* He snorted and flicked his tail. *Your ancestors called them crossings, as if they could take the elementals of the Mother and breed them like they would horses.*

Had he read anything about crossings before? The term seemed familiar, though he didn't know why that would be the case. The ancient shapers had many terms that sounded harmless when taken out of context, but Tan had begun to understand the depths of the horrors they attempted, often in the name of curiosity. The harnessing of the elementals was one such thing. These experiments—the crossings—were another, and probably worse.

How many crossings were there?

There were not many that were successful. You have seen what happened with kaas. The creature was to have been banished. I do not know how it was returned to these lands.

And the hounds?

Asboel paused. Tan felt him questing along the fire bond and followed along with it, reaching with a shaping of fire and spirit, stretching out his senses much like Asboel did. The draasin was more skilled at drawing along the fire bond, but Tan had grown more comfortable with each attempt.

Through the bond, he sensed the draasin now away from the den. There was a sense of joy from Asgar and the other hatchling, an unbridled excitement for the hunt as they circled high above the ground, watching for movement. Sashari watched with pride, letting them hunt, guiding them. Asboel should be with them, reveling in the hunt as they did, joining and teaching, instead of trapped within the den, unable to do anything more than watch.

Beyond the draasin, there was the sense of saa. Saa flowed all around the city, a wispy sense from the elemental, but taken together made it incredibly powerful. There was a new sense to Tan, that of an elemental that he had no name for, that crawled in dark spaces along the streets above. Tan wondered if it might be inferin or saldam, finally drawn to Ethea now that the barrier was down.

Outside the city, he sensed other sources of fire. Many of the same elementals were there, but scattered. A bright light drew Tan away from Asboel's questing, pulling him toward it, until Tan recognized it as the hound. She prowled the hills of Ter, the cool wind of ara ruffling her short fur and the scent of deer heavy in her nose.

Asboel pulled him back, dragging Tan along the bond. They quested beyond the border with Incendin, reaching into the Sunlands, until Tan sensed the great burst of fire that came from kaas as it slithered beneath the ground. The fire bond showed him other bright lights, that of the dozen hounds Tan had healed, who raced across Incendin. It was here that Asboel paused, lingering and holding Tan's focus.

You see their connection? Asboel asked. His voice seemed to come differently now as he surged through the bond, a deeper sound, one that carried with it a sense of the centuries he'd lived. Tan had always known that Asboel was vast and ancient, but connected to the fire bond as he was and listening to his friend, he had a sense of how truly connected he was to fire.

As Asboel instructed, Tan focused on the connection of the hounds to the fire bond. They surged brightly, the heat of their connection strong and powerful, but different than so many others that he'd seen. They were fire… but they weren't.

You see it, do you not? Asboel asked.

How was I able to heal them?

These creatures are a crossing of fire and earth. Only the fire was twisted, pulling them away from the Mother. I had not thought they could be restored.

Tan recognized the significance to what Asboel said. Asboel might have known what the hounds were, but even he hadn't thought what Tan had done was possible.

How did I do it?

Instead of answering, Asboel pulled him along, drawing along the fire bond, sending them questing farther and beyond Incendin. They moved through the southern tip of Chenir, where the elementals had once lived and now were pulled away from the land, until they drifted over Doma, the remnants of the Par-shon attack still leaving the land scarred. Udilm washed along the shores and mixed with the elemental Elle had bonded. In time, they would heal the land. Even through the fire bond, he recognized that.

Then Asboel paused. They drifted above the ocean, the vast swell of blue with swirls of white splashing over it. Tan was surprised to note blooms of fire even within the ocean, elementals that he hadn't ever known existed. The bond told them that they lived deep beneath the ocean, a place Tan thought would be nothing but cold and darkness.

It is dark, but fire burns even there, Asboel said.

Tan focused on the elementals he sensed. They clung weakly to the fire bond, but they were there, swirling around a jet of hot water. *Water and fire?* Tan asked.

The Mother has no need of your kind to create crossings. She has made all that are required.

Asboel drifted on, pulling Tan with him.

They are more water than fire, Tan noted, still straining to reach the strange elemental deep within the ocean.

As those creatures you healed are more earth than fire. As the draasin are more fire than wind. Many of the elementals could be considered a crossing, Maelen.

Asboel moved farther out to sea, pulling him past a series of islands peaked with wide, sloped mountains. Fire burned within them as well. The draasin followed the fire bond further, and Tan began to feel a strain as he struggled to maintain the connection. Asboel might be able to trace along the fire bond, but he didn't have the same strength as the draasin, nor the experience to know how to search the way the draasin did. He'd done something like this before, but hadn't that been spirit?

Tan pulled on fire and spirit, shaping more strength to keep up. The sense of the draasin grew increasingly distant until he faded almost completely from Tan.

Tan pushed out, questing as far as he could with the fire bond. It felt vague and indistinct, almost like something he was never meant to reach. As he considered releasing the bond and returning to the den, he sensed another draw on fire.

It came to him distantly, an indistinct sense of fire burning far from him. Something about it seemed different, though Tan couldn't quite place what it was. Tan focused on it, letting the sense of fire draw him, but he could not go any farther along the bond. This was his limit.

Do you sense it?

This came from Asboel, though Tan had the sense that his voice came from all around and filled his mind. The draasin was not limited in reaching the fire bond.

I sense something. What is it?

You sense the crossings.

Crossings? Like kaas and the hounds?

Asboel pulled back toward him, becoming a more distinct sense along the bond. The sense of him surged all around, powerful and full of the might of Fire. *Kaas should not have returned. I thought it banished, or that it had perished in that time.*

Kaas is no longer a threat, Tan reminded him.

Only because of you, Maelen. My time in the den has allowed me to explore the bond more fully than I have ever attempted. I see now why kaas returned, as I see that there are now others, much like kaas and equally dangerous.

I don't understand.

Let fire show you, Asboel instructed.

Tan turned his attention back to the fire bond, straining through it and drawing on fire and spirit with everything that he had remaining. Asboel lent him strength, as he had so often done, giving him the additional power that he needed to push outward. As he did, he felt what Asboel intended him to find.

Fire burned, but fire that was not pure, fire that was like the lisincend and the hounds had been, twisted from the source of Fire. It was dangerous and unstable. And it sensed him watching.

Par-shon has created these crossings, haven't they?

That is the only reason I can learn that kaas returned. Kaas was a difficult crossing in your ancestors' time, and one that nearly destroyed everything. The draasin did what we could, but we were hunted.

Is that why the artifact was created? Tan asked.

I don't know. The Mother aided in its creation for a reason. It's possible that it was because of the crossings.

Asboel pulled back, dragging Tan with him, receding from the connection and back toward the kingdoms. Tan resisted a moment, letting his sense of the fire bond pull on him a little longer as he tried to understand what it was that he sensed out there, but Asboel was too strong and forced him back.

They skimmed across Incendin, where Tan sensed the Fire Fortress burning, the shaping the lisincend worked still compelling him to join, and then deeper into Incendin, where he sensed kaas burrowed far underground. There were other elementals that caught his attention, but nothing like kaas or even the scattered hounds that he detected. And then they were back in the kingdoms, where the draasin flew high over Galen, when saa joined with fires scattered in homes and cities, and the single hound still watched from just outside Ethea.

Then they returned to the den.

The effort of the shaping left him exhausted. Asboel watched him with his deeply intelligent eyes, the golden color almost glowing with an inner light. Tan's shaping of a ball of light had failed, leaving them otherwise in the dark.

He should move and return to Amia, or any number of the dozens of other things that he knew needed doing, but the effort of stretching that far along the fire bond had taken too much out of him.

Asboel snorted as he shuffled to the side. His long tail wrapped around Tan. *Rest, Maelen. I will watch over you.*

CHAPTER 11

A Complicated Responsibility

TAN PRESSED ON HIS RING, which vibrated on his finger. Its summoning had surprised him; Roine rarely used it. Roine was usually too busy with the daily requirements of keeping the kingdoms running to worry about what Tan was doing. Most of the time, Tan made a point of coming to Roine if there was anything that the king regent needed to be informed about.

He was better rested after a night spent in the draasin den. Lying on the hard stone shouldn't be comfortable, but curling up next to Asboel and feeling the warmth radiate off the draasin had helped him sleep more soundly than he had in days. For the first time in a while, he hadn't worried about what would become of Incendin or how he would reach the Chenir shapers to convince them to work with the kingdoms. He hadn't had one of his recurrent dreams where he saw the Utu Tonah descend from the sky, surrounded by dozens of elementals, all bound to him and filling him with incredible power. Tan had simply slept.

When he'd left the den, Asboel had been sleeping. The other draasin hadn't returned from their hunt, or if they had, they didn't bother Tan and Asboel. The great draasin had barely moved, only his massive sides expanding with each breath. Tan used a combination of earth, water, and spirit, combining them in a sensing to try and determine what else might be wrong with him, but he was not skilled enough to understand what he sensed. He'd left Asboel there with a request to the nymid to do what they could to heal him, knowing that the water elemental had been unable to do anything so far.

The summons drew him toward the university grounds. The last few weeks had allowed the kingdoms' shapers to make significant progress on the repairs to the university. Stone rose three stories high in most places, with the central tower already six stories tall. Tan hadn't been involved in the plans for the repairs and didn't know how tall Ferran intended to make it. Before, it had been a massive and sprawling expanse, but when the destruction from the draasin and lisincend attack had left much of it broken into rubble, the masters had taken the opportunity to redesign it. Golud was strong within the walls of the university, filling the stone with nearly as much strength as what Tan had sensed deep beneath the city, drawn by Ferran's request and his connection to the elemental. With golud, the air was left with an earthy scent, like a mixture of fresh rain and dirt, and—strangely—a hint of pine.

Shapings went on all around him, the strength of their work putting pressure within Tan's head. When he'd first started noticing the pressure from shapings, he hadn't known what it was. Over time, he'd grown accustomed to it and barely noticed anymore, other than to recognize when shapings took place around him. That he'd pay attention to it now told him how powerful the shapings were.

The rebuilt university spread out around the grassy plaza, where the shaping circle remained. It was one of the few things that had survived the attack on the university, and a remnant from a time long past, back when dozens of warriors used it to travel to and from the city. The walls of the university arched around the circle, like arms on either side, with the massive tower rising from one end. An archway led away from the university and out to the street.

Ferran stood atop one of the arms. He worked with a dedicated focus, shaping stone up the sides of the building until set in place and sealed with another shaping. The power from his shaping was more than Tan had ever known him to use, and he managed it with ease. The connection to golud had made him incredibly strong.

A few other shapers—all earth shapers, Tan noted—worked with Ferran, though Tan didn't recognize most of them. Together, they drew up the university, one enormous block of stone at a time.

"They harvest stone from the hills to the west," Roine said, stopping and following the direction of Tan's gaze as he watched the earth shapers.

"The entire thing will be more impressive than before," Tan noted.

"A chance for a new start, I suppose." Roine pulled on the hem of his dark green jacket, letting his fingers linger on the embroidery that ran along the edge. "How are you feeling today, Tan?"

Tan noticed an unusual hesitancy in Roine. Normally, the king regent was a confident man, and he'd always displayed a certain bravado from the moment that Tan first met him in the forest outside of Nor. He had to, in order to search for the artifact despite the risk to himself.

"What is it, Roine?"

Roine forced a smile, though it appeared pained. "I wanted to keep you from leaving the kingdoms again, especially after you have only now returned. It seems you've been spending so much of your time traveling outside of our borders lately. First to Doma to help Elle, then chasing all over after the elemental, and now you've only returned from Incendin a few days ago."

"I do what I'm supposed to do," Tan said.

"Yes. And as Athan, I think you've been asked to do more than most in your position. Not that I'm complaining. I can't, not really, because if you didn't follow your heart and do what you knew was right, you wouldn't be the man that I know you to be, the man who has made his mother proud."

The way that Roine said *mother* told Tan that something more was going on than Roine let on. Only the other day, Roine had not wanted Tan to leave the kingdoms, thinking that Tan needed to remain in Ethea to help provide stability for the people.

"What is it?" Tan asked. "What happened with Zephra?"

"Zephra," Roine started before sighing, "sent a summons. You know your mother, Tannen. You know that she rarely asks for help. That she would call to me when she is in Chenir, especially since we know that Par-shon continues to move, tells me that she has found something that worries her."

Possibly more than worried her, if she had summoned. Tan noted that she hadn't summoned *him*, only Roine. But his mother didn't like asking for help, no more than Tan did. In that way, they were much alike.

"She's still in Chenir?" Tan asked.

"She went with the Supreme Leader. They offered to help demonstrate their shapings, and she thought she could learn what else was happening there."

The fact that his mother had gone and now summoned told him all that he needed to know: Par-shon had attacked. Chenir had shapers and the ability to call to the elementals that shapers in the other kingdoms had never learned, but they didn't have numbers. If Par-shon attacked, they would be in real danger. Zephra was a powerful shaper and bonded to one of the wind elementals, but she had limits, the same as other shapers.

"What did her summons imply?" Tan asked.

"It's not clear," Roine said. "The rune doesn't work quite like that."

"It could, if she wanted it to." Tan had learned much of runes since working with the First Mother. Runes were at the heart of what Par-shon did, the power that they manipulated, the way they forced the bonds onto the elementals. Without the runes, there would be no bond. There was much power to them, and Zephra had learned nearly as much about the runes as Tan.

"Now isn't the time for your frustrations with your mother," Roine said.

"That's why you summoned? You want me to find out what happened to her?"

"There is no one else, Tan. I can't risk you, but I can't risk losing Zephra, either."

With their growing relationship, Roine worried more about Zephra than he would another shaper. And if there was anyone who could travel to Chenir and find out what Zephra had discovered without being in too much danger, it was Tan. He could reach Chenir and be back in moments, if needed.

"If I do this, you will meet with Incendin," Tan said.

"Tannen—"

Tan raised his hand and shook his head. "No, Theondar," he started. "You hate Fur. I understand that emotion as well as any. But I know that he will be needed to defeat Par-shon." More so, now that he'd had the vision of the fire bond while with Asboel. "We can't do it alone. If what I've learned is even remotely real, then neither can Incendin. Doma and Chenir will be afterthoughts, destroyed along with the rest of us. We *have* to find a way to work together."

99

"Fur can't be trusted," Roine said softly. "You know about the last peace treaty we had with Incendin. I told you how long that it lasted."

Tan remembered what Roine had said. That the treaty had lasted barely more than a month before Incendin attacked again. "This is different."

"That was Fur, Tan. He was the reason the treaty failed. Do you really think that your shaping changed so much about him that he can be trusted? What happens if he chooses to forge a treaty with Par-shon? What happens if he decides that he will simply let Par-shon claim the kingdoms in order to keep Incendin safe? Do you really think that we can trust a creature like that?"

"Yes." Tan had seen the intensity of Fur's desire to keep Incendin safe. In that way, Fur and Theondar were much alike. Both recognized the threat that existed. Both understood that they needed to do whatever was necessary to keep their people safe. And neither was willing to accept the possibility that the other could be trusted.

Roine turned back to the university, his gaze lifting to where the earth shapers pulled rock high onto the wall. "The university will be stronger now than it was before it fell. Ferran tells me that golud answers his request to give strength to the stone. In another few weeks, the students can return. The university will once more be an example of the power of the kingdoms."

"Roine, I fail to see—"

Roine turned and started toward the street, motioning for Tan to follow. When they reached the stone archway that led out into the cobbled street in front of the university, he paused, pointing in either direction. "The kingdoms need a place like the university. Knowing that our shapers watch over the city, knowing that the masters are unrivaled in their skill, gives the people a sense of peace."

"But we're not unrivaled. Not anymore." And perhaps not ever, though Tan didn't think that Roine wanted to hear that.

"My role as king regent is to provide stability. What will happen if word spreads of a treatise with one of the lisincend? What will happen if others learn that I have bargained our safety on the word of Fur?"

This street had been as damaged as any in the attack. Rock had heaved, leaving piles scattered throughout, forcing anyone who wanted to reach the university to do so by shaping or by crawling over the debris. Some of it had been shaped back into place, but not all. Hundreds of men had worked to clear the rubble. Now, dozens of people made their way along the street. Most paid Tan and Roine little mind. A few glanced their way, though few recognized Roine, and those who did simply bowed and scurried on their way. Carts loaded with supplies traveled along the street, something that would have been unthinkable only a month before. The city had finally returned to what it had been before all the destruction hit. There was a sense of normalcy that had returned, and with it, a sense of purpose.

"What happens when Par-shon attacks?" Tan asked. "What happens when they lose another crossing?"

Roine arched a brow at the question.

"Kaas was their doing. At least, it was theirs as much as it was ours. The ancient shapers thought to breed elementals, forcing them to combine."

"That isn't possible, Tan."

"You've been in the tunnels beneath the city. What do you think they were used for?"

"You told me the ancients harnessed the elementals."

There was a hint within his tone of voice that led Tan to wonder if Roine had considered harnessing the elementals as well. "Harnessing led to other things, worse things. I called it an experiment and had

101

thought that kaas was the only one, but there have been others. The hounds. Probably more. Now Par-shon replicates the mistakes of our past."

Roine stood straighter and turned to Tan. "Mistakes? Look around you, Tannen. All of this, the entirety of the kingdoms, is built upon those mistakes. Think about the life you've been afforded because of those mistakes."

"It's one thing to make mistakes, Roine, but you should learn from them, not make the same one over and over again."

His friend smiled at the comment. "And how is trusting Fur and the lisincend any different? We have tried that once before and failed. We lost many shapers because we believed they were willing to make a real change. If they have truly changed as you say, I am willing to let Incendin prove themselves against Par-shon. Let Incendin be the barrier that keeps our peoples safe."

Tan said nothing. He could think of nothing that would sway Roine, that would convince him that he was not thinking clearly. When it came to Incendin, Roine struggled to look beyond what had happened decades ago, letting it cloud his judgment. Tan wouldn't make the same mistake.

"I will go to Mother," Tan began. "But then you will at least meet with Fur."

"I make no promises. My duty is to the kingdoms."

"As is mine," Tan said.

Roine smiled sadly and shook his head. "Tannen, we both know that yours is more complicated than that."

CHAPTER 12

Into Chenir

FOLLOWING THE SUMMONS took Tan well beyond the Gholund Mountains. He traveled on a fury of lightning mixed with the flash of bright white that always accompanied a shaping of spirit. The summoning rune given to him by Roine vibrated with the rune for wind stamped onto it.

When Tan landed, a wide, rocky plain spread all around him. Tents were spaced with regularity, several hundred in total, and the chaotic sounds of the settlement rang out around him. Someone screamed nearby, and Tan realized that there was the stink of blood and death, mixed with the heat and char of fire shaping. Over all of it was the steady beating of drums, the rhythmic calling that he'd learned was part of the way Chenir had learned to shape.

Chenir was at war.

Tan had expected, at worst, to find Chenir readying for a fight, but this was much more than simply preparing. And if Par-shon had already invaded, the time they had was limited.

He readied a shaping but saw nothing that he could shape. Men and women moved with organized purpose as they hurried between tents, some carrying the injured. A few moved more slowly, with limps or missing limbs, and wore a dazed expression that Tan had seen before. Shapings took place all around him, including one that he recognized.

Tan walked rather than shaping himself through the camp. He didn't want to risk getting attacked by one of the Chenir shapers, though they sounded too preoccupied to worry about a single shaper moving through the camp.

He found his mother sitting on the edge of the expanse of tents. She perched on a shaping of wind, staring out at the Chenir camp. A bruise swelled one of her eyes, but she was otherwise unharmed. Ara and her bonded elemental, Aric, swirled around her loose hair, sending strands of black and gray hair flipping into her face.

"Theondar was not to send you here," she said as he approached.

Tan snorted. "Nice to see you too, Mother."

She relaxed her shaping and landed next to him, crossing her arms over her chest as she did. "The summons was for Theondar, not for you, Tannen."

"And Theondar made a point of sending his Athan."

She took in a quick breath. Tan recognized her frustration, even if her face didn't change. In spite of what had happened between them over the last year, he still knew her well and remembered the agitated way that she could be when she didn't get what she wanted.

"Why did you summon him, Mother? What's happening here?"

Tan took in the tents and the people hurrying through the campsite. He listened to the shapings, recognizing a similarity to what Incendin used within the Fire Fortress. This wasn't an attempt to defeat Par-shon. This was only an attempt to hold them back.

"They're already here," he said.

"Why do you think that I'd summon Theondar?" Zephra snapped.

Tan bit back the sharp retort that came to mind about the closeness he'd seen between Zephra and Roine. That wasn't of his concern. Then he sighed. "Are you going to tell me what you've seen here, or do I have to go and search for answers on my own?"

Her brow furrowed, and for a moment, he thought she might admonish him much as she once did, but now there was a different tension between them. Tan was Athan to Theondar, the king regent. In that, he outranked her.

"Fine. I will show you, and then you will tell Theondar what you saw. After that, you will tell him that he needs to come himself when I summon."

Tan suppressed a laugh and waited for his mother to catch the wind, lifting into the air.

Her shaping swept her away from the camp, taking her north. Tan followed, using wind and a hint of fire to remain aloft. In the past, he'd summoned Honl to assist him, letting the wind elemental carry him. Since Honl's change, the elemental hadn't been as available, but Tan didn't summon him for reasons that were different than just that. Honl was different, and he wasn't certain that the elemental always *wanted* to be summoned. In some ways, Tan suspected that was a good change. It made Honl more independent and confident. In other ways, he missed the ability to call on the wind and draw strength from the elemental to preserve his shaping strength.

Only, that wasn't even necessary anymore. Tan's shaping pulled on the elementals, even when he didn't intend to do so. His ability was so mingled together with the elementals that he often didn't think about whether he was shaping through himself or if he was using elemental power. In that way, he was more like the Utu Tonah than he cared to admit.

They reached a series of small, jagged peaks covered with dark green pine trees that rose toward the clouds. His mother stopped, letting the wind hold her in place. The bitter bite of char and ash mingled with the pine scent. The air stagnated, not gusting as it had closer to the Chenir camp.

"Do you sense anything here?" she asked.

Tan stretched out with earth sensing, mixing spirit with it. The combination allowed him to detect even more than he would otherwise. Wolves prowled in far-off trees but moved away, drifting to the west and south. A few birds lingered, but they too preferred to stay away. There were none of the other creatures he'd expect in a mountainous place like this. The land was empty, almost barren. As if abandoned.

"No," he said. "There is life, but it moves away from here."

"What else has moved away from here?" she asked.

Tan frowned, wishing she would simply get to her point, but that was not his mother's way. Arguing would do no good, especially if she thought that whatever she'd seen was important enough to summon Roine. It would be a risk to call him out of the kingdoms, a risk that the king regent shouldn't take lightly.

Tan listened. He used the skills that his father had taught him long ago, focusing on the way the earth called to him, letting his senses roll away. He was stronger now than he'd been then, his ability with shaping giving him more earth sensing than he'd ever managed when learning with his father. It was during times like these that he missed him the most. He'd never had the chance to see what Tan had become, to learn of the shaper his son had become.

Earth sensing didn't reveal anything more, but maybe that wasn't what his mother intended to show him. Tan shifted his attention, listening now through his elemental senses, straining for water and earth, knowing that the stagnant wind would prevent the elementals from coming through here and that the fire bond hadn't revealed any sign of fire here.

There was nothing.

Even in the most barren land—places like the center of Incendin or the high rocks of Galen—there had been *some* evidence of the elementals, even if it was nothing more than a gust of wind or the heavy sense of the earth elemental. There was nothing here.

This was what his mother had wanted to show him.

"Is this Par-shon?" he asked.

"Some," she said. "Chenir as well. They call the elementals away, thinking that withdrawing them keeps them safe. They do not see the effect of their actions."

Tan found it interesting that his mother would use the term *withdrawing*. When Enya had attempted her attack on Incendin, she had attempted to withdraw fire. Tan hadn't known what that meant at the time, but Asboel had opposed her, preventing her from completing it. That had weakened him, leaving him vulnerable to the Par-shon attack.

Then there was what he'd seen in Doma when Par-shon had trapped the elementals. The landscape had quickly changed, as if without the elementals, the land had died. Did Par-shon know that would happen?

How could they not?

"Why does Chenir pull the elementals away?" he asked.

His mother turned toward him. "They fear for the elementals' safety. They think it better to release the elementals than to risk their capture by Par-shon."

Tan shaped himself forward, moving away from his mother to search the rock around them. The slope gradually made its way higher, and he watched for movement, for anything that would be a sign of others moving along the rock, but he found nothing.

Tan closed his eyes, focusing on what he could of the elementals. Now that he knew they were gone, he strained to determine if he could find any of them. Tan was given the gift of reaching the elementals and speaking to them, but what he needed now was a way of locating them. The fire bond would help him reach elementals of fire, but that wasn't what Tan wanted. He knew that fire had withdrawn. He needed to know about the others and understand where they might have gone.

Would spirit help him reach the other elementals?

Spirit pooled deep within him. When he focused, he could reach for the connection, pull on it, and use it to give him even more strength with his shapings. He'd never attempted to use spirit to help him search for elementals other than how he'd used it in the fire bond.

Tan reached for spirit, while at the same time questing out with a sensing for water, much like he did when he reached for the fire bond. If there was a bond within fire, wouldn't there be something similar with the other elementals? Shouldn't he be able to reach them as well as he reached fire?

Only, he didn't have the same connection to the other elementals that he had with fire.

Could he reach for wind? His bond with Honl was strong, in some ways as strong as the one with Asboel.

Tan shifted his focus, releasing water and grabbing onto his connection to the wind elemental. The sense of Honl drifted in the back of his mind. Tan called to him, trying to make it clear what he wanted from the elemental.

Is there a connection to wind as there is with fire? Tan asked.

The awareness of Honl drifted closer. *Wind is everywhere. Without wind, there is no breath, no life.*

Is wind connected?

You breathe out and another breathes in. That is wind.

The air shimmered faintly with a hint of dark smoke. Honl was here, but he chose not to reveal himself. Tan wondered if Zephra would even recognize him, or if she'd be frightened by the change.

Can I use that to reach for the other elementals?

Why would you search for wind?

I would know if Par-shon has trapped them. I would know if Chenir has pulled them away, Tan answered.

How does that change what you must do? Honl asked.

Tan didn't know if it changed anything about what he needed to do. *Can you come with me?*

Honl coalesced for a moment into a darker cloud. Tan looked past Honl and saw Zephra frowning, her forehead wrinkling as she stared at where Honl had been.

"Return to the camp or the kingdoms. I will see what I can learn and then return."

"I don't think you understand what this means," Zephra said.

"What does it mean, Mother?"

She shaped toward him on a cloud buffered by Aric, her bonded elemental. Zephra moved with tight control as she came toward him. She stopped where Honl had been and studied the air for a moment, sniffing softly in a way that reminded Tan of the lisincend.

"You can shape well, Tannen, but you are not a strong shaper on your own." He arched a brow at the comment and she shrugged. "You have grown stronger with your shaping, but you have always been able to rely on the elementals to assist. If you go out there—"

"I'm bonded to the elementals, Mother."

"And you intend to draw from their strength? Do you really want to risk that without knowing what you'll find?"

He knew that she was right, but he needed to know what Par-shon and Chenir had done, and learn if there was any way to restore the land. "I'll be fine," he said.

Her eyes flickered to where Honl had been. "Then I will go with you."

"Mother—"

"No, Tannen. You often forget the limitations you have, mostly because your limits keep changing. I will not risk you endangering yourself without good reason. I will go with you for this."

Tan considered arguing, but it wouldn't do him any good, not when Zephra got it in her head that she needed to do something.

Distantly, he thought he heard Asboel laughing within his mind. Tan pushed it away.

"Fine, you may come, Zephra, but you will remember that I am the Athan to the king regent."

Her mouth tightened. Tan couldn't tell if it was irritation or amusement that tugged on her face.

CHAPTER 13

Zephra Falls

TAN TRAVELED ON A SHAPING of wind, using fire with it as he flew above the desolate lands of Chenir. He had been within Chenir only one other time, and that had been when kaas had attacked the elementals here, forcing Tan to come. Had he not, how many elementals would have been lost to the twisted one?

And now, the land had changed, partly because Chenir thought to withdraw their elementals. Once green lands had gone brown, leaving everything with a desolate and dreary appearance. Tan sensed nothing moving below, no life and nothing from the elementals that should have called Chenir home.

Honl drifted in a trail of smoke alongside him. Tan made a point of not pulling on his strength, using a shaping of his own rather than anything that was borrowed from the wind elemental. Zephra trailed him.

Is there anything here that you can see? Tan asked Honl.

This land has changed, Tan. There is much lost here.

Was it Par-shon, or is this all the effect of Chenir?

I don't know.

Honl drifted away, more like a smudge of darkness. As he did, Zephra approached and touched Tan's arm. "What happened with your elemental?" she asked.

Tan's breath caught for a moment. "Nothing happened."

"Tannen, I can *see* him. That alone tells me that something changed. More than that, Aric tells me that your elemental is more than only wind now."

More than wind. That was an interesting way of describing what had happened with Honl. "You know that the elemental kaas destroyed other elementals," Tan said. Zephra nodded. "When we were chasing him, trying to keep him from injuring any other elementals, my bonded wind elemental was trapped, pulled toward kaas. As I tried to save him, I had to use spirit and wind. Since then . . . "

Tan didn't know how to finish. How could he explain that since he'd saved Honl, the elemental had seemed less in touch with ashi than he'd been before? How could he explain that now Honl seemed to have insight that he'd lacked before? Or that he could speak, where before he'd only communicated through the bond.

"The bond changes both bonded," Zephra said. "That much is inevitable."

"I don't think it's ever changed the draasin."

"Hasn't it? Don't you think that your draasin acts differently now than he had before you'd bonded?"

"He sees the need to help save the elementals," Tan said.

"That's all that you've done? You might have cleared Doma and tried to free the bonded elementals, but you've done other things that should not matter to the draasin. Without the bond, why else would he assist you when you rescued the Aeta?"

Has the bond changed you? Tan asked Asboel.

The response came distantly but clearly. *There is always change, Maelen.*

And what of you? What of the change within you?

I have learned to appreciate the bond. Once I would not have said the same.

Tan took solace in that.

"And you, Tannen. You have changed more than I ever would have imagined. It's more than your ability to shape. It's what your connection to the elementals has done to you."

Tan frowned, thinking about the implications of what she said. "You were not bonded for most of my life," he realized.

She shook her head. "I've told you how I lost my bond. I wasn't even certain that the wind would answer when I summoned again. It had been so long. Losing that bond the first time . . . It was painful, Tannen. I did not think I would ever want another bond, even if it were possible. Alyia suited me. But Aric . . . " She sighed, and her voice took on a distant note. Her eyes unfocused, as if she were seeing something that only she could see. Likely Aric, though Tan wondered if she was remembering what it had been like for them when they'd lived in Nor. It had been a peaceful time for them all, a peace that had been broken when Tan's father had been summoned to serve along the border and push back an Incendin attack. "Aric suits the person I am now."

Anger at Incendin had filled him for a long time, but he understood now that his anger had been misplaced. Incendin hadn't been the problem. They might have been the reason that his father had died, but they had attacked because they sought to have enough strength to oppose Par-shon. Had Incendin only been willing to ask for help, much might have been different—or maybe it would have changed nothing. There was so much distrust, built over the centuries of Incendin's anger at the splitting of Rens, that could either side have been willing to see that they needed to work together?

Could they find that common ground now?

It is these questions that show how much you have changed, Maelen. They are the same questions that have proven how much I have changed. There was a time I would have destroyed all of what is Incendin for what they have done to the draasin, but I see what you do and can understand the need for restraint.

"When you bonded to Aric, it changed you again," Tan commented.

Zephra's eyes narrowed slightly. "I am your mother, Tannen. The bond has not changed that, nor could it."

Tan wondered what it *had* changed. Since her return, his mother *had* seemed different. He'd never really understood before, but he had never really considered the fact that she had bonded at the same time as the attack that leveled Nor.

More than that, Tan had formed bonds about the same time. First to Amia, and then to Asboel. "You are my mother," Tan said. "And I would see you happy. Whatever—and whoever—it takes."

Tension that he hadn't known was in her face eased, letting some of the hard lines around her eyes soften. "That is all I've ever wanted for you as well."

"When we finally push Par-shon away, maybe we'll both be able to find happiness."

She twirled on the wind holding her, strands of hair coming loose and blowing in her face. "I don't think we can wait to find happiness, Tannen. We face too much already; any chance we have to be happy, we should—"

A blast of lightning struck, sending Zephra tumbling before she could finish.

Tan readied a shaping, drawing it around him, creating a buffer of wind and healing water, readying for whatever had attacked. There was no evidence of another attack.

Honl!

The wind elemental slid toward him on a cloud of dark smoke, materializing into the shape of a man floating alongside Tan. "I saw nothing."

Tan glanced at Zephra, who was sprawled across the ground. Earth sensing told him that she lived, but he didn't know how much time she might have. If he waited to reach her, the shaping that had struck might have been enough to kill her.

Unsheathing his sword, he started toward her, streaking toward the ground with Honl racing along next to him. As he did, he felt the shaping building before he could see anything. Tan changed the angle of his approach, shooting off to his left. The ground exploded beneath where he'd been.

"Can you check on Zephra?" Tan asked.

Honl shifted into nothing more than dark smoke and raced toward her. He stopped right before he reached Zephra and through their bond, Tan could feel pain. There was a barrier around his mother, and even though Honl tried again, he could not penetrate it.

Tan reached the ground barely a dozen paces from his mother. The ground around him swelled as he took his first step. Tan pushed out with a shaping, but he didn't have the strength needed to completely undo the shaping. He reached for elemental strength, but there was only Honl, and if he borrowed from his bonded wind elemental, Honl might be trapped.

Asboel, Tan said. *Can you help?*

The draasin pushed through the bond, lending what strength he could spare. Tan breathed deeply with the borrowed strength from the draasin, letting it fill him, and shaped each of the elements together through the sword, binding them with spirit. When he released them, it came as a violent explosion away from him.

The shaping revealed five Par-shon shapers, but only briefly. Tan didn't have the chance to see how many stolen bonds they carried, but the fact that they were this deep into Chenir meant they would have many, including a powerful bond to earth that obscured them.

Anger surged through Tan. They had attacked Zephra. They had attacked his mother.

Tan unleashed another attack, using the combination of the elements through the sword in a surge of power. The first two shapers disappeared with the flash of light. Their bonded elementals were freed and quickly disappeared.

Assist me, Tan urged, before they had gone too far. He had done the same when fighting Par-shon while in Doma, using the freed elementals to increase his strength.

The call for help didn't work this time. They were drawn away, toward the steady summons of Chenir, leaving Tan facing three more bonded shapers.

Zephra lifted from the ground, shaped by one of their shapers. She started floating away from Tan. If he failed, she might be taken from him. Tan would not lose his mother to Par-shon.

With another combined shaping through the sword, he struck down the nearest remaining shaper. As he turned his attention to the next, fire and wind attacked. Tan caught the shapings with his sword and turned them away, deflecting them into the ground. A series of attacks came quickly, more quickly than a single shaper could manage.

He'd missed others.

"Honl!" Tan cried aloud.

The wind elemental swirled around in a torrent of wind, sending dust and debris flying. Through it, Tan saw nearly a dozen other shapers coming at him from different angles. The shapings were too fast, and he wasn't strong enough to deflect them and still rescue his mother.

Tan managed to stop three more shapers, but still the attacks came, unrelenting. Two more fell to his shapings. Each time, Tan attempted to call the elementals to his aid, but each time they failed, drawn by Chenir, dragged away from where they could help him.

As Zephra was pulled away, she rolled her head toward him and her eyes flickered open. With a knowing glance, she sent a whisper that carried on the wind. "Go," she said.

"No!"

Tan pulled on elemental strength, fighting for power from the bonded elementals. Power flowed into him again, filling him with the elemental strength, and he shaped again and again, loosing the blinding white shapings that struck down one Par-shon after another.

For a moment, Tan thought he might succeed.

But then he felt the shapers take control of their elementals. A shaping started to swirl around him, one that he'd felt before, one meant to separate him from his bonds and his ability to shape.

His mother mouthed another word, sending it across the distance between them. "Go, Tannen. Know that I love you."

Tan spun in place, releasing his deadly shaping at as many as he could, but there were too many. More appeared as he continued to fight, and Tan was only one shaper, and in a place where his advantage had been neutralized. This was not a fight he could win.

Screaming, he used the last of his strength and pulled a traveling shaping. As he did so, he released the last of his energy on the shapers surrounding him, striking at bonds that he couldn't see, determined to free as many elementals as he could before he disappeared.

He felt the surge of the released elementals as his shaping carried him away.

CHAPTER 14

A Call for Water

TAN LANDED BACK IN THE UNIVERSITY yard in a heap. Honl had helped as much as he could, and now swirled around Tan in a protective cloud. Tan sensed him more distantly than he should have, as if something had changed about the bond. He felt a moment of terror, worried that he'd lost his connections, that the Par-shon shapers had somehow managed to sever those connections before he could escape, and strained for Asboel. The sense of the draasin was there, but weakened as well.

There came a series of shouts, and for a while Tan knew nothing more than a jostling series of movements. Each time he opened his eyes, he saw that he was somewhere new. First along the streets, with tall buildings rising up on either side. Then again within a darkened hall. And then with a bright fire blazing in front of him.

Then a hand touched his neck and he smelled Amia's familiar floral scent. "Tan," she whispered to him, leaning into his ear. Her voice was edged with concern that he felt weakly through their bond.

He managed to open his eyes and keep them open so he could look around. He didn't quite know how he'd managed to get into the palace, but he recognized the room. The walls held pictures depicting ancient shapers. Carvings of the elementals were etched into columns. A warm hearth roared with fire, and Tan sensed saa working within the flames.

With each passing moment, he felt his strength returning. The elementals within Ethea restored him, but too slowly, far too slow for him to help his mother.

"What happened?" Amia asked.

Tan licked his lips. "Get Roine," he said, struggling to sit up.

She cupped his face and held him down, not letting him move. "Don't move, Tan. Not yet."

He shook his head and struggled against her. "Amia, I need to reach Roine. He needs to know—"

"Ferran already summoned him, as well as Wallyn."

"Wallyn?" Tan asked. "Why would they summon a water shaper?"

Amia touched him again, running her hands along his cheeks. As she did, he began to understand why everything seemed so distant and faded. Amia shaped him, soothing him.

"How injured am I?" he asked.

Amia held his eyes. "Wallyn will be here soon."

Tan reached for a shaping of spirit, but he was exhausted and it nearly failed. When he managed to hold onto it, he used the shaping to help him understand what had happened to him, questing within himself. He could see what Amia did to him, how she shaped him, easing spirit over him. Without the bond they shared, he wondered if she would have been able to shape him. His spirit shaping normally protected him.

As he did, Tan recognized the injuries. Shapings must have gotten past him. Both legs were hurt, one shattered. His arm was badly damaged. Suppressed pain shrieked in his back. The tiredness he felt might be more from blood loss than from his elemental shaping.

His mother would have seen his injuries. That was why she'd told him to go.

"I need to be healed," he whispered.

Amia ran her fingers though his hair. She fought to suppress the pained look he could see all too clearly. "You need rest, Tan."

A hidden door thundered open and Roine hurried into the room. His gaze seemed to quickly take in the injuries, and he stopped in front of Tan. Ferran followed Roine, the earth shaping he held ready filling him.

"What happened, Tannen?" Roine asked.

The way he said his name reminded Tan of his mother. "They have her, Roine," he said.

Roine's demeanor changed in an instant. His back stiffened and he clenched his hands into tight fists. "Chenir?"

"Par-shon. I found her in Chenir. They're withdrawing the elementals from Chenir, but it places them in even more danger."

"I don't understand. She went to Chenir to secure our agreement. There should have been nothing more."

"Chenir was camped," Tan started. Talking was making him tired and he blinked, letting his eyes drift closed. "I needed to see the effects of what they did when they withdrew their elementals. I told her to return, but she wouldn't. She came with me, and we were attacked."

Tan sagged into the bed and his eyes fell closed. He heard whispered voices around him as he drifted into a dark slumber. When he opened his eyes again, Wallyn had his thick hands on either side of his head. The top of Wallyn's bald head had beaded with sweat.

"Shh, boy," Wallyn soothed.

"That boy is your Athan," Tan heard Roine snap.

Wallyn kept his focus on Tan as he answered. "And he is still a boy, though one with much experience and strength. Even you should see that, Theondar. Like most boys, he forgets that his body has limits. Had he been any other, he might not have survived. I think his youth sustained him when his body would have failed."

"Not my youth. The elementals," Tan said.

His entire body ached, throbbing with a painful intensity that hadn't been there the last time he'd been awake, telling him that Amia's shaping was gone, likely lifted from him so that he could undergo whatever healing that Wallyn felt he needed.

Tan tried to push himself upright, but he found that his arms and legs wouldn't move. He strained again, recognizing bindings of earth wrapped around him, and pulled on the shapings, freeing himself from them.

"Easy," Wallyn warned. "You convulsed during your healing. They were for your safety."

At the mention of convulsions, Tan reached for the bonded elementals, fearing that something had happened to them. Awareness of them came slamming back into him, filling him with the sense of Asboel, Honl, the nymid, and lastly, Amia.

He let out a shaky breath as relief washed over him. "Are you finished?" Tan asked Wallyn.

"This is a complex healing, Athan. You must have patience if you expect to be fully restored."

"I don't have time for patience. Par-shon has Zephra, and I need you to heal me so that I can save her."

"Healing takes time, Athan. You have never suffered anything like this before, so you won't understand. You have much strength with your shaping, but you must trust my experience."

Tan focused on his breathing. Every moment that he delayed, every moment that he simply lay injured, was another moment that Par-shon would have to separate Zephra from her bond. Once separated, he didn't think that she would survive. The last time she'd nearly lost the bond, she had nearly died. Had Tan not been there, she *would* have died. He was not about to lose his mother after she had managed to survive everything else. He was not about to let Roine lose his mother.

"Roine," he said. "Send shapers to Chenir."

Roine stepped into his line of sight. Heavy lines twisted his face, leaving his eyes drawn. "Tannen, we have so few shapers remaining. We can't risk the last of us to save even Zephra."

The pained way that he spoke told Tan how hard those words were to say.

"So she's lost?"

"That was always a possibility. She knew that, Tannen. She understood what she risked by continuing to scout, but she was one of the few who could."

"Cianna can. Ferran too."

"Cianna does," Roine answered. "And Ferran has another task that is more important."

Tan grunted. "The university? If Par-shon reaches the kingdoms, it won't matter that he's rebuilt the university."

"Having trained students will."

"Then let me go," Tan said. "I will do what I can to save her."

Hope flickered through Roine's eyes for a moment, but then faded again. Even Roine thought that Zephra was lost. "Tan, you're too weakened. Trust that Wallyn knows what he's doing. Your injuries will require time to recover and heal."

"Not Wallyn," Tan said.

Roine frowned.

The healer's hands pressed on the sides of Tan's face as he continued his healing.

"I mean no disrespect," Tan said to him. "But Theondar knows that I can be healed by other means."

"You don't know that the nymid will help."

"I'm bonded to the nymid. They will help."

* * * * *

Tan could barely move with his arms bound to his sides and his legs wrapped in shapings of air. Wallyn claimed it was for his safety as they made their way down from the palace into the tunnels beneath the city, but Tan wondered if he was getting even for Tan's request to have the nymid help him.

The air warmed immediately as they descended. Roine led the way and Wallyn followed, letting the king regent hold the shaping that carried Tan down the steps and past the dungeons, finally into the tunnels. Roine had been down here before, but Wallyn had not. With each step, the wide shaper made a worried cough until they reached the solid stone of the path beneath the palace.

"Toward the archives," Tan instructed.

"I remember," Roine said.

He hurried toward the pool that lay halfway between the archives and the door that led up into the palace. Warm water, tinted with the bright green of the nymid, swirled there. Tan could sense the connection to the nymid growing stronger as they came closer. Though it shouldn't, a nagging doubt set in that the nymid wouldn't heal him. They had healed him so many times before that he wondered if the elemental would eventually decide not to.

Roine stopped, lowering Tan to the ground and releasing the bindings of air wrapped around his legs and arms.

"This? You intend to climb into this filthy water?" Wallyn said.

Tan crawled forward, not waiting any longer. The sense of urgency racing through him compelled him forward. Pain jolted through his legs and arms, and his back felt like it was on fire. He wished that Amia had come with him and soothed him with a shaping of spirit, but Roine refused to have her watch the healing.

"This filthy water is nymid," Tan said, reaching the edge of the pool. He stretched his hand into the water, feeling the warmth surge up his arm, and then he tumbled forward.

Wallyn gasped as he disappeared beneath the surface.

Warmth flowed over him, almost as if the nymid mingled with the draasin. Tan was again aware of how all his bonded elementals seemed pulled by fire, as if fire ruled over them all. Yet he knew that was not true. Each of the elements was needed for different reasons, and all were needed for spirit.

Nymid.

He Who is Tan.

Can you heal me?

You would save Zephra.

How could he explain to the nymid that he *had* to save her? If he didn't, Par-shon won. He'd lost so much; he wasn't willing to lose her, too. *She is my mother.*

Water swirled around him for a moment, sending him into a spiral. A green-tinted face appeared out of the water, coming into focus in front of Tan. *You serve the Mother.*

I've done much on behalf of the Mother and will serve still, but I can't serve well until I know that she's safe.

You will find saving her dangerous, He Who is Tan, even for one such as you.

And Roine wouldn't allow him help. Tan understood. Roine *couldn't* allow Tan any help. Doing so risked the safety of the kingdoms. He would have to find a way to do it on his own.

The Mother has seen that you are never alone, He Who is Tan.

There are places where the elementals withdraw. That is how I was injured.

Even in those places, there is life. One such as you can see it returned. The elementals leave by choice.

Is that what you think, He Who is Tan? The Mother would not see her work undone. She would not see the elementals destroyed. You could return them.

And I can't do anything unless I am healed.

Water swirled around him again, leaving Tan spinning. The face reappeared and seemed to smile. *You were healed when you entered water, He Who is Tan.*

Tan realized that he no longer felt the pain racing up his arm and his back, and that his legs felt restored to what they had been. Through his connection to Amia, he sensed her relief. *Can you help? The nymid once provided armor.*

When you serve the Mother, you will have our armor. Go, save Zephra, and serve the Mother.

The water calmed, and Tan remained floating for another moment before surging from the pool on a shaping of water.

Wallyn stared at him, his eyes widening as Tan emerged from the pool. The wide man took a step back and nearly stumbled.

Roine stood fixed in place with his arms crossed over his chest. When Tan came free from the water, he hurried toward him. "Are you . . . " Roine began. "Did it work?"

Tan rested his hands on his legs, taking slow and steady breaths. Water dripped off him and ran back into the pool with the nymid, leaving a sheen of shimmering green coating him. "It worked," he said.

Roine traced a finger over Tan's shirt and pulled it away. He pursed his lips as he studied his finger, his brow furrowing into a tight line.

"Not only healed, though." Roine looked up and watched Tan. "What else did you ask of them?"

"Only what had been given to me in the past. The nymid will keep me safe."

Tan started to make his way down the tunnel. While here, there was something else he needed to see. He would rather Roine and Wallyn not be with him when he went to the draasin, but if they were, he would seal them out.

Roine caught him by the arm and spun him around so they faced each other. "Tannen," he began. The hesitancy in his voice made it clear that he wasn't sure how to say what he needed. "I know that you want to help your mother, but we can't risk losing you. You're the only connection we have to the elementals."

Tan glanced at Wallyn, now crouched in front of the pool where the nymid swam. One arm touched the water, twirling through it, and he lowered his head down toward the surface, inhaling deeply. "I'm not the only connection. Not anymore, at least," Tan said.

Cianna could reach the draasin. Ferran could reach golud. Others within the kingdoms would learn to speak to the elementals. They would have to, or too much would be lost.

Roine squeezed his arm, and he seemed like he wanted to say something more but didn't. Finally, he let go of Tan. "I should be going with you."

"We can't risk your coming," Tan said.

"I hate that. I should be with her. I shouldn't have allowed her to go on her own."

"Would you have been able to stop her?"

"No. That doesn't change the fact that I should have tried. This role—this title—chafes at times." Roine inhaled deeply. His jaw clenched and he touched the sword hanging from his side, briefly gripping the hilt. "Promise me that you'll bring her back safely," he said.

"I will bring back my mother," Tan said, leaving Roine standing in the tunnel with Wallyn still crouched in front of the pool of nymid.

CHAPTER 15

Fading from the Hunt

THE DRAASIN DEN FELT COOLER than the last time Tan had been there. Asboel lay with his head down, his tail curled up and around him, and his chest expanding slowly with each breath. The hatchling, Asgar, lay in front of his father, larger than the last time Tan had seen him, nearly as large now as Enya. There was a fetid odor within the den, and Tan wondered whether it came from the recent hunt or from something else.

Asgar turned as Tan opened the door to the den, making a point of closing it securely behind him and sealing it with a shaping of fire and spirit. Wallyn was still down in the tunnels, and Tan didn't want to risk him accidentally coming upon the draasin. While he didn't necessarily hide the fact that he'd given the draasin permission to use the tunnels as their den, he also didn't want to risk word spreading about it. Too many might grow frightened.

Asboel? Tan asked, reaching through the bond to connect to his friend. The sense of him was distant, as if the injury Tan had sustained had weakened the connection.

Asboel didn't move.

Tan started toward him, but Asgar moved to block him, stepping in front of Tan and keeping him from reaching the other draasin. *What is it?* Tan asked Asgar through the fire bond.

He is unwell.

Asgar's voice sounded deeper than when Tan had last spoken to him, coming through the fire bond more easily. There was still a hint of youthfulness to it, but now he'd taken on more of a confident air than he had before.

Tan reached for Asboel again, straining through the fire bond and the spirit bond between them. As he did, he sensed the slumbering draasin and realized where the odor in the den had come from. The wound to his wing that kaas had inflicted was worse than Tan had realized. It festered, and even with fire burning within him, Asboel was unable to heal from it completely.

How had he missed the extent of the injury? Had Asboel really managed to keep it from him so completely?

Let me see to him, Tan demanded through the fire bond.

Asgar snuffed and a streamer of flame and steam shot from his nostrils, striking harmlessly at Tan. The younger draasin pawed at the ground and shook his head at Tan, who stood his ground, arms crossed over his chest as he waited.

Then Asgar stepped off to the side, giving Tan a chance to make his way to Asboel. When Asgar moved, the stink from the wound filled Tan's nostrils. He had to cover his mouth to keep from gagging, and he forced himself to look at the injury. It had been his fault that Asboel had been there, and his fault that the draasin was injured.

Asboel's eyes opened and he let out a soft breath of warm air. *Maelen, you can be so foolish at times.*

Is it foolish to wish you wouldn't have come to help?

Do you think that you could have restrained me? Asboel stretched out his legs, which moved weakly. *Kaas roamed because of the draasin. The Mother assigned us the task of removing him. In that, I failed her.*

You didn't fail. You helped me.

Yes. Now he sits within the fire bond. Perhaps the Mother knows best after all. Asboel lowered his head again, resting it on the stone. *Soon enough I will sit among her again, and then I can ask.*

Tan swallowed. After everything that Asboel had been through, for him to be injured by another elemental seemed a cruel twist of fate. *Isn't there anything that can be done?* The nymid had healed him; why couldn't they help heal Asboel?

The nymid serve water, not fire.

They healed me.

Because you sit within water. Not as much as with fire, but enough that it matters.

Can Fire heal you?

Asboel snorted something like a sneeze. *Fire burns regardless of me, Maelen. You should know that by now.* His gaze turned to Asgar, who crouched, watching Tan. The younger draasin sat mostly on his hind legs, and his head brushed the top of the den, the long, thick spikes atop his head now scraping at the stone much as Asboel's did. *Fire will not stop burning simply because I no longer do. When my fire snuffs out, another will be kindled. That is how it always has been.*

Asboel—

Do not mourn what is inevitable for us all, Maelen. Each of us rejoins the Mother. Soon it will be my turn.

131

Tan swallowed the lump that formed in his throat. *I would like to have hunted with you one more time.*

As would I, Maelen. Yet I have watched the hunt through your eyes. You have grown much stronger than when I first met you.

I hope that I have been worthy of the bond.

You have served fire better than any shaper who has lived. The Mother chose well for the bond.

I wish that I could have been stronger. Had I known how to restore kaas to fire sooner, you would not have suffered.

And had your ancestors not have forced the others to help, I might not have survived to hunt alongside you. The Mother saw what must be done. I accept her terms, as must you.

Tan rested his hand on Asboel's side, feeling the smooth scale that was so much cooler than it had ever been before. What would happen when he lost Asboel? It wasn't his ability to shape, or his bonded connection to the elemental that he cared about. It was losing his friend that hurt the most.

You are strong, Maelen. You will survive this, as you have survived the hunt so far. And the hunt remains. You must finish the task that the Mother has asked of you.

What the Mother has asked. Tan wasn't sure what that was. Did that mean returning the elementals to Chenir as the nymid suggested, or was there more? Even if he managed to do that, would they be able to keep Par-shon out?

And if I can't?

Asboel shifted his head so that he could fix Tan with a golden-eyed stare. *You will.*

I made a mistake in the last hunt. I nearly died.

But you did not.

I need to return for my mother. The Par-shon bonded have her. They might already have separated her from the wind elemental. I need to stop them.

The nymid have seen that you will not go unarmed.

Tan glanced down and saw the slight glow to the nymid armor that coated him. *I asked for their aid. They protected me once before.*

And did so willingly.

Tan hesitated and heard Asboel's clucking sort of laughter distantly in his mind.

Ask your question, Maelen.

Tan forced a smile. With the connection, likely Asboel knew the question without Tan needing to ask. *How much longer do you have?*

Asboel let out a huff of steam. *If the Mother allows it, long enough to watch you complete the hunt.*

Tan rested his hand on Asboel's side, feeling the heat from the great draasin's side. He hated the change, and what it meant for his friend. Once, he had been terrified of Asboel, scared of the connection between them. Now, he was terrified that he would lose it.

* * * * *

The wind blowing around him was cool and crisp, biting at his flesh. Tan was aware of it as a distant sense, one that left him not uncomfortable at the presence of cold ara. Amia stood next to him, both of them surveying the field where Par-shon had once attacked the Aeta.

"I could come with you," she suggested.

Tan breathed out softly, wishing that were true. For so long, he'd had Amia at his side, the two of them fighting against impossible odds. This time was different. He still wasn't certain that he knew how he'd manage to reach his mother, not without shapers to help. Roine couldn't risk the kingdoms' shapers going with him, and there were no others that Tan dared to ask.

"Your place is with your people," he answered.

She glanced over her shoulder toward the walls of Ethea rising up in the distance. "They are your people too."

He smiled. The bond between them had been formalized, but neither of them truly needed it to prove what the other meant. "They are mine, too," Tan agreed.

"What if you can't reach her?"

"Then I will accept that the Great Mother did not intend for me to reach her. I do not believe that, though."

Amia rested a hand on his arm, holding it as they stood there. "You won't take another with you this time?" She didn't say Cianna's name, but she didn't need to.

"Roine asked that I not."

"That didn't stop you when you went to Doma."

"This is different."

Amia pulled on him. "How? You went to Doma for Elle and you're going into Chenir for your mother. How is this different?"

Tan sighed. "Maybe it's not different. Maybe I only want it to be different."

"I know that she's the only family you have remaining—"

"Not the only family," Tan said.

Amia arched a brow. "You have her and Elle—"

"And you."

Amia smiled and lovingly touched his face. "I would do no different if I could," she said. "I'm not saying that you shouldn't go, only that I wish that I could go with you."

"I almost didn't make it out the last time. I wouldn't have you risk that with me," he said.

"And you will risk it?" Amia asked. "What if you don't make it back? How will I know?"

"You'll always know."

Amia sighed. "And if I don't? What happens then?"

"Then you will support the People. You will be First Mother."

"That's not what I want anymore," Amia said. Her voice caught as she said it.

Tan felt much the same way. Once, the idea of becoming a warrior would have seemed an impossible dream, but now that he was a warrior, now that he could speak with the elementals, all that he wanted was peace. Since discovering his abilities, he'd known nothing but fighting and constant struggles to stay alive. All that he wanted, really, was a chance to simply be with Amia. With every passing day, that seemed less and less likely.

"If we make it through this," Tan began, "maybe then we can have time to ourselves."

"Or maybe Roine will find something else that you need to do," Amia said softly. "I'm not sure his Athan will ever have real peace."

"Then I will have to let someone else serve as Athan," Tan said. "The title doesn't suit me that well anyway."

"I think it fits better than you realize," she said with a laugh.

Tan pulled her into a tight embrace and they stood for a moment with the wind blowing around them, the heavy, earthen scent of rain lingering in it. "Why did you want me to come here with you?" he asked.

"For a request," she said. "With your pull with the king regent—"

"I think you have the same pull."

She smiled and shook her head. "Not the same, and you know it. But with your pull, I was hoping that you could see if Roine would mind if the People remain here."

"I think we know his answer. They have already set up outside the walls," he said. The wagons were only a few miles from here, set in the wide circle they had again established. "Do some of the families want to resume their travels?"

"Some do. Not all, though. Those who want to move on have been convinced of the dangers by the others. I think that in time, that might not be enough. These are people who are accustomed to wandering, to traveling. And now they stay in the same place. Most have adjusted well enough, but there are some who still struggle. They remember what it was like when they were able to travel through places like Vatten and Galen, or even all the way to Doma and Chenir. They remember the challenges of the road, but also the rhythmic way the wagons felt as they slowly lumbered on, the steady creak of the wheels, and the sweat of the horses. The life they have now is not the one that most wanted. But there is safety here, and that is what matters. That's what I would ask of Roine."

Amia eyed the flat clearing. This was where the Aeta had gathered when summoned by the First Mother before her passing, the area where the Aeta had been attacked when Par-shon sought to claim spirit shapers to force the draasin bond. This was where Tan and Amia had begun to be pulled apart.

"And that was the only reason you wanted me out here?" Tan asked.

Amia smiled playfully. "Well, maybe not the only reason," she said and kissed him. For a moment, Tan was able to forget everything that he had to do. For that moment, he was able to find peace.

CHAPTER 16

Return to Chenir

THE EDGE OF THE KINGDOMS flowed into Chenir, the steady swells of mountains rising out of the flat plains of Ter. To the east, Tan could make out the start of Galen, the sweeping slopes of the Gholund Mountains rising high into the sky, leaving the hint of the white-capped peaks that were visible through dark clouds. The ancient nation of Ter spread out to the west, mostly flat and covered with simple grasslands. The wide Bristal River flowed out of the Gholund Mountains and created the border between Chenir and the kingdoms, running out into the sea near Vatten.

Tan hovered above the border, listening for the residual effect of the barrier. As Roine had promised, it had been abandoned. Once, Tan would have sensed the barrier as a vibrating and tingling sense across his skin as he traveled between the kingdoms. When the barrier had first fallen, he had felt it as a residual sense, one that barely registered. Over time, as Roine had rebuilt the barrier using the remaining shapers, Tan had gradually begun to notice it once more. Now, he barely sensed anything. Only the border's presence told Tan where he should listen.

All around him, he sensed the presence of the elementals. When he crossed into Chenir, he expected that sensation to change, especially as the shapers of Chenir used their unique summoning to draw the elementals to them and used that summons to create powerful shapings. How had the kingdoms never known of Chenir's ability with the elementals? How many years had they been partners, trading openly, with none of the kingdoms's shapers ever learning the tricks of Chenir's?

Now that summoning technique placed Tan in danger. If he could convince their Supreme Leader to release the elementals, he might be able to reach his mother. Tan could use the power of the elementals as he rescued her, drawing strength from them. Had the elementals still existed in Chenir, he might have found a way to save his mother rather than nearly dying.

Honl appeared to him, sweeping in on a dark cloud and a warm breath of wind. He stepped out from the cloud with more form than before. Each time, he managed to create features, drawing a sharp nose and thin lips. Deep hollows for his eyes made his face look weary. He even had gradations of color where before there had been none.

"You will return here, Tan?"

Tan focused on what he could sense on the other side of the border. Chenir spread out from him, a vast and mysterious sense. "I have no choice."

"Did you not teach me that there's always a choice? Is this the choice the Mother would have of you?"

"I need to help the elementals," he said.

Honl actually appeared to smile. "That's not the entire reason you go."

Tan sniffed. "No. I can't leave her behind. She's family."

Honl stepped toward him, the wispy smoke form trailing slightly with each step, as if he struggled to maintain his form. Heat radiated from him. "You continue to think so narrowly, Tan."

"Narrowly? I've lost my father and my entire village."

"It seems to me that you have gained more than you've lost."

Tan couldn't argue with that. "Are you here to tell me I shouldn't go?"

Honl tipped his head to the side and raised his hand, almost as if to scratch it. "I don't think I am intended to convince you of one decision or another, only to counsel you."

Tan laughed softly. "Is that your purpose now?"

Honl's smoke shape shimmered a moment. "I have not determined my purpose. There are no others quite like me."

"No, Honl. I think that you are now unique among the elementals." Honl had bonded to Tan to seek understanding, but what he'd gained was something much different than Tan suspected the elemental intended. "Is that where you've been? Have you been searching for your purpose?"

"I have been searching for understanding. I think that my purpose will come as I further my understanding."

"And what have you learned?"

"That you aren't entirely correct, Tan. There are other unique elementals."

Tan's breath caught. He thought of the Utu Tonah and what he knew the leader of Par-shon attempted with the elementals. If he could force them to bond, and then force the crossings, how long until he happened upon something even worse than kaas? Hadn't that elemental been bad enough? Without his ability to reach the fire bond, Tan would not have been able to stop kaas. He didn't think that he could do the same with another elemental, one that didn't use fire. What if there were a forced crossing between air and earth? Tan would have no way to assist the created elemental.

"Similar, but different. They come in such numbers, Tan. The shaping of the Fire Fortress holds them back, but I can see the winds shifting. In time, even that shaping will fall."

"And then what?" Tan asked.

Honl appeared to take a breath. Tan almost laughed at that, considering he was an elemental and one of wind. "Then the Mother's task for you will come to fruition."

Tan shook his head. "I don't know what you mean."

The wind elemental stepped forward, crossing the border. For a moment, he shimmered, as if some lingering effect of the barrier weakened him. "You have been chosen for a purpose, Tan. The Mother asks much of you, but has given much in return. Soon it will be time for you to complete your task."

"How is it that you know so much about my task? I don't even know what I'm meant to do."

"You have always known, Tan. From the very beginning, you have known."

Honl stood in place for a moment and then shifted into a cloud of dark smoke, blowing away from Tan, who stared after the elemental, uncertainty swirling within him. He pulled a shaping of lightning toward him and traveled into Chenir.

* * * * *

The shaping took him into the heart of the country. He let it bring him to where the people of Chenir had camped when he last saw them, and he landed amidst the rock. The landscape around him was barren and dry, with nothing but cracked ground spreading out. Had he not known where he'd traveled, Tan might have assumed that he'd ended up in the wrong place. Devoid of life as it was, it appeared more like Incendin than Chenir.

Tan immediately prepared another shaping. In the time since he'd been here—barely more than a day—so much had changed.

He reached out with earth sensing, straining to determine if there were any Par-shon shapers nearby. His senses gave no sign of anyone around him. Nothing moved. Even the plants that had grown here seemed desolate and dying.

Did Chenir know what it did when they withdrew the elementals? Tan couldn't see how they did not, not with the way that everything changed, but why would they have forsaken the land, abandoning it to Par-shon? Pulling the elementals away from here would not starve Par-shon; it would only weaken those connected to the elementals—people like Tan.

Where had Chenir gone?

Tan shaped earth in an attempt to sense as far out as he could, straining with the effort of it. As he did, he found the first signs of life far to the south, much closer to the kingdoms than he would have expected.

With a traveling shaping, he brought himself there.

The camp that had been orderly and neat was now chaotic. Tents were thrown up in places, but not in the familiar lines he expected. A massive fire burned in one part of the camp, with shapers of fire circling around it, stoking the flames. Earth shapers worked to lift an enormous berm into place, creating a protective rim around the camp. Shouts rang out and mixed with the cries of injured people. Above all was the steady and rhythmic sound of the call to the elementals.

Chenir retreated, and what would happen when they reached the borders? Would they continue to withdraw? Would they think to retreat all the way beyond Chenir and into the kingdoms? As Athan, Tan couldn't allow them to do so, but as one intended to serve the elementals, could he do anything less, especially if it meant that the elementals were safe?

A shaping nearby caused Tan to turn. The tiny water shaper that he'd seen in Ethea stared at him, watching him with an intense gaze. She held a shaping prepared and nearly unleashed it. Tan waited, thinking that the nymid armor would protect him much as his connection to the draasin protected him from fire. Would that change when Asboel passed on? Would Tan find another bond to replace Asboel?

He didn't think that any elemental would be able to replace the connection that he shared with the draasin. And Tan didn't want any to even try. He'd shared so much with Asboel, they had been through so much, that Tan didn't think he could ever have another connection as meaningful as the one that he shared with Asboel. Except, was it the same for his draasin? He had lived much longer than Tan could even fathom. He'd been alive when the ancient shapers still hunted and harnessed the elementals. He'd survived a thousand years frozen beneath the ice. Perhaps the bond wasn't as important to Asboel as it had been to Tan.

"Why are you here, warrior?" she asked.

"You're calling the elementals away from Chenir," he said. "Do you even know what it is that you're doing to your lands?"

She touched a finger to her chin, tapping lightly as she did. The tapping summoned water, much like the heavy drumming called to earth. The fire stoked and blazing would likely be calling fire. He had no sense of the wind. Had Honl been there, Tan might have been able to understand what Chenir did that called to wind.

"You think we don't know? You think that we haven't seen what happens to the elementals if we leave them? The Supreme Leader will not abandon the elementals that way. He would see that we drag them away if needed, but that we see the elementals to safety."

Tan briefly stretched out with an earth sensing. He was able to detect countless elementals around him, with enormous power stored up. This much power would have allowed him to keep his mother safe. It would have let him stop Par-shon and prevent them from taking her from him. And Chenir forced them away.

"Do you really think they are safe this way? If you fall, what happens to the elementals that you've summoned? Leaving them free would give them a chance. Now?" Tan wondered how what Chenir did with the elementals was different than what Par-shon attempted. "Now you have forced them away from safety and away from their lands."

The water shaper ran a finger through her black hair. Her other hand adjusted the heavy wool jacket she wore. Both hands continued to tap, giving her a constant sense of movement. "Have you ever had to sit by, watching as the great strength of your home is torn away, forced to bond and fight against you? Have you ever experienced that, Warrior?"

"I've felt the pain of my bonds separated from me when Par-shon tried stealing the draasin bond."

Her eyes widened for a moment, and then she turned toward the fire blazing to the side of the camp. "You are outside the kingdoms, Warrior. Why is it that you've come?"

"Zephra was captured. And the elementals of these lands suffer."

She frowned. "When Zephra didn't return, we suspected that something had happened. Then the wind no longer gusted as it had with her presence." She turned back toward Tan. "We don't command the wind with the same strength as Zephra. She was able to help and gave us a chance to escape."

"Zephra was aiding your retreat?" Why hadn't his mother told him what she'd been doing?

"Zephra was helping. She said the borders were open."

Tan wondered if Roine knew what his mother had promised. For Chenir to retreat all the way back to the kingdoms would put everyone at risk, unless the retreat was part of his plan. Had Roine *asked* Zephra to help? Was that the real reason that the barrier had been lowered? If so, when did Roine intend to raise it again? Would it even matter to Par-shon? They had already attacked within the borders of the kingdoms, but the barrier had been weak, barely anything. If Roine could raise the barrier with Chenir and her elementals on the other side, could the kingdoms mount a defense?

Was that what Roine had wanted him to see when he sent Tan to help Zephra?

He didn't know. But Roine didn't know what happened to Chenir as the elementals were withdrawn. He would not have seen the way the lands changed, much like Roine had not seen what had nearly happened in Doma when the elementals had been trapped. Tan began to suspect that it would be like that anywhere Par-shon visited, tearing away that which was meant to be a part of the land.

"Par-shon attacked when she showed me," Tan said softly. "I wasn't able to stop the attack." The memory of what she had whispered to him was burned into his mind.

"Why have you returned?"

Tan reached for his sword and felt the solid and reassuring grip of the hilt. He squeezed it briefly, thinking of what he intended. Would Chenir try to stop him? He didn't understand enough about their plans for him to really resist, but what if rescuing his mother put what they intended in danger? What if Chenir thought to prevent Tan from trying to reach Zephra? He didn't dare risk delaying any longer, but he also couldn't risk fighting his way free.

"I've come to restore your elementals," he started, feeling the power of the rhythmic calling that Chenir's shapers used. Would he be able to counter that? "And I've come to rescue Zephra."

The woman laughed, a soft and fluid sound. "You think that one shaper can survive against Par-shon?"

Tan didn't know, but he'd done it before. Maybe not against the might that Par-shon now had on the shores of Chenir, but he'd faced Par-shon enough times that he wasn't going in unprepared.

The only problem was that he needed the elementals to help. Always before, Tan had been able to call to the other elementals, to draw on the strength that they could lend him, granting him enough strength that he was able to oppose Par-shon, but the way that Chenir had withdrawn the elementals from the land, leaving it barren, Tan wasn't as certain that he had the strength that he needed. He might be able to shape, but how was that any different than what any of the bonded Par-shon shapers could do? Without his connection to the elementals, Tan's ability wouldn't be enough to survive.

"You need to release the elementals," he said to her. "Let them return to the land. I will do what I can to oppose Par-shon."

She laughed again, this time pointing out and into Chenir. "You might be powerful, warrior, and the Great Mother knows that I saw how you attacked the elemental, but even you cannot stare down the might of Par-shon alone."

"Not alone. I will work with the elementals."

"The elementals will not be released."

Tan turned to see Tolstan Vreth, the Supreme Leader of Chenir, standing behind him. He wore a long wool jacket embroidered with the crest of Chenir, and loose-fitting pants that did nothing to hide his muscular frame. The shaping he held pressed upon Tan's ears, leaving pressure in his head. One hand tapped his thigh while the other hand drummed across his abdomen. Tan hadn't learned whether the movements and the rhythm would also allow them to use the strength of the elementals, or if they could simply summon them.

He bowed his head slightly, keeping his eyes on the Supreme Leader. "You understand what you're doing here?" Tan asked. "You see what happens to Chenir when you draw away the elementals?"

"I will not allow Par-shon to harm them, Athan. More than anyone else, you should understand how important it is to protect them."

Tan considered what he'd sensed in Chenir when he'd stood on the empty expanse of land. "What you're doing doesn't protect them," he said.

The Supreme Leader's eyes narrowed. "You are not of Chenir, Athan. You cannot understand."

"And you don't speak to the elementals."

The Supreme Leader stared at him and said nothing. His shaping built, continuing to call to the elementals.

"You won't help?" Tan asked.

He shook his head. "Theondar has promised safety were we to need it."

"You're withdrawing into the kingdoms?" Tan didn't know what would happen to the elementals of the kingdoms once those of Chenir appeared. Would it even matter to them? But he knew that it did. The elementals migrated over time, but doing so changed them. Would those of the kingdoms change as well? Would Chenir's elementals change?

"We do what is necessary to keep our people and the lands safe."

"You could fight Par-shon—"

The Supreme Leader cut him off with a wave of his hand, gesturing to the camp around them. "Do you hear these sounds, Athan? Can you hear the cries of my people? We are a hardy folk, but there are limits.

To keep my people safe, I am willing to retreat. I am willing to give up our homeland, if it means my people will survive."

Tan wanted to ask what would happen when Par-shon crossed over into the kingdoms. He wanted to know whether Chenir would fight then. But he didn't. The pain on the Supreme Leader's face was too much.

"How many have you lost?" Tan asked.

"Chenir is not a large nation, not by the standards of the kingdoms, and now we are a tenth of what we had been."

Tan surveyed the camp, trying to take a count of how many people were there. Through his earth sensing, he detected nearly five thousand camped along the rocks, but if what the Supreme Leader said was true, far more had been lost.

With so many gone, wouldn't he do the same in the Supreme Leader's position? Wouldn't he fall back and try to find a way to safety?

And with so many dead, how did Tan expect to reach his mother? Why could he succeed when so many had failed?

Tan didn't think that he could. Not against the might of Par-shon, and not with the lands as barren as they were, devoid of elementals that could help. He could try to overpower the Chenir summons and try to force the elementals to ignore Chenir, but doing so would weaken these people even more. Already they had lost so much.

But if he couldn't reach the elementals, then his mother was truly gone. Worse than that, though, all of Chenir would be lost.

Had Par-shon already won?

CHAPTER 17

A Plan for Rescue

WITH A SHAPING THAT WAS MORE WIND and fire than anything else, Tan traveled away from Chenir as he tried to think about what he should do. The shaping brought him to the south, floating above Galen, and then even farther. As he traveled, he had the sense that he was drawn on his shaping, pulled along in a way that he had not been since he'd first encountered the nymid.

Tan let the shaping be guided, wondering where it would pull him. As he veered farther east, he wasn't surprised to realize that he made his way toward Doma.

Taking control of the shaping, Tan focused on guiding himself beyond the mountains, along the border with Incendin. Once within Doma, a distant voice began calling in the back of his mind, and he added earth and water to the shaping already carrying him and traveled with a burst toward Falsheim.

Tan landed outside the city. Massive walls surrounded Falsheim, with only the slate-covered roofs visible above them. Dark scorch marks stained parts of them, a reminder of the Par-shon attack. Tan wondered if those marks would ever be removed or if they should remain, a reminder of what had happened to Doma.

Soldiers patrolled atop the wall, several along each section. Tan felt them shaping, most pulling on water. He used earth to mask himself to them, not wanting to risk an attack.

Falsheim was not accustomed to warrior shapers and had no traveling circle for him to use, so he didn't want to simply appear in the midst of the city and risk further damaging already fragile buildings. The Par-shon attack had left Falsheim in nearly as bad a shape as Ethea had been in when attacked by the lisincend. Tan's arrival the last time had leveled other parts of the city, leaving entire buildings destroyed. He would not repeat that if he could help it.

Three stunted trees rose along a wide river leading into the city. Near the trees, Tan found his cousin. She wore a plain white cotton dress and had her long brown hair pinned behind her ears. One hand tapped on her arm and reminded him of the Chenir shapers summoning water.

"It took you long enough," she said, stepping toward him. She moved fluidly, sliding across the ground. A shimmery mist sprayed up from the river and followed her.

Tan suppressed a laugh and released the earth shaping that obscured him. "It's good to see you, too."

"You don't listen anymore, do you, Tan?" she asked.

"I listen just fine."

Elle started toward the city, waving for him to follow. "Zephra tells me that your draasin is injured."

"You've spoken to my mother?"

Elle looked over her shoulder, a frown pursing her lips. "Zephra is of Doma. She has not forgotten that."

Tan wondered what that meant. She might have grown up within Doma, but she'd learned at the university and had spent her entire life serving the kingdoms. By that measure, it made her more of the kingdoms than of Doma.

"You didn't think that you could ask for healing?" Elle asked.

She paused, both of them looking out to sea, and Tan realized what she wanted to show him. The sea arced around Doma as it jutted into the ocean, surrounding the entire nation with water. From the maps Tan had seen, Doma had once been much larger, but had changed over time. Whether that was something the kingdoms had done as they claimed land from the sea, or whether it was due to natural erosion, Doma was much smaller now.

Their shapers were still powerful. Tan had never realized quite how powerful they were, and he wondered how much of it was because the elementals had been freed from the Par-shon bonds. Tan sensed the shaping, but he didn't need to be a water shaper to know what they did and why Par-shon had left Doma alone since Tan had freed them. Much like what the lisincend did with their shaping of fire, Doma and their water shapers now did with water, creating massive waves that washed *away* from the city. The effect of the shaping created a driving sense out and away from Falsheim.

"Did they learn that from Incendin?" he asked.

Elle's eyes narrowed slightly. As a child, she'd lost her home to Incendin. In that, she and Tan shared much. "Incendin can be a harsh instructor, but our people learn," she said.

Tan wondered what the shaping did. Incendin had changed in some ways as their shapers pressed out and away from their shores with their shaping of fire; would it be the same with Doma? And now

Chenir, pulling their elementals *back*. It had definitely changed the lands.

Elle motioned for him to follow, and they circled around before reaching the wall. She guided him toward a small hidden door along one side. With a shaping of water—more tightly controlled than even the last time he'd seen her—the door came open. Once inside, Elle shaped the door closed again, sealing it.

Tan studied what she'd done. He might be able to repeat the shaping, but even that wasn't guaranteed. Elle had learned exquisite control over water in a short period of time. "Did you learn from your water shapers or the elemental?" he asked.

She crossed her arms over her chest. "You're surprised that I can shape water?"

Tan ran his fingers across the invisible seams of the door. He could sense where it was, but had he not known, he doubted he would have managed to find it. "Not surprised that you shape, but impressed with your skill." He turned back to her. "You might be more talented than most of the kingdoms' water shapers now."

Elle tipped her head, the slight crease to her brow making it appear that she listened to some distant voice. Likely she spoke to her water elemental. The elemental that Elle had bonded was different than udilm, different even than the nymid, yet there was power to what she did, and a strength to the elemental that few would have once believed.

"Whatever skill I have comes from the fact that I listen," she said.

Tan smiled. Asboel had once said the same about him. "It's that way with fire for me. There aren't many shapers with my skill." He wasn't boasting, but it still felt strange to admit. "The other elements don't come quite as naturally."

Elle's face relaxed, the lines around her mouth softening. "I can try to help, Tan. With healing, that is."

She led him down the narrow streets and veered onto a side street that was slicked with water and coated with a brackish grime, as if the sea had managed to overflow the walls and spray along this street. Elle moved quickly along the street.

"I don't think there's anything that you can do," he said, keeping pace with her. "The nymid have already attempted to heal him, but even they can't do anything more than what has been done. It's delayed now, but in time, he will move on and return to the Great Mother."

Elle paused as she sucked in a quick breath. "The nymid might have attempted, but perhaps masyn can succeed where they failed."

Tan doubted that another elemental would be any more capable than the nymid, but he nodded anyway. "Why did you summon me here?" Tan asked.

"Because you're needed, Tan. Why else would I summon you?"

They stopped at a small building with a door made of oiled wood. A sloped roof hung over the edge, leaving the door covered and protected from the wind and rain, but still the door had a weathered appearance, the wood faded and chipped in places. Corrosion and a thin green film, much like that on the street, coated the handle. Elle pushed the door open and motioned for Tan to follow.

The other side of the door led into a small room. Inside was a long bench, a chest with the top thrown back to reveal stacks of clothing, and a simple shelf lined with books. A vase with cut flowers tucked within gave off a sweet floral aroma, covering the musty odor that seemed so prevalent within Falsheim.

"This is your home?" he asked.

"This is where I stay," she answered. "Home is all of Doma." She said the last with more force than Tan would have expected, but then she smiled.

Tan took a seat on the bench and scanned the shelf, curious what books Elle found appealing these days. When she'd been in the university,

she'd focused mostly on the elementals, taking texts that would reveal anything that might be useful to her so that she could learn shaping. But she'd
never really managed to learn to shape while in the university. She hadn't
learned how to reach the elementals, either. All that had happened since
the udilm had restored her, bringing her to water. He still found it surprising that she hadn't bonded one of the udilm, but rather an elemental that
Tan had never before heard of.

"Elle," Tan began, "Zephra was taken. Par-shon has her." And there
might not be anything that he could do to reach her. There might not
be anything he could do to stop Par-shon.

Elle nodded. "I know."

"You know? How?"

Elle took a seat next to him. This close, her skin was cool and clam-
my, leaving her dress damp. "Water speaks to me, Tan. Water flows
through everything. It is life."

Tan wished he understood which elemental really was the source
of life. From speaking to the elementals, each felt that *they* were the
source of life. Maybe that was the answer. Maybe they were all needed
for life.

"What does that have to do with knowing what happened to
Zephra?" he asked.

Elle tapped his chest painfully and Tan pulled back. "You think you
are the only one with any talent, Tannen Minden?" she asked. "You
are skilled with fire, and you can use the other elements, but you can
sometimes be obtuse."

"Elle," he began slowly, not wanting to upset her again. Elle had a
temper. He'd seen that when he first got to know her when they were
both at the university, but since then, he didn't really know her. Like
him, she'd changed much. Whatever she'd gone through had made her
stronger and more independent. "Can you find my mother?"

"Why else would I have called you here?" she asked.

Tan shook his head. "I don't really know, to be honest. And I don't think that I have much time to find her. They might already have stripped her bond from her. If they managed to do that . . . " Tan didn't want to finish. He couldn't think of what would have happened to his mother if they'd managed to tear her bond away, or whether she could even survive it.

Elle closed her eyes and tipped her head to the side. "The bond remains," she said. "I don't know how, and neither does masyn, but the bond is intact."

Tan sat upright and caught Elle's wrist, pulling her around so that she faced him. How could the bond still be in place? Could it be that Par-shon didn't want to separate the bond, or was there something more to it? Had the healing changed something about the bond? "Wait, are you able to sense her *now*?"

"That's why you're here, isn't it?"

"I don't really know *why* I'm here, but if you know where my mother is, I need to reach her."

"You can't. At least, not easily."

Tan sat back, letting out a frustrated breath. "How can you sense her?"

Elle smiled and laughed to herself. "Par-shon doesn't even know that masyn exists. They think all of water is udilm or the nymid."

"But they've bonded to water. How could they not know?"

"I think it's their way of resisting. Water doesn't like the bond, Tan. They do all that they can to resist, but there's only so much that *can* be done."

Tan suppressed the surge of excitement within him. How many elementals were like masyn; how many would Par-shon not know about? Tan remembered what he'd seen of the Utu Tonah, the way that he'd been so heavily bonded that it seemed impossible for him to not know of any elemental, but would Tan have thought to look in the mist for elemental power? Would *he* have known, if not for Elle?

Possibly, he had to admit. His connection to the elementals gave him a different understanding, one that the Utu Tonah could never know. And somehow, he would have to use that to stop the Utu Tonah. Only, Tan didn't know how he would be able to do that.

"Can you tell me where she is?" he asked. If he only knew that, he might be able to figure out some way to reach her.

Elle grabbed a book from the shelf and flipped it open, folding out a page inside it to reveal a carefully drawn map. Doma was large on the map, leaving Incendin and the kingdoms depicted much smaller to the west and the south. Only Chenir rivaled Doma in scale.

"There's something wrong in Chenir," Elle said, pointing to the map. "Masyn tells me that this part"—she motioned to an area along the middle of the country—"has changed. I'm not really able to understand why. Par-shon controls the rest. If not for udilm and our shapers, I think that Doma might have been attacked again."

Tan wasn't sure that it was the Doma shapers that kept her people safe, or whether it was some residual effect of Incendin's shaping. That shaping was powerful and pushed away the other elementals. In that way, it was probably much like how Chenir called the elementals away.

He hadn't really considered it that way before, but it made sense now that Incendin would be as barren as it was. If they used shapings as they did, if they were forced to push away elementals, then they *would* end up much like Chenir with the elementals withdrawn. It wasn't quite the same; Incendin still had elementals, but he wondered if that difference was due more to the fact that they used fire in their shapings, and thus allowed the fire elementals to remain.

They were questions for scholars, and Tan wasn't one. He barely had time to understand the elementals well enough to help them. And now he had to find some way to reach his mother, and rescue her, before Par-shon stole the bond from her.

He studied the borders, noting the mountains that separated the kingdoms from Chenir, as well as Incendin from Chenir, effectively isolating the entire country. Doma shared a flat piece of border that he'd never visited, but the map claimed that it was mostly swampland between Doma and Chenir, making that way more difficult to traverse.

"Chenir has retreated to here," Tan said, pointing to the map.

They were much closer to the border with the kingdoms than he had realized. They would still need to pass through the mountains, and doing so would be difficult, but Tan figured that with shapers helping—and possibly the elementals that were called away from the land—they had only another week or two before Chenir reached the kingdoms. How much longer before Par-shon's attack moved beyond Chenir? How much longer before they attacked Doma again?

"Why have they retreated so far?" Elle asked.

"They're pulling back, calling the elementals with them," he answered. "Think of what Doma was like when Par-shon invaded. Do you remember how your land changed as the elementals were taken from you? It's much the same in Chenir, only they are calling *all* of the elementals away as they retreat into the kingdoms."

"They think the barrier will protect them and the elementals?" Elle asked.

She had a quick mind and had picked up on what Chenir intended faster than Tan. "That's what they think," he answered. "But once they retreat, their lands are lost and the elementals will change."

Elle tapped a point on the map and made a circle with her finger. "All of this is Par-shon. They have countless elementals bonded here,

Tan, more than even masyn can report. I can't even tell you how many people are there, only that it's more than when Par-shon attacked Doma." She looked up at him, her eyes reddened. "I know that you want to save your mother, but I don't think there's any way that you can even reach her."

Tan sighed, understanding what Elle said. "Without the elementals, there's not much that I can do. I won't be strong enough otherwise."

There was a knock on the door, and Elle pulled it open. Vel stood on the other side. Dressed now in a dark green jacket with his gray hair slicked back, he looked different than the last time Tan had seen him. The madness in his eyes was gone, leaving them clear and bright. He pulled on the hem of his jacket as he stepped across the threshold and into the house.

"You've told him about Zephra?" Vel asked her.

"He knew that she was captured."

"Then you've shown him where she is?"

Elle nodded.

"You need to find some way to reach her, Tan," Vel said.

"I was with her when she was captured. I nearly died, and without the nymid, I might have. I don't know that there is any way that I can reach her."

Vel stopped and leaned toward Tan. "There's a way that you haven't considered," he said. "You might be the only one who can use it."

"I can't use the artifact, Vel. It's not meant for—"

"You don't *know* what it was meant to be used for. You've seen it used by Althem, but do you really think that someone like him was ever meant to control power like that?"

"No one is meant to control power like that," Tan said. "There's a reason the ancients hid it. I think they discovered just how dangerous it was and made certain that no one could use it. That might be the

157

only good thing that they did." He said the last bitterly, thinking of how much his ancestors had betrayed the elementals.

Vel moved back and leaned against the wall. He rubbed one hand across his head and his mouth pursed. "You think that the ancients knew so little that they didn't intend their device to be used?" he asked.

Tan faced Vel. "I've seen what the ancients knew, Vel. I have seen the way that they sought to harness the elementals, the experiments they worked when they crossed the elementals. It's because of them that we had creatures like kaas or the hounds."

Vel stiffened and stood away from the wall. "What do you mean by the hounds?"

Tan sighed. "They're elementals of earth and fire. They're like kaas in that, but more of earth than fire. I've done what I can to restore them and bring them into the fire bond. It's changed them, I think."

Vel glanced at Elle. "Did you know of this?"

"I only knew of Zephra. I hadn't had the chance to talk to him about the other yet."

"What other?" Tan asked.

Vel tapped on Tan's shoulder and started toward the door. "Come on, Tannen. For this, I must show you."

CHAPTER 18

An Ancient Connection

TAN FOLLOWED VEL OUTSIDE the city, where he used a shaping of water to fly above the land, much like the Par-shon shapers. Even Elle managed to shape the same way, practically gliding across the sky, using a shaping of pure mist that glistened in the air. Tan thought that he could do something similar, but it might take a deeper connection to water than he possessed. The nymid might help, but he wasn't sure that he could use them in the same way that true water shapers managed. Tan could use fire and wind to fly, and he could travel on warrior shapings that combined each of the elements, but using only a single element like water would be difficult.

They stopped to the north, and Vel pointed into the distance. From Elle's map, Chenir would be beyond the wide swamp. Vel hung as if suspended above the ground, his feet sliding above the surface of the water. Elle used her shaping of mist to stay in place.

"What is it?" Tan asked.

"Don't you sense them?" Vel asked. "Can't you see them?"

Tan wished that Asboel could be with him, that he could use the draasin's sight to see where Vel pointed. As he did, he realized that he hadn't heard Asboel's voice in his head since leaving Ethea. The draasin was weakened and sick, but Tan prayed that they still had time together. He needed the chance to help Asboel hunt once more, even if he had to shape the wind to allow the draasin to float above the ground. His friend deserved that much.

"I don't see anything," he said, stretching out with an earth sensing, reaching away from him, straining to determine what Vel might have noticed. Earth focused strangely here, and Tan didn't quite know why. He added water to the sensing, calling to the nymid, and felt the draw of the water, suddenly aware of much more than himself.

Fire burned across the swamp.

Tan released his sensing. Reaching for the fire bond, he quested out. What elemental was out there? It wasn't the draasin. Cora remained in Incendin, and as far as Tan knew, Cianna was still within the kingdoms. Both would keep their draasin close by.

The hounds. He sensed a pack, each pulling on the fire bond. There was one that was not, and the others trailed it.

Tan shaped himself toward the hounds.

Lightning brought him to the ground on the other side of the swamp. He sensed the water spreading out behind him, and could vaguely detect Elle and Vel following him on their shapings. The hounds clustered around another, as if seeking to contain another hound. As Tan appeared, one of the hounds turned his attention to Tan and briefly flashed his fangs.

Tan kept himself in the air to stay away from a possible attack. Unsheathing his sword, he focused on the hound still outside the fire bond and pulled on the shaping of earth and fire that was needed to bring it back. As he dragged on the shaping, pulling with incredible effort, he found the hounds granting him their strength. When the hound was brought into the fire bond, there was a flash of light and a surge of spirit.

He sagged, dropping to the ground, the shaping that had been holding him aloft failing.

One of the hounds bounded toward him. A shaping of water built from behind him with incredible strength. Tan turned and saw Vel hovering over the ground, readying to attack the approaching hound.

"No!" Tan shouted, diving toward the hound as Vel unleashed his shaping.

A powerful burst of water struck him and deflected off the nymid armor. The force of it sent Tan spinning, spiraling away from the hound and sprawling in the middle of the collected pack. Tan lay in place for a moment, staring upward and trying to clear the ringing in his head. Fire flared around him as flashes of light.

He struggled to sit, and as he did, one of the hounds crouched in front of him. The creature was massive, larger than any other Tan had seen, and radiated a sense of size. Tan quested toward it with a sensing, cautiously wanting to ensure that the hound had been healed, brought back into the fire bond. The connection was there, blazing with fire, but also with the heavy rumbling weight that he'd associated with earth.

Vel dropped next to Tan, holding a powerful shaping at the ready. Above Vel, Tan sensed Elle waiting, careful not to approach too closely. "Get up," Vel urged.

"Vel, I told you that they're elementals."

"I saw the way that creature attacked you."

Tan rubbed at his temples, trying to clear the throbbing in his mind. He considered asking Vel to heal him. The water shaper would be able to find some way to clear the pain, but seeing the tension in his body and the way his jaw clenched as he spun in place, Tan wasn't sure that Vel was in any mindset to try to heal him.

He used a shaping of earth to stand and took a moment to steady himself. The large hound still sat in place, watching him. The others circled around them. It took Tan a moment, but he realized that he'd seen the enormous hound before. She was the same one that had followed him out of Incendin and then tracked him toward Ethea.

You've gotten bigger, Tan said to her.

Her lip curled and she flashed a mouthful of sharp teeth. *This form changes.*

She sounded like a deep rumbling, like that of an earthquake rolling downhill, mixed with a steady hiss of steam. It was a unique sound, a voice unlike anything Tan had ever heard before.

You have formed a pack. When he'd last seen her, she had been alone, but the hounds had always been found in packs. Tan wondered if that much had stayed the same, connected to whatever crossing had created the hounds.

We have formed a family.

A family?

Is that not what your female called her grouping?

Tan tensed. Next to him, he sensed Vel doing the same. The shaping he held continued to build. Tan rested a hand on his arm. "Easy, Vel. I will take care of this."

"I saw how you were nearly taken care of, Tan. Come. This was not what I wanted to show you."

Tan frowned. If not the hounds, then what had Vel intended for him to see?

What else could there have been that Vel needed him to see? The hounds would have caught his attention, unless there was something else that Vel feared. Whatever it was would have to wait.

You followed us? Tan asked her.

You are an interesting creature.

Tan almost laughed, but doing so would probably upset Vel. The water shaper already seemed to struggle with what he was seeing. How would he react to Tan laughing about the hounds?

Why have you come here? Tan asked.

For one of the Lost. The hound turned toward the one that Tan had healed.

You came to claim him?

The Lost are not to blame for what happened.

Did you know that I would come?

The hound growled, the sound deeper than any animal that Tan had ever heard. *The Mother knew that you would come.*

Tan wondered how much the Great Mother really influenced what happened, and how much was chance. *What will you do now?*

We hunt.

The hound held Tan's gaze for another moment, and then she loped off, the others following behind her. She moved quickly, disappearing into the swamp. Tan watched for a moment, uncertain what to do, and then finally faced Vel.

"What was that?" Vel asked. His voice took on a high-pitched quality, leaving him sounding slightly panicked. "You said the hounds were elementals, but that is no hound—"

Tan squeezed the hilt of his sword, briefly drawing a shaping of earth, letting it quest out from him so that he could sense the pack. They had moved away, but one remained nearby, just beyond a circle where Tan could easily detect her. Without his connection to earth and fire, he might not have been able to. She waited, as if lingering to see what Tan and the others would do.

"The hounds are different now. The return to fire has changed them."

"Changed?" Vel asked. His voice settled, but the panicked expression in his eyes, one that reminded Tan of how he'd appeared when he'd been rescued from Par-shon, remained. "How did they get so big?"

"Earth, I think," Elle said, lowering to the ground on a shaping augmented by a shimmery spray. "I feel something deep and vast to them. I've never known anything quite like it."

"Like I said, they are earth and fire."

"How? The hounds aren't new creations. They've been around for as long as Doma!"

Tan closed his eyes and sighed. "Blame the kingdoms. The shapers from long ago thought they could experiment on the elementals. These experiments led to creatures like kaas, and to the hounds, creatures that have not managed to reach fire."

"I've been chased by hounds, Tan. I know how the hounds use fire," Vel said.

"Not true fire. What they did was twisted, like the lisincend. And like the lisincend, they've been restored to the fire bond. I hadn't expected the hounds to be elementals. It makes a certain sort of sense, though." He turned to Elle. "This wasn't what you wanted me to see?"

She glanced past him to Vel. "Not this. I don't think that Vel knew about the hounds," she said.

"Vel didn't, but did you?" Tan asked.

Elle wouldn't meet his eyes. "I knew there was something different to them. They've never moved beyond the borders of Incendin without the lisincend before. Over the last few days, I've detected them moving, mostly to the north. Some have remained in Incendin, but . . . "

Tan wondered what it meant that the hounds had been moving toward Chenir. Were they answering the summons that the Chenir shapers were sending to the elementals, or was it something else?

"If it wasn't the hounds, then what is it, Vel?" Tan asked. "You wanted to bring me here."

Vel shook his head and smoothed his hands down his jacket. One corner of his eye twitched slightly and he sucked in a quick breath, his attention turned in the direction the hounds had gone. "You traveled too far, Tan. This was not what I needed to show you. The hounds . . . well, I didn't know they were there. Elle is more skilled with things like that, you know. My talents are different."

Vel shaped himself aloft again and started toward the swamp.

Elle's brow creased as she watched him disappear. "He still struggles with this bond. I think udilm claimed him again, but something about it is different."

"It's the same for Cora," Tan said. "She had bonded to saldam, but when the draasin needed bonding, she claimed it. I don't think it's the same."

Elle tipped her head, shaping herself after Vel. Tan followed, moving quickly on a shaping of wind and air. He added a hint of earth to it and felt a slight connection through the earth shaping to the hound still watching him. How long would she stay there after him?

"Zephra had bonded before," Elle noted.

"But she had my entire life between one bond and the next. That might be a difference. Even that is challenging for her, I think. Wind reacts differently to her. *She* is different."

Elle nodded to herself. "Maybe that's all it is. The bond changes the shaper, so maybe that's all I'm seeing."

"You're worried about him."

Elle glanced over. Wind pulled on her dress, letting it flap as she made her way after Vel. It was a cool breeze, one that had more dampness than any found in the kingdoms, almost as if the air itself was filled with water. Tan recognized the wind then, understanding that it was a different elemental, that wyln blew through Doma.

"I'm worried how he's handling the change," Elle admitted. "You've told me about Cora, and Amia shared how difficult the healing had been, but I don't remember you telling me anything about Vel."

Tan considered sharing with Elle how Vel had reacted when released from Par-shon. He had attacked the Par-shon shapers with a sort of unrestrained joy, and had a dangerous glee to him as he had done so. But without his help, Tan wasn't sure that he would have escaped.

"Vel didn't need the same type of healing as Cora," he said. "At least we were able to help her. Our healers have barely been able to do much for Theran." The third bonded shaper that he'd rescued from Par-shon had been entirely silent since the rescue, only answering when asked his name. None recognized it so far.

"You never asked for my help," she said. There was an edge of hurt in her words.

"You've been busy with helping Doma. And the kingdoms have water shapers, Elle. They might not have the same connection to the elementals—"

"You do."

Tan shrugged and went on, "But they are skilled healers. Besides, I think it's more like what happened with Cora. The healing needed is something more than simply of the body, but of the mind."

"And Amia?"

"She's tried, but with her new responsibilities, there is only so much time that she has to help. I don't think she trusts anyone else to do it, either."

They caught up to Vel, who had stopped near what Tan suspected was the center of the swamp. All around, large reeds protruded from the water. A thin film of green and brown coated the surface. Patches of land were visible in places, but it was otherwise a murky mess. Without shaping, Tan wouldn't have been able to cross the swamp.

In the midst of it was a simple wooden building propped up on long wooden legs. It was this that Vel hovered above, one arm extended as he pointed.

"What is this place?" Tan asked.

Vel shrugged. "Don't know. None had ever seen it before. If not for this new talent," he said, waving his hands in the air as if trying to mimic flying, "we might never have seen it."

Tan studied the hut. Other than its location, there was nothing particularly impressive about it. "Any of your people live here?"

"None from Doma," Elle said. "The swamp has long been thought to be impassable."

Vel nodded. "Some try. You get a few crazy enough to think to bring one of the shallow-keeled fishing boats through here, but none have ever been able to make it across. That's why it's been an effective barrier between us and Chenir."

Tan saw and sensed nothing about it that made him think that Par-shon had anything to do with the hut. The swamp would be a good place to hide, otherwise. As he sensed, listening to water around him, he realized that someone else was there.

Not someone, but definitely something.

He dropped to the small wooden porch in front of the hut door. Vel shouted something after him, but Tan ignored it. He pushed the door open, not sure what to expect. The other side was dimly lit and smelled of damp air. Heat pressed on him and he sensed a heaviness, much like he'd detected with the hounds.

This was a place of elemental power.

Tan quickly shaped the door closed, not wanting Elle or Vel to risk entering. As he did, he shaped a hint of fire, only enough for him to see and not enough to do any damage to the hut, not until he knew what he might find.

Spread out around the hut were signs of elemental power, but nothing like anything that he'd ever seen before. A large, smooth stone of deep black rested on the wooden floor. Tan sensed fire and earth from it, a combination that should not exist, but then again, neither should kaas or the hounds. A small crack in the floor let some of the light trickle out. Through this, Tan noticed a thick, greenish-tinted mist that swirled around it. Wind and air. The combination was not as surprising as fire and earth, but still uncommon.

Other combinations were present here as well. In a corner was an obsidian bowl, much like the one that he'd seen the archivists possess. Water slicked its surface, leaving it steaming. Water and fire, Tan suspected. A simple iron pot contained a slurry of water and mud. A few similar pots were empty.

This was something like elemental power, but not elementals.

A layer of dust coated everything. How long had it been since someone had been in this hut? And *who* had been here?

He made his way around the room, searching for anything else that would explain what he found, but there was nothing but a thick book angled against the wall. Tan grabbed this and glanced at the cover. His breath caught. Runes for each of the elementals were marked on the surface, much like the books that he'd found at the university.

He flipped through the book. Written in a tight script were notes. Whatever this was, it was similar to those left at the university archives.

As he read through a few of the pages, he felt as if a weight were lifting from his chest. Written here in *Ishthin* were the writings of an ancient shaper. That wasn't what gave him relief. It was the concern he saw for the elementals, the recognition that what the other shapers had done was wrong. And this, everything around him, was an attempt to correct it.

Even better, there must have been others like this scholar. The book was written for someone else, telling Tan that there had once been others like him, others with the same concern for the elementals, and others who had wanted to do what was needed to protect them.

Since learning about the ancient shapers and the steps they'd taken to damage the elementals, he'd been troubled. How could shapers as connected to the elementals as they had been think that harnessing them was acceptable? Worse, how could they have thought it acceptable to force the crossings between elementals?

He had hoped that there had been those who'd thought differently, but now he knew. And maybe there would be answers within this book about how they had stopped the harnessing at that time.

Tan pocketed the book and glanced around the hut. There was power here that he didn't fully understand. Finding it, learning of that power, left him feeling more hopeful than he had in some time. Maybe he would find the answers he needed to stop the Utu Tonah. Maybe he could even find something that would help him repair the artifact.

As he stepped back out of the hut and lifted to the air on a shaping, Elle studied him with a worried look creasing her brow. "How did you get through?" she asked.

Tan frowned. "What do you mean?"

She pointed to the hut. "We couldn't get through. There's something here that prevents us."

Tan didn't detect anything, but then again, he was a shaper more like the one who had built the hut and placed it here. Maybe he was meant to find it.

"What did you find?" she asked.

169

Tan thought of the book and the messages within. Not all the ancient shapers had wanted to harness the elementals. Not all wanted to cross them. Maybe there *had* been some like him. Could that be why the artifact had been made?

"Tan?" Elle said. "What was in there?"

He smiled. "Hope."

CHAPTER 19

The Bond Forms

THE BORDER BETWEEN DOMA and Chenir quickly sloped from lush grasslands scattered with towering trees down to the hard, barren rock of Chenir. A wide, cracked valley blocked foot travelers; it was the reason that travel from the kingdoms to Chenir had typically been done by ship.

Elle stood next to him and stared into Chenir with a quiet intensity. Vel had returned to Falsheim, determined to continue to patrol the borders around the city, using udilm to ensure the safety of the people within. "They're moving the wrong way," she said.

Tan looked at her. "What do you mean?"

Elle shrugged and tucked a loose strand of hair back behind her ears. "You're the one who suggested it to me. Incendin pushes out with fire. Doma does the same with water. Look at Chenir. They have strength in earth, much like our strength in water, but they sacrifice it as they draw back. Retreating to the kingdoms isn't the answer."

Tan couldn't believe that he hadn't seen it before. The first thing he'd noticed about Chenir had been the powerful drumming that they used to draw on the earth elementals. Their other shapers were strong, but there was something about the rhythmic drumming that called on earth the best. Would they be able to alter their shaping, use the strength of the earth to push Par-shon back?

If they did, it left only one place left for Par-shon to attack. The kingdoms wouldn't be ready. They didn't have enough strength to be ready.

Not without Zephra. Tan needed to free his mother. Seeing what Elle pointed out, he thought he understood a way that Par-shon could be kept from the shores—not just of the kingdoms, but of all the Kingdoms. Fire. Water. Earth. That left wind for the kingdoms.

Would it work?

"What is it?" Elle asked him.

The hope that Tan had felt when he had first found the hut and understood what it was began to spread through him. It was different than what he had thought would be necessary to defeat Par-shon, but at the same time, it was *exactly* what he had thought. The nations, each working together, each with the same risk. Fighting individually had not worked, but together? *Could* they make it work?

Only if others would believe him. It would have to start with Chenir.

Even more than that, it would have to start with Zephra. He would need not only her, but her wind shaping and her connection to the elementals to be able to create a shaping that rivaled what he'd seen in Incendin and now in Doma.

And if he could save Zephra, he might even be able to convince Chenir.

"There has to be a way to rescue my mother," he said.

Elle shook her head. "Tan, I don't think you understand what you're saying. Masyn tells me that Par-shon has her in the middle of—"

"I know where you've seen her, but I think I know how to exclude Par-shon," he said. More than that, it might even be enough to stop the Utu Tonah. Tan almost didn't dare let himself hope that something could be done. The possibility seemed unlikely, but then, so too would it once have seemed unlikely that he could work with the lisincend, or that the hounds were elementals.

"Tan—"

"It's going to be dangerous. I know that, but what Chenir does is dangerous, too. Pulling away the elementals doesn't stop Par-shon, it only weakens them. We need to find a way to strengthen these lands, and then use that to push back Par-shon. It starts with reaching Zephra."

"No, that's not what I was getting at," Elle said. "Look."

She pointed into the distance. Tan had to squint, but he could see what she indicated. Streaks of darkness moved in the distance, crawling across the rough Chenir rock. These were lands where the elementals had been withdrawn, but elementals were returning—except they weren't elementals native to Chenir.

"What are they doing?" Elle asked.

"You'd said they were moving north. I thought that Chenir . . . " He'd thought that they were drawn by Chenir, but that didn't seem to be the case. The hounds moved *toward* lands where the elementals had been withdrawn, as if to fill the void. "This is where they are going," Tan said. If they could do that, then maybe Tan would be able to borrow from their strength.

"That's not what I mean," Elle said. "Can't you see?"

"Clearly not as well as you can," he said.

"Here." She shaped water and created something like a lens for him to see through, using her hands to hold it.

The shaping augmented what he could see, and he realized what Elle wanted him to see. The hounds were perched atop the rock, as if waiting. There were dozens, probably as many as Tan had healed, and possibly a few dozen more trapped in a valley below. From those, Tan could tell that they were still twisted, and that the remaining hounds watched, as if herding them onward.

Or, he realized, holding them, preventing them from moving farther into Chenir.

"Stay here," Tan suggested.

"If you're going after those hounds, then I'm coming with you."

"I'm not going after them. Do you see the two dozen or so down in the valley?" Elle nodded. "Those are Incendin hounds. The ones surrounding them are healed."

"How can you tell? You couldn't even see them without me helping with your shaping."

Tan suppressed the smile. It was good to see Elle confident in her shaping ability, even if it was somewhat disconcerting. She'd been shaping for less time than him, and he hadn't been shaping all that long. Somehow, the safety of the kingdoms rested on their ability to find a way to keep Par-shon from moving any further.

"I can reach the fire bond."

With that, he shaped himself to the hounds.

* * * * *

Healing the remaining hounds had taken considerable energy, but less than the last time he'd healed so many. Then, he'd been trying to pull lisincend back into the fire bond at the same time, and now all he had to worry about was the hounds. There was an additional advantage, and one that Tan wasn't certain would have helped. As he'd worked his healing, he'd needed to reach for fire and earth elementals to assist him. While he hated doing so with Asboel injured, the draasin had willingly added to his shaping, though he'd remained distant and in the back of Tan's mind. The earth shaping had come not from golud or another elemental that had once lived in these lands, but from the hounds themselves.

Elle had watched, remaining above him, as if ready to rescue him if things went awry. Possibly, she would have pulled him free, but Tan didn't think that the healed hounds would have let the others harm him. There was a willingness to what he did, and a sense that they longed for it as much as he did.

The massive hound bounded down from the upper rocks to stand in front of him. The others deferred to her, backing away. Tan wondered how she had managed to claim authority so quickly, and he wondered why there should be a hierarchy within the hounds. The draasin had something of a hierarchy, but it was led by Asboel, the head of the family. Tan had never had the sense that ashi or the nymid had much distinction.

We keep seeing each other, Tan said.

The hound circled him. Tan sensed unease from Elle and focused on trying to connect to her as they once had. *I am fine here, Elle.*

The discomfort he detected from her eased somewhat, receding to a mild anxiety.

You are an interesting one, the hound said.

As are you. Did you bring them here, or do you keep them from moving away?

She bared her fangs briefly. *They would remain in the sun. That is not the place for our kind.*

You are of earth and fire.

As are you.

Tan smiled. *I am of each of the elements.*

The hound sat and studied Tan with eyes that seemed to glow. *Of all, but you serve fire.*

Why would you say that?

You have restored balance to the bond. Doing so serves fire.

I serve the Mother above all. She is the reason that I restored fire.

The hound stood and paced around him again. *You are troubled. These lands disturb you.*

Tan hesitated. How would the hound know that he was troubled? *This is not how the Mother would have the elementals.*

She would see this land returned. The pack returns.

That's why you come here?

The hound peeled back her lips again and a low growl rumbled from her. *I come because you are troubled. The pack comes because of me.*

Why would you come because of me?

She dipped her head and pawed at the ground. The earth split with the movement and rock tumbled away from her. Tan took a step back, uncertain what she intended. *You restored fire. You restored me. This connects us.*

I restored all of the pack, Tan said.

The hound met his eyes. *This connects all.*

Tan had the sense that he was missing something. *Do you understand what I must do? Will you help?*

The hound tipped her head back and bayed. The sound echoed off the rock, like the sound of a mountain avalanche, the kind of sound Tan had once feared. There was a reassuring weight to it now. As one, the other hounds picked up the call, answering in kind. It reverberated, building louder and louder, something like a drumbeat that was determined to overpower the drumming of

Chenir. With the power that built from the hounds, Tan wondered if it might be possible.

The ground vibrated with their voices and cracked in places, splitting open. Then, slowly, the sound died out again, and only the female standing in front of him still bayed. Finally, she stopped as well.

Tan could tell that something had changed, though not what. The rumbling didn't seem to ease, continuing like a steady peal of thunder from a distant storm. It took Tan a while to realize that the rumbling came from *within* him, the sound of the voices of the dozens of hounds, faint but distant.

What is this?

You ask for help. It is freely given. The pack agrees.

Tan blinked, feeling suddenly woozy. The steady rolling thunder within his mind continued unabated. What did it mean that the pack agreed? And why did he hear *all* of the hounds in his mind?

I am Maelen, Tan said. In many ways, the name Asboel had chosen for him suited him better and fit the connection he shared with the elementals. Asboel had been the first of the elementals that he'd bonded, and the most ancient. It was fitting that Asboel had provided his name.

The hound waited, her eyes locked onto Tan, her nostrils flaring with each breath. She sat ready, as if expecting something of him.

Tan understood. She had no name, not yet, and not until *he* gave her one.

You have formed a pack. You have found the purpose, he said, trying to think of what name suited her. To all things, names were important, but possibly even more so to elementals, creatures of the Great Mother bonded to the elements. When he'd named Asgar, he had relied upon Asboel and Sashari to help, using their memories of the draasin. He'd pulled from his knowledge of *Ishthin*, finding a name that seemed well-suited to the young draasin. The one that Tan had chosen felt fitting.

With this hound, he had nothing but his own memories of her. She had been an Incendin hound, a fearsome and terrifying creature of twisted fire, but now she was something more. She had unified the hounds, pulling them together, making her an earth elemental of much strength. That strength allowed her to lead the others, but she had curiosity in her as well. Tan had sensed that when she first came to him, seeking the connection.

Kota, Tan said.

In *Ishthin*, it meant something along the lines of *Strong One*, but there was a deeper element to it than that, a reflection of what he saw in her.

There was a flash of spirit drawn from Tan as the bond formed.

Kota tipped her head back and howled.

CHAPTER 20

A Race for Zephra

TAN RAN WITH KOTA, racing after her with a shaping of wind and earth, each step fueled by an additional shaping. Elle surfed along next to him, somehow drawing water out of the air that she slid upon. When he focused on what she did, he thought he understood, but he still marveled at her newfound control.

The ground around them changed quickly as they made their way through Chenir. Rocks dropped off quickly, and Tan used shapings to guide himself down. Kota leapt, taking a single bounding jump each time, bouncing from rock to rock. The rest of the pack roamed on either side of them, racing ahead, having no more trouble with the changing elevation than Kota.

The sense of the hounds as a deep rumbling in his mind hadn't changed. Every so often, they bayed, a steady and rhythmic calling. It took Tan a while to realize that their howls served to disrupt the drumming of Chenir that sought to call them back. He wondered if the hounds would be able to call the other elementals back into Chenir, but doing so would take an understanding of the calls that Tan didn't possess.

The bond to Kota was a solid sense within him. As with the other elementals, bonding to her had changed something inside of him. With fire, it had burned in his mind. The bond to Honl had given him a connection to wind, and increased his strength and ability there. Water had come next, but then he'd always had a certain connection to the nymid, even if there hadn't been the bond. Now that he'd bonded to an earth elemental—and one of the hounds—he wondered how that would change him. What would it mean that he'd bonded to an elemental from each of the elements?

The ground sloped steadily down. The rockiness to it never changed, only the elevation. From the map that Elle had, Tan knew they must be nearing the borders where Par-shon had their shapers. Surprisingly, he didn't feel that he would be outnumbered this time.

"Are you sure that you want to be here?" Tan asked Elle. "I plan to rescue my mother and then return the elementals."

Her expression clouded briefly. "Do you know where to find Zephra? Can you speak to masyn?"

"Probably," Tan said.

"Fine, then you go ahead. When masyn answers, I'll return to Doma. Until then, you need me to guide you."

Tan didn't tell her that he'd already tried, but speaking to water required a distinct touch. The nymid protected him—he wore their armor—and he'd spoken to udilm in the past, but he had only the vaguest sense of the elemental that Elle had bonded. It was wispy, much like the wind, and there only at the edge of his senses. Tan suspected that he could reach it, but could he guarantee that he could, especially if his mother depended upon it?

"Is she still alive?" Tan asked.

Elle nodded. "She lives. I know little more than that."

At least there was that. If she lived, and if he could find a way to reach her, then there was a chance that he could get her to safety.

He reached through his connection to earth, sensing the elemental strength of the hounds around him. Tan found that he used Kota instinctively, reaching through the new connection that he shared with her. It was a potent and powerful bond, almost as strong as the one that he shared with Asboel. Could it be that the process of healing her and bringing the hounds back into the fire bond had made the connection even more solid? There seemed to be more of a connection to spirit within the bond than he would have expected, though that might only be imagined.

Through Kota, Tan was able to detect the other hounds around them and was able to know exactly where they were through a combination of earth sensing and the keen sense of smell the hounds possessed. They ran easily, their cries occasionally echoing out and filling Chenir with the rumbling roar of the hounds.

Elle touched his arm after a while.

Tan hadn't needed her to point out what she detected, though he was impressed that her connection with water was so potent that she knew as soon as he did that they'd reached the edge of the lands claimed by Par-shon. Tan had sensed shapers here. Always before, the connection had been tenuous, especially when Par-shon used earth to obscure their presence. This was different; this time, Tan simply *knew* they were there.

Kota, Tan said, reaching for his new bond.

The pack knows.

Can you hunt?

She looked over at him and bared her fangs. *You think that we have forgotten?*

Tan smiled. There was a part of her that reminded him much of the draasin and the way Asboel chased the hunt. *It should be done quietly.*

Rather than letting out a howl, Kota sent a low rumble through the earth. *There are others of earth bonded here, Maelen.*

Tan knew there would be. With Par-shon, they would have bonded earth to enough shapers that they would be able to hide. If they discovered the hounds, and if they learned that they were elementals, there would be a new danger to them. They would become the hunted, with Par-shon seeking to trap them and force a bond. Tan would not allow that.

That is why it must be quick.

It is already done.

Tan almost lost his shaping and stumbled. *Already?* Even as he asked, he reached through earth, borrowing from Kota and using the earth sensing that he possessed. Through it, he detected the fallen Par-shon shapers, their bonds now freed, released back into Chenir where the steady summons pulled them back. At least they would be safe for now.

"What happened?" Elle asked.

Tan smiled. "The hounds. They've made sure that Par-shon won't know we're here."

Elle's eyes tightened. She squeezed her hands, as if readying to make a fist. "But they *will* know, Tan. They're connected in that way."

As she said it, he became aware of a new attack. Three of the hounds that had roamed the furthest were attacked by fire and wind. Connected to fire as they were, they ignored the fire, but the wind was difficult for them. They jumped and snarled but were thrown back.

Can you draw them back? Tan asked Kota.

You wanted the hunt.

Not like this.

Another three hounds were attacked as well. Tan barely had time to marvel at the fact that he could practically *see* the attack in his mind, that the connection to Kota had given him the ability to follow the sense of all them. Water and wind mixed, attacking these hounds. They separated, attacking the shapers, but they didn't have the element of surprise as they had before.

Worse, more shapers were coming.

Tan sensed them as they made their way toward him. Dozens. Dozens of dozens. Would they be strong enough to fight Par-shon back?

"How much farther is she?" Tan asked.

Elle shook her head. "Tan, we're only on the outer edge of what Par-shon has claimed."

"Show me what you know," he demanded. He needed to see where Zephra was held. He needed to know how far he had to reach.

"I don't know how—"

One of the hounds fell and didn't move. The others howled and pulled the fallen one back.

Tan couldn't wait. He wouldn't have these elementals sacrifice themselves for him. "I'm sorry, Elle." With a shaping of spirit, he reached into Elle's mind, surging through her, and found what she knew of masyn. As he did, his understanding of the elemental changed. He could almost hear it, but it came through Elle's connection. Through that, he was able to locate Zephra, and knew how much farther they had to go.

He considered what he'd seen of Chenir from the map. Too far, at least too far with only the two shapers and the elementals. They would need more help if they were to push Par-shon back from here.

He needed help. Using the summoning rune, he shaped a request and not a demand. Only those who wanted to help would answer.

Another hound fell, but it managed to get up weakly. Through his connection with Kota, he was able to reach it and sent a shaping drawn of water, healing it.

The hounds howled again. The sound echoed off the rock, filling the air.

For a moment, the Par-shon shapers were pushed back, creating a new hesitation to their attack. Kota seized upon it and sent the hounds charging forward, racing into the attack, striking at the bonded shapers, who fell before the onslaught. The hounds howled each time another fell.

As they did, Tan realized something. No longer were the freed elementals pulled away. The hounds' call held them in place, as if disrupting whatever effect the rhythmic sounds of Chenir had on the elementals.

Renewed hope surged within him. Could he use those elementals?

"Stay back here and be ready," Tan told Elle.

"Tan—"

He shook his head as he readied a shaping, pulling on the strength of the elementals around him, feeling them fill him with energy. "Elle, this might be more than you can handle."

She placed her hands on her hips and glared at him. "You think that I did nothing the entire time that Par-shon attacked Doma? Do you really think that I'm so helpless?"

Tan struggled with thinking of her in any way other than the young girl he'd met at the university, the one who'd worn dresses far too large for her and kept herself buried in books. The same girl who had relied on him to save her when the archivists attacked. But now she *was* different. Whether that came from bonding the elemental, or whether it was the experience that she had, Tan couldn't deny the fact that Elle was capable.

He nodded, taking a deep breath as he did. He couldn't do the same thing to Elle that his mother had done to him. Elle had to make her own choices. With what she'd done to keep Doma safe when Falsheim was attacked, she'd certainly earned that right.

"Elle . . . just be careful," he said.

Her mouth tightened, and she tipped her head toward him. "Parshon thinks they know the elementals, but they don't know masyn. They don't know your hounds, either." She lifted from the ground on a shaping of water, mist spiraling around her. "Let's go reach Zephra."

CHAPTER 21

Help Arrives

T AN FOLLOWED KOTA AS SHE RACED across the rocky ground. Chenir changed the farther they went, the rocky slope leveling out and leading to a flatter ground. It was colder here and covered with a thin layer of frost. Dried grasses remained, the only remnants of the summer season that had long since passed.

Elle stayed above the ground, but Tan ran alongside his new bond. The hound jumped with such lithe grace, moving like no creature he'd ever seen. Had these hounds chased him when he'd first encountered the lisincend, he might never have managed to escape.

The pack raced along with them. They encountered other shapers from Par-shon, but not nearly as many as they had before. The hounds continued baying, their near constant and steady call continuing to distort the effect of the Chenir shapers. Each time elementals were freed from their bonds, Tan summoned them, calling them to help. Most answered.

Would other shapers answer? The rune in his pocket glowed, but he couldn't expect anyone else to follow him here, not this far into Chenir, where Par-shon had completely laid claim to the lands. But Tan had no intention of ousting Par-shon. He might not be able to do so on his own. With the elementals, he had a better chance, but what he wanted was simply to reach his mother and find a way to rescue her. If he could do that, *then* he would be able to attempt the next part in his plan.

The awareness of other shapers came to him through the bond with Kota. Tan reached over and patted her. *I will take to the air. Let us hunt.*

Kota snarled and raced forward.

With a shaping of wind and fire, Tan jumped into the air, shooting high above the ground. Connected to the hounds, he was able to sense what they sensed and could tell where they encountered other shapers. Elle stayed closer to the ground.

A pocket of five shapers approached the leading edge of the hounds. Tan streaked toward them, using all of the elements, drawing not on his own strength, but that of the elementals around him. He would save his own strength, hold it back in case the elementals were drawn away. He landed amid the shapers as they battled the hounds.

It was the first time Tan had actually *seen* the hounds attacking, at least in this form and as elementals. They worked together, moving as if connected by the fire bond, or likely something of earth, leaping around the shapers. These shapers were talented, and all had bonded more than a single elemental.

As Tan arrived, they turned their attention to him. Within moments, they began shaping a pattern intended to separate him from the elementals. He'd known this shaping before and had survived it in the past.

Tan raised his sword and sent a shaping of spirit at the nearest shaper. Bonds were separated from him, and the elementals were freed. He turned to the next shaper and did the same. Again, the Par-shon bonded fell.

Three remained. They cornered Tan, ignoring the hounds.

That proved to be their mistake. The hounds came at them from behind, all snarls and teeth. When they turned, Tan sent his shaping after them, having no regrets for doing so from behind.

They fell forward, sprawling onto the rock, as the shapings struck.

The hounds pounced and finished their attack. Tan felt only a fleeting recognition of the fact that he felt no remorse at their passing. They would have done that much and worse to him. He had yet to learn what they had done to his mother.

Maelen.

The call came from Kota, and there was urgency mixed into it. Tan sensed her through the bond and leaped to her on a shaping of lightning, landing next to her. At first he wasn't certain why she had summoned him. Her hackles were raised and her stubby tail pointed straight back from her. She sniffed at the air with her wide nostrils, swiveling her head as if to search for more shapers.

Then Tan realized why she'd called him.

Above him, Elle faced nearly a dozen shapers. Par-shon shapers had realized that the hounds couldn't reach them in the air. The hounds could leap and nip at them, but they were elementals of earth, not meant to be in the sky. Elle fought with more skill than Tan would have suspected her capable of, holding them back with a swirling mist of thick green water.

The shapers pushed back with incredible strength, their own water shapers drawing Elle's effort away and sending it streaming back toward the ground.

Can you shift the ground? Tan asked Kota.

I don't know.

Try, he suggested.

Tan took to the air and pulled on a shaping of the combined elements, drawing through the sword as he did. The sword blazed brightly. He pulled on the strength of the elementals around him, borrowing from the hounds but also from unnamed elementals of earth that had returned to Chenir when released from their stolen bonds. Tan sensed the damp, heavy air of wyln, and there was the heat of saa. The nymid, through the armor they had lent him, gave him additional strength.

Tan shaped, striking three of the bonded with his first attack. As he did so, the other shapers turned away from Elle and began to focus on him. He pulled upon his connection to the elementals, drawing more, and demanding more as he shaped the next three shapers. That left five. They surrounded him, but now Elle had recovered enough, and she wrapped her shaping of water around them in such a way as to separate them from the connection they had with their elementals. Using spirit, Tan severed the bonds placed on them. As he did, he summoned the elementals to him.

More shapers were coming. Through his connection to the hounds, he could sense them. They might be able to fight the coming Par-shon attack, but one after another would wear on him and would be more than he could handle even with the elementals helping.

Lightning crackled and Cora appeared, landing next to him on a streamer of fire. With a glance, she took in the fallen shapers, the hounds circling them, and Elle floating on a cloud of shaped water. "You summoned. I didn't know that it would be for *this.*"

"Where is she?" Tan asked, not wanting to use Enya's name. Having one of the draasin here would be helpful, but also risky.

Cora flickered her eyes to the sky. To the south and the east, a dark shape circled far overhead, and Tan sensed Enya as much as he saw her.

189

"Have her be careful. Chenir summons the elementals, and Par-shon . . . "

"She will be careful, Tan." Cora nodded toward Kota. "Impressive creature."

Kota bared her fangs and sat to Tan's left, eyes fixed on the new-comer. "She is."

"Another bond?"

He nodded.

Cora shook her head. "You have all the fun, you know that?"

"Talk to the hounds. See if they answer."

Cora's mouth twisted, as if the thought disturbed her. "I'm not certain that the hounds and me are on the kind of terms that would allow us to work well together."

Tan wondered what she meant by that, but he let it drop. He'd summoned, but only Cora had answered. More and more Par-shon shapers were approaching, but even with three shapers and all the elemental help from the hounds, they still might not be able to get through to Zephra.

"What of Fur?"

Cora shook her head. "Fur will not come. He protects the Sun-lands, and . . . "

She didn't need to finish. This was Chenir. How long had Incendin faced Par-shon alone? They no longer needed to, but Fur was much like Roine in his reluctance to work with others.

A massive shaping built, and Tan glanced up to see another bolt of lightning, followed by another.

Theondar landed next to Tan, holding his sword and with a shaping prepared. A short, green cloak flapped in the damp air. Like Cora, he quickly surveyed the ground.

Following Theondar was the Supreme Leader of Chenir.

Now there were four warriors, the only four that Tan knew of who remained in these lands.

"You found Zephra?" Roine asked.

Tan tipped his head to Elle, who lowered herself to stand next to them. "She did. She senses where she is, but she's too far into Chenir."

The Supreme Leader looked at the ground, at his lands, with his shoulders sagging. "So much is lost already," he said.

Tan faced him. "I warned what would happen. By withdrawing the elementals, you weaken the land. Without the hounds, I wouldn't have made it this far." Tan nodded toward Kota. "They're able to disrupt what you do, the drumming and whatever else your shapings are, but they can't restore these lands. You need to release your elementals. You need to shape earth to push *out*. Let Doma teach you, or Incendin, but it must be with earth. If we don't, then whatever else happens, Par-shon will succeed."

"Why earth?" Roine asked.

Tan wasn't sure how to explain, but it felt right. "Each nation has a predominant element, much like most shapers have a predominant element. Even warriors."

A pair of Par-shon shapers that had made their way too far ahead reached them, and Tan pressed out a shaping through his sword, knocking them down.

"I need help if I'm going to reach Zephra," he said to Roine.

A pained expression crossed Roine's face. "Tannen, if *you* can't get to her, then no one can."

"We need her."

"I know, but we can't risk you—"

"You don't understand, Roine. We need her to help lead the shaping of wind. That's what the kingdoms must shape. Incendin has fire. Doma has water. Chenir, if they will do it, must shape earth. I think they can use their drumming and augment their shapings with that. That leaves wind."

"For what?" Roine asked. "What purpose is there in using each of the elements to hold back Par-shon? They will continue to come. We need to get behind the barrier—"

"That won't work," he said. He strongly felt that was true. "We can work together, push Par-shon off these shores—"

"And if we can't?"

Tan sighed. "Then we will have failed. At least we will have tried. If we don't do that, then the Great Mother will no longer look upon us with favor."

The Supreme Leader took in the way the land had changed, the effect that Tan sensed through his connection to earth. The connection was potent and filled him, granting him a clear sense of everything spread all around him. Tan could tell how much had been lost by withdrawing the elementals, much like Asboel had feared how much would be lost when Enya attempted to withdraw fire from Incendin. All of Chenir had changed because of what their shapers did. Did it leave their lands any safer? Did it leave the elementals any safer?

"I need a distraction," Tan said. "I will go past Par-shon. If Chenir releases their elementals, I can make it in to Zephra and back out without capture. But I need you to draw their shapers away," he said to Roine and Cora.

Roine glanced at Cora. For the old warrior, agreeing to work with Incendin was difficult. It had been difficult since Tan had first suggested it, but they had no choice. If they didn't find a way to work together, then all of them would fall. Cora also struggled with the kingdoms, but she had spent enough time with Tan that she understood his motivation—probably better than others. She knew that he wanted nothing more than to see the elementals protected. He hadn't hesitated when she had bonded to Enya, knowing that the bond would keep the draasin protected even a little longer.

"You will help?" Cora asked.

Roine nodded. "For Zephra, I will help."

"This isn't about Zephra," Tan said. Maybe at first it was, and maybe there was still a part of Tan that would attempt to reach his mother anyway, but he needed to get through to reach her to do all that he could to save the kingdoms. If they couldn't stop Par-shon now, if they couldn't figure out some way of pushing them back, they would have already lost. "We do this for each of our homelands. Work together, as we should have been all along."

They nodded. The shapers were getting close. Tan could sense them through the hounds. Not much longer, and they would be upon them.

"Please," Tan started, talking to the Supreme Leader, "your shapers need to change their focus. They can't withdraw the elementals. They need to push out Par-shon. We can't do that with what your people do."

The Supreme Leader watched Tan for a moment, and then he disappeared with a bolt of lightning.

Kota, Tan started. *Can you remain hidden and come with me?*

The hound shifted. Tan had no other word for it. She was there, and then she was not. Without his ability to sense her through the bond, he wouldn't have known she was there.

Can the others hide like this? he asked.

As one, the other hounds disappeared from view. Bound to elementals, the Par-shon shapers might know they were there anyway, but it could limit their ability to easily find them. Anything that limited Par-shon gave them a chance.

"Nice trick," Elle said.

"You be safe," Tan told her.

Elle pulled him into a quick hug and let him go. "You too. I can't have my cousin go dying on me."

Tan forced a smile. "I'll get her back. I promise."

Elle shook her head. "Not her, you dummy."

A pair of shapers appeared. Cora shot after them, and Tan sensed Enya joining the fight.

"Go, Tannen. Save Zephra," Roine said.

He nodded, and as he readied a shaping that would take him away, he reached into the distant part of his mind where he could hear the hounds. Their steady rumble was there, filling his mind as he drew the sense of them forward.

Hunt well.

As one, the hounds bellowed with a roar that shook the earth.

CHAPTER 22

Within the Hidden City

THE SHAPING PULLED HIM deeper into Chenir. Tan didn't quite know where to find Zephra, only what he saw from his shaping of Elle. He used a traveling shaping without spirit, letting it keep him above everything, but not moving so quickly that he couldn't see below him. Kota raced across the ground. With each leap, she picked up speed, having no difficulty keeping up with him.

Honl. Tan sent a request out to his wind elemental, needing every advantage that he could have. Asboel rumbled in the back of his mind, weak and thready, but there. The nymid armor kept him connected to water. Hopefully, with his elementals, he would be able to find Zephra quickly.

The wind elemental drifted toward him on a cloud of black smoke, coalescing into the form that Honl had begun to take. He traveled along with Tan, moving with the same ease that Kota managed.

"You have bonded another, Tan," Honl remarked. "She is powerful. The timing might be early, but I think that you have chosen well."

Tan grunted. The ground streaked past him. Through Kota's senses, he saw no sign of other Par-shon shapers. Tan wouldn't have stopped if he had. He needed to be drawn into the battle with the hounds and the other shapers. There might not be enough to fully battle Par-shon, but all Tan needed was time. Enough time to reach his mother and pull her free.

"I don't think she gave me much of a choice."

"You named her. There was choice in that."

Tan scanned the ground. Was that a tent in the distance?

Kota raced ahead to check on what Tan had seen.

"There was a choice," Tan agreed. "But she deserved a name." Honl moved to float in front of him, facing him. The elemental's features had become more pronounced, making it so that Tan could pick out clothing and what appeared to be a cloak flapping in the wind behind him. Tan smiled at that. "You saw how she created the pack?"

Honl tilted his chin. "She has followed you since you healed her. I think the bonding was inevitable. The Mother chose well with her, I think."

"How much is the Mother, and how much is chance?"

Honl shrugged.

"What if I never would have answered the summons to the lisincend? The hounds would have remained twisted, drawn away from fire."

"Yet you answered the summons. Was it not kaas who summoned?"

"On behalf of Fur."

Honl's smoky face pulled into a smile. "Was it Fur, or was Fur influenced by kaas?"

Tan sighed. "Does it even matter? Would I have done anything different? The hounds needed to be returned to the fire bond."

"Is that still what you think that you did?"

Tan frowned. "That *is* what I did."

"They are of earth, Tan. You brought them to the fire bond, but you did so with earth. Why else do you think that it took such strength to heal them?"

"But they were of earth *before* I healed them."

"As are all creatures."

Tan's shaping slowed. Kota had found something and was circling around a wide wall of rock. The fur on her back was raised. Whatever she'd found had made her uncomfortable.

"Are you implying that *I* created the hounds? That they're only elementals because of me?"

"Not at all. The crossing that created them was between hyacan and isaln, but so long ago that the elementals that led to their creation no longer exist. They were joined, but it was incomplete. That is why fire remained twisted, and why they were never able to fully join into fire."

"Then what *are* you saying?" The Honl since he'd been healed was so different than the one Tan had first found, the ashi elemental that had been afraid to get too involved in fighting Par-shon. He seemed more aware but was able to share knowledge that Tan didn't have access to otherwise.

"You think that you only sealed the hounds to the fire bond, is all. You did much more than that, Maelen. You brought them back to earth as well."

Kota suddenly howled.

As she did, Honl drifted apart, moving in cloud form toward the hound. Kota remained hidden, but her thunderous cry would be heard for miles. She pawed at the ground, and as she did, a shaping failed briefly before reforming. For a moment, there was a walled city, with heavy stone buildings within. Then it was gone.

This was where his mother would be. Par-shon had an entire city hidden, obscured by a shaping of earth. Without Kota, Tan would never have found it.

If there was enough strength to hide the city, there would be powerful shapers here.

Tan wasn't sure that he would be strong enough to reach the inside of the city, let alone find a way to reach his mother, but he would try.

Kota, can you disrupt the shaping and find whoever is masking the city?

I will try, Maelen. There is strength here.

I know. Are you not strong enough?

She roared again, and this time she leapt to the air, coming down with her front paws digging into the earth. As she did, the shaping flickered again. Kota didn't wait and jumped again, roaring with the motion, dropping down to the ground once more. Each time she jumped and crashed to the ground, the shaping revealed more and more of the city.

Honl swirled through as a cloud of inky smoke. Through the bond between them, Tan sensed him searching for Zephra. Like the hounds and masyn, Honl would be an elemental that Par-shon had never seen before. Could they use that to let them reach Zephra?

Could *he* use an elemental that Par-shon had never encountered? Masyn would be here, or else Elle would not have been able to find Zephra. But what? How could he reach the elemental?

He focused on water, pulling on his connection to the nymid. The nymid moved like the powerful current of the river, strong and steady. Reaching udilm was different. They were powerful, but more like the waves, strong enough to overwhelm and attempt to force a shaper to alter their focus. But masyn was the mist, the heaviness of the air, the dampness of the fog.

Tan pulled in a breath and let it out, thinking of how to reach masyn. *Masyn, help Maelen find Zephra.*

Tan sent the request out on a shaping of moist air, mixing it with a shaping of water and wind, combining them in his attempt to reach the elemental. He'd told Elle that he thought that he could reach masyn, and now he had to prove it.

A voice drifted into his mind, thick like fog. *He Who is Tan.*

Tan almost breathed out a relieved sigh. He hadn't been sure that masyn would answer, and even if they had, would he be able to hear them? How long had it taken him to understand golud? Even now, Tan could speak to golud but struggled to hear and understand a response from the elemental. There was a part of Tan that worried that speaking to masyn would be the same.

The Child of Water claims you know where to find Zephra, Tan said.

She is here. She is sick.

Tan tensed. What had Par-shon done to his mother? *Her bond?*

Ara remains, but something is wrong. Zephra fails, He Who is Tan.

A surge of anger came through him, but he tamped it down. He couldn't allow himself to be overcome by emotion. To help his mother, he needed clarity of thought. He needed to remain calm and reach her, or she would suffer. Tan wouldn't let that happen to her, not when he was close enough that he could almost reach her. All that he needed was to reach her location.

Honl swirled toward him on a dark cloud. Without taking any form, Tan heard him through the bond. *She is down there, Tan. There is another, much like the Bonded One.*

Tan hadn't heard the elemental refer to the Utu Tonah by that name before, but it was fitting. Without seeing the shaper, Tan worried that it might be the heavily bonded shaper that he'd faced twice before. Each time, he'd barely survived. Those times, he'd had Asboel with him. Now, without the draasin to assist, would he be strong enough to get through this shaping and rescue his mother?

He had to try.

But he didn't want to attempt to reach her without saying something to Amia first. There was a part of him that wished that she was with him, but her place was with her people. The Aeta needed her, much like the elementals and the people of the kingdoms needed him. If he couldn't rescue his mother quickly, then the other warrior shapers would be in even more danger. They bought him time, but Tan didn't think they could hold out indefinitely.

Amia, he sent, straining through the spirit bond between them, uncertain what more he could say to her. They had shared so much in the time they had known each other. All that he wanted was a chance to be with her, a chance for the two of them to know peace, but maybe they weren't meant to find that kind of peace, at least not until he managed to stop Par-shon and prevent another attack.

Her response came quietly, building steadily. It came as a sense of warmth that washed over him. *I know.*

It was all that she needed to say.

Tan took a deep breath. *Take me to him.*

Honl's face appeared briefly, concern creating something like wrinkles across his brow. Then he nodded.

Tan pulled on the elemental energy that he sensed around him. There was power here, at least more than he'd sensed when he'd been attacked by Par-shon before. He could call upon that strength, could borrow from it. The elementals wouldn't have to sacrifice themselves, and neither would Tan.

Power flooded into him, but he pulled on more, calling to the connection he shared with Kota, to Honl, and to the nymid. Tan didn't dare borrow from Asboel any more than needed. Weakened as he was, the draasin didn't need Tan destroying him.

Then Tan shot toward where Honl led.

He erupted with shapings building all around him. There was power that rivaled what he could draw, enough that had Tan *not* pulled on the elementals, he would have been overwhelmed. It threatened to separate him from his bonds, but Tan pushed through it, forcing the connections to remain.

Par-shon would *not* take his bonds from him.

Tan raised the warrior sword and lashed out with a combined shaping, sending it out in a circle of power that quickly expanded away from him. He continued to draw on the power, continued to pull, and felt resistance as his shaping washed over Par-shon shapers.

Kota howled. Wind whistled around him. The air was damp from the mixture of masyn and the nymid. Only fire was missing.

Tan reached for the fire bond, bypassing Asboel. Connected to the bond, he found fire that he could reach, and borrowed from nameless elementals all within it.

With this, he pressed even harder.

The shaping that obscured the city fell.

Tan stumbled. He stood in the middle of a street with homes made of thick stone. Straw roofs sloped to a high point on each. He saw no other shapers on the cobbled street but sensed those who had already fallen.

Kota, keep me safe.

The hound howled.

Masyn, where is she?

The elemental appeared in a cloud of mist that thickened, guiding him forward. It stopped at one of the nearby houses and Tan listened, pausing long enough to sense who might be on the other side. There, he detected his mother. As masyn had told him, something was wrong.

Tan shaped the door open, and it exploded with a splintering explosion.

The room inside was small. There was nothing but a mattress within. Tan's mother lay upon the mattress, but she didn't move. She wore a dirty gown, and her arms and legs were unbound, but there was nothing else that seemed to hold her in place.

Zephra didn't look up as he entered. What had Par-shon done to her?

Tan glanced around and noted the runes carved into the walls, one for each of the elements. As he considered each, he realized that there was something different about them than what he'd seen in the testing room, different even than the runes he'd seen when he was in the place of separation. Mixed within the runes was the mark for spirit.

Par-shon had learned of the runes' weakness.

Tan focused on the first rune that he saw, the one for wind. With a combined shaping, he pressed into it. Destroying it took more strength than he'd remembered, and he had to draw upon the elementals once more, borrowing from their strength. The rune split with a soft crack.

He turned his attention to another rune, this one for water. With another shaping, it cracked. Like before, the effort to destroy the rune was more than Tan had expected.

Pausing to collect a breath, he was tempted to step further into the room and go to his mother, but concern for how the runes might affect him prevented him from moving any further than the doorway.

Somewhere behind him, Kota growled.

Tan spun. A bald shaper covered with glowing runes stood at the end of the street. He wore only leather pants, leaving his chest exposed. Dark tattoos streaked across his chest. The runes extended down his chest and coated nearly the entirety of his uncovered body.

He was the same shaper Tan had seen before, the one who had twice nearly separated him from his bond, and a shaper who had nearly enough bonds to rival the Utu Tonah.

"You are predictable, Warrior," he said.

Tan stepped back into the street, not willing to risk being too close to the building with runes, fearing what might happen were he forced into it. Water and wind might be available, but not earth or fire.

"Zephra returns with me," Tan said.

The shaper tipped his head and Tan realized that he must be listening to the bonded elementals. Tan counted dozens of bonds on him, so many that even were Tan able to separate even a few, the shaper would remain powerful.

Can you do anything with him? Tan asked Kota.

The hound gave him a rumbling response.

Tan reached for Honl but couldn't find the wind elemental. There was a distant sense of him, but nothing more than that. Even the nymid had faded from his connection, though he still had the armor.

"He thought you would be drawn by her. The resemblance is clear. And the others will soon join you."

"You won't capture the others."

The shaper took a step toward Tan and his smile spread. "How many do you think your shapers can stop? One hundred? Two? A thousand?"

Tan's heart fluttered. There was no way that Roine, Cora, and Elle would stop even a hundred shapers. "You don't have a thousand stolen bonds."

"Stolen? Is that what you fear? These creatures are no different than the dog you brought with you. They are no different than the cows you raise for meat. They are gifts, meant to be used by those with the capacity to understand how those abilities *should* be used."

The shaper took another step toward him, moving leisurely. He walked with an impossible grace, one that Tan had only seen once before, and that from the Utu Tonah. "You think that you can stop me by yourself?" Tan asked.

The shaper paused, and then his smile spread more widely across his face. "Bold, warrior, even for one such as yourself. Yes, you have slowed me once, and you have delayed Him before, but can you stop us both, especially while your friends are separated from you?"

Tan sucked in a quick breath, suddenly understanding why the shaper delayed. He waited for the Utu Tonah to arrive.

How much time did Tan have?

Maybe not enough.

Tan pulled on the elementals around him. As he did, the shaper's eyes narrowed. He had sensed what Tan did.

Tan pulled harder, reaching for earth, binding what he could from Kota, demanding the nymid help as he used water, and reaching for wind, straining for whatever help that Honl would grant him. Power filled him, but it would not be enough.

The shaper started toward him again, runes glowing brighter with each step. Like Tan, he must have been pulling on his bonds, drawing strength from the elementals. With each step, he glowed brighter, soon becoming something like Tan's sword when he mixed the elementals.

Tan reached for other elementals. In this part of Chenir, with most of the elementals drawn away, there was little for him to reach. He found an earth elemental that he couldn't name. There was the hint of ara—maybe from Aric—that mixed with the thickness of masyn, an elemental that Tan recognized as water *and* wind. There was the distant pull of fire, though he couldn't tell which elemental. Tan pulled on them all.

Strength flooded him, and he called more through the sword. Even with all of that, it still wouldn't be enough. Tan sensed the shaping the Par-shon warrior created, and knew that he wouldn't be able to stop it.

He needed more. He needed fire.

Asboel—

Take what you need, Maelen.

For the first time in days, Asboel's voice came through with strength and vibrancy. Asboel's power filled him, called by their connection, but added to it through the fire bond. Tan screamed out, pulling on a massive shaping, one greater than any he'd ever attempted alone.

The Par-shon shaper paused.

Tan bound his shaping together but didn't have enough spirit to bind. Reaching again through his bonds, he called to Amia and borrowed from her. Spirit strength filled him—enormous stores, and more than Tan had known Amia possessed.

With this, he called to the elementals. Even those bonded to the shaper responded, dragged away from him. Tan pulled on the shaping, binding each of the elements together, securing it with spirit. This he turned on the shaper.

Light brighter than any bolt of lightning shot toward the shaper. He was illuminated for a moment, surprise etched on his face, and then his bonds exploded from him.

He screamed and ran toward Tan.

Tan's strength faded, the effort of the shaping draining him, but he raised his sword.

It would be too slow.

After everything, he would still fall.

A streak of brown fur bounded over Tan and landed atop the shaper as Kota quickly tore him apart.

Tan felt another shaping building in the distance. He didn't have to use his connection to the elementals to sense that it was the Utu Tonah, summoned by his warrior. Tan was exhausted, but he reached toward the elementals, hoping those that he'd freed from the warrior would assist him, as they had once assisted him when he battled in Doma.

Strength came back to him, but slowly. Through it, he sensed that hundreds of shapers came toward him. Not only the Utu Tonah, then, but the rest of the Par-shon shapers.

He needed more power. This would be his opportunity to stop the Utu Tonah and finally be rid of Par-shon shapers. He could end the war with Par-shon. If he could summon support like he had summoned when facing the other shaper, he might have enough.

Only, he had no strength remaining to do so.

Tan sagged to his knees. A black cloud swirled across his vision as he fell.

And he knew that they had lost.

CHAPTER 23

The Price of the Rescue

TAN AWOKE SURROUNDED BY SHAPERS he knew. Zephra sat in the plush chair of his home, hands folded in her lap as she watched him. A fire crackled in the hearth, saa swirling around within it, moving strangely and with something like lethargy. Zephra's hair was cut short, more wrinkles lined her brow, and her back had a stoop to it from the way her shoulders slumped forward, but it was his mother.

"How?" he asked, trying to sit up. He was still weak, but it was a physical tiredness, not the fatigue of shaping.

Zephra took a slow breath. "You risked much coming to my rescue, Tan."

"I had to do it," he said. "Not just for you, but to try and return the elementals."

She breathed out. "I'm not sure that you did. What would have happened had you been captured? What would the kingdoms have lost without you alive?"

"There are others," Tan answered.

She nodded slowly. "There are others. And we have you to thank." She straightened her back as she looked to the fire. "You know that Alan has bonded to ara?"

Tan shook his head.

"And Wallyn. He said you guided him to the nymid. They have bonded him as well."

Tan smiled at the thought of Wallyn binding to the nymid. The nymid were different from other elementals in many ways. They were strong and had healed him many times, but there was not a single distinct nymid like there was with the other elementals that Tan had encountered. Maybe it was the same with masyn for Elle, and even the udilm. He'd never really considered if all water was the same.

"It's good that the elementals have resumed the bonding," Tan said.

"I can't help but wonder if it is too late," she said. "Will it matter if Par-shon forces bonds and takes all of our elemental strength?"

"They won't be able to take it all," Tan said. "Not if we've bonded to them."

Zephra looked over at him. "Those bonds can be stolen, Tan. You know that."

Tan managed to sit up. The window was open to the street, and a cacophony of sounds filtered through. He was struck with the realization that most of those on the street knew nothing about what was going on. How many would be surprised to know that Par-shon had reached Chenir? How many would even know about Par-shon?

"I couldn't let you fall to Par-shon," Tan said. He swung his legs off the bed and leaned forward. His head swam for a moment and a warmth flashed within his pocket.

"Again, Tan, I'm not any more important than any other shaper. I was mistaken staying in Chenir. I know that now. Par-shon is unlike anything we've ever faced before. I don't know if we are strong enough to stop them. That's why you should not have come for me."

Tan took a deep breath, his mind clearing. "That's just it. For this, you might be the more important one."

She dropped the bunched-up cloth she held in her hand and frowned at him. "What do you mean?"

Tan took a moment to tell her what he planned, and how he thought that the kingdoms needed to shape wind. "Now that Alan has found wind, I think it might work. I wasn't sure before. With Incendin, Fur can use kaas to shape. It makes the shaping even more powerful. Doma has Vel using udilm, and Elle. There might be others, but I don't know. Chenir might not have any bonded shapers," he said, realizing that he didn't know whether they did or not, "but they can summon the elementals, earth especially. The kingdoms need to work with wind."

"Tan—"

He stood and went to the window. "This has to work. We can push them back. If the nations work together like that, it will work."

Zephra sighed. "Chenir has been forced to withdraw. Par-shon came with more numbers than we could counter. There is nothing more we can do."

"What?"

"When you fell, you'd freed me. I don't know how, but you did. Something came over me, a thick fog that left me refreshed and restored my connection to Aric. I came out of that building and found you on the ground. Par-shon shapers were returning, so I escaped on the wind. As we did, I summoned Theondar. I didn't know that you'd already summoned him. They were pushed back and barely escaped."

"What of Chenir? The Supreme Leader was going to have them stop summoning the elementals."

Her face tightened. "I don't know what they were doing. The barren lands are unchanged, if that's what you mean. Chenir did that to protect the elementals." His mother shook her head. "It doesn't matter. They will cross the barrier and then Theondar will replace it. We will be safe."

"Safe?" Tan asked. "You think that holding the barrier up will keep us safe? What of Doma? The rest of Chenir? What of Incendin?"

"The kingdoms can't be concerned with them. We need to keep *our* borders safe. We can't do that if we're trying to help all those other nations."

Tan glanced over at the flames, noting the way that saa swirled within them. How could his mother still think that they only had to worry about themselves? How could she still not think that they needed to look beyond their borders? If Par-shon remained on the continent, everyone would suffer. Not only the nations that fell, but the kingdoms would be in danger, and there would be no way to avoid the eventual attack.

"Where are the others?" Tan asked.

Zephra stood and planted her hands on her hips. "I'm not the only one who feels this way, Tannen."

He shook his head. "Where are the others?"

"Roine is in the palace. He's meeting with the Supreme Leader."

"And Cora?"

"What about her?"

"She answered my summons for help when I went to save you."

"I didn't see Cora."

"Then Elle returned to Doma?"

Zephra nodded. "She returned. Vel summoned her to assist with a shaping."

Tan snorted. The shaping that Vel would have needed Elle's help with was the same type of shaping that Tan wanted his mother to attempt. In his frustration, Tan went to the door, not looking over at her.

"Where are you going, Tannen?" she asked.

"To see what I can do to stop Par-shon."

As the door closed, her voice followed him. "You can't stop Par-shon. Our best hope is to keep them out of our lands."

* * * * *

Amia caught Tan as he exited the house. Worry lined her face, and her eyes had dark rings around them. Her golden hair was spiraled atop her head, twisted with a thick braid. The gold band on her neck caught the sunlight. One of her fingers ran around the edge of the band.

"You intend to return," she said.

Tan inhaled deeply. "I intend to help Chenir. We have to push Par-shon back, and the only way is to stop them from withdrawing the elementals."

"But you're not certain."

Tan hugged her, swallowing past the lump in his throat. "When I faced the warrior, I had to use every ounce of strength that I could summon, and even then I almost wasn't strong enough to stop him."

"You did stop him."

"I had help. The elementals came to my aid, but they might not be strong enough against someone like the Utu Tonah." He hesitated and faced Amia. "I can't stop him, Amia. He's too powerful of a shaper. But we *can* push Par-shon out. Incendin and Doma have done it. Chenir can. The kingdoms can."

Tan reached for the sense of Kota and found her roaming the mountains along the border with Chenir. The other hounds were there as well, connected to him distantly. Honl drifted faintly in the back of his mind, and the nymid were like a steady, rhythmic sense deep within him.

One sense was missing.

Not that Tan couldn't sense Asboel. There had been many times when the draasin simply was too far away for him to reach, but this was different. All sense of the draasin was gone, as if he simply wasn't there.

"No . . . "

Asboel!

There was no response.

Tan tried again. *Asboel!*

Again, he heard no response.

He ran toward the lower level of the archives, moving more on a shaping of wind and bounding steps of earth. When he reached the archives, he raced down the steps in the darkness, not pausing to light any of the shapers lanterns. At the bottom of the stairs, he shaped open the door to the tunnels and continued running, sprinting through the tunnels, finally reaching the door to the draasin den.

Tan shaped it open and ran inside.

Asboel was there, but he no longer breathed.

Asgar and the other hatchling sat on either side of him. Asgar glanced up as Tan entered and breathed a streamer of flame at Tan, but he did so without much strength behind it. The flame fell away from Tan harmlessly. The other hatchling backed away.

Sashari poked her head through the hole in the den, her glowing eyes catching Tan. *Maelen,* she said, reaching Tan through the fire bond. *He has returned to the Mother.*

It is my fault, Tan said. He remembered needing additional strength and the willing way that Asboel had given of himself, lending Tan all the strength that he had remaining.

He did not blame you. You brought him peace, Maelen.

Tan ignored Asgar and stepped up to Asboel, moving around until he could see the draasin's face. His eyes were closed, no longer to look upon the world, no longer able to hunt. Tan rested his hand on Asboel's cool nose. Tears streamed down his eyes and he blinked them away.

He had lost so many that he'd cared about over the years, but in some ways, losing Asboel was the hardest.

I would like to have hunted with him again, Tan said.

You did, Maelen. This came from Asgar. The draasin stood, and his head brushed the ceiling. He'd grown larger in the few days since Tan had last been here, now equal to Enya. *He hunted through your connection.*

It brought him comfort, Sashari said.

Tan sensed Amia at the doorway. She hesitated before coming in and slipping her arm around him. She mourned with him, feeling the loss nearly as acutely as he did.

What will you do with him? Tan asked.

Sashari snorted. *He will remain in the den. We will find a new place.*

I will seal it, then, Tan said.

It is fitting that it should be here, Sashari said.

Fitting how?

This is where the Great One hatched, she said. *This is where he will rest.*

With that, Sashari snorted and the two hatchlings followed her, leaving Tan alone with his friend. He stood with his hand resting on Asboel's nose for a long time, remembering when he had first met the draasin, the terror he'd felt, and how different that was compared to now. If only he would have had the chance to soar with him one more time, to hunt with him one more time. If only they would have had more time.

"He would not want vengeance," Tan said.

Amia embraced him. "I don't think that he ever wanted vengeance."

Tan wiped away the tears on his face. "No. He wanted only to serve the Mother. In everything, he was a faithful servant of fire." Tan lifted his hand from Asboel and took a deep breath. "His work—*our* work—isn't done. No matter what my mother thinks, Par-shon must be stopped." For Asboel, he would find a way to do it.

Amia was silent. He shared the uncertainty she sent across their bond. How was he to stop Par-shon now that he'd lost one of his bonds? How would he be able to withstand the Utu Tonah without fire?

CHAPTER 24

Decisions

THE SHAPING TOOK TAN AND AMIA to the palace courtyard. Tan shaped through his ring, summoning Roine as he
landed and waited. Tan was surprised to learn that it was early. The sun
was barely to midday, and cooler than he'd known in some time. The
air gusted with the strength of ara. Honl rarely mixed in these days, so
changed since Tan had healed him. Perhaps Tan had already lost that
bond as well. When would he lose the bond to the nymid? To the hounds?

Ara, Tan called to the wind, *you must convince Zephra to shape the
wind away from these lands.* He sent an image of the shaping he'd seen
in Incendin as well as in Doma. In order to keep the kingdoms safe, ara
would need to complete a similar shaping, but Tan suspected it needed
to be guided by a shaper, someone like Zephra, or Alan.

Roine appeared as Tan finished sending his request to ara.
He appeared from a smaller door in the palace and was dressed

in simple pants and a dark green shirt. His sword hung from his belt.

"Tannen. Your mother didn't think that you'd be up for days."

Tan debated telling Roine about what had happened to Asboel, but what would it change? He had never shared the connection to the draasin, had never understood the true importance of the bond. "My mother doesn't understand the connection to the elementals," he said.

Amia tugged on his hand, but the hurt from losing Asboel burned within him.

"Zephra is bonded to one of the elementals, Tan. I think that she understands them as well as any."

"She *should* understand them, but I wonder if she listens."

Roine smiled, and it diffused some of the frustration that Tan was feeling. "Your mother has never been particularly good about listening, Tannen. I doubt that you will change her now."

"She thinks that the barrier should be replaced as soon as Chenir withdraws."

Roine glanced toward the palace and then sighed. "That is my suggestion. I think she is only offering what I have suggested that we do."

"But you know what will happen if Chenir withdraws," Tan began. "You know how much will be lost if we allow that to happen."

"That was before I saw what Par-shon brought to these shores. Tan, I don't begin to know how they have managed to trap and bond so many shapers, but they have numbers that we can't even begin to dream about. Even when the university was at its strongest, we didn't have that many. And each of their shapers is bonded to at least one of the elementals. Do you have any idea how powerful that makes them?" Roine touched the hilt of his sword. "When you left, we were barely able to hold them back. Cora and Elle helped, as did the hounds, but we were overpowered. We had to withdraw. Without the separation that Chenir created by their shaping, we wouldn't have made it. The Supreme Leader—"

"What of the Supreme Leader?"

Roine shook his head. "He did not make it back to his people. Another was chosen. At my urging, they continue their separation. That was their price for taking refuge in the kingdoms. It gives them—and us—the time we need to prepare."

"That *separation* is how they withdraw the elementals," Tan said.

"Isn't that what you want?" Roine asked. "Don't you want to keep the elementals safe? If they're withdrawn from Chenir, we can get them beyond the borders, and then they *will* be safe. The barrier can keep Par-shon's shapers on the other side."

"For how long, Roine?" Tan asked softly. "How long until they attack us from the sea? How long until they've conquered Doma and Incendin, too?"

"This will buy us time," Roine said.

"No, it gives them a chance to become stronger." That was the greatest risk. With every elemental that was lost, with every forced bond, Par-shon became stronger. They had nearly a thousand shapers now; what would happen when they had two thousand? Ten?

It wouldn't stop. Tan understood that now. He didn't know what lands were out beyond the sea, but he could imagine Par-shon continuing to push their influence, capturing more and more elementals until there was no one able to oppose them. Those peoples would suffer, but so too would the elementals.

Tan would find a way to keep them from these lands—*all* of these lands.

"Is the Supreme Leader still here?" Tan asked.

Roine glanced to the palace and shook his head. "He has returned to his people. We seek a treaty. The kingdoms will grant safety, but not lands, and they will be beholden to our laws. It's much like what we've done with the Aeta," he said to Amia. "Why do you ask?"

"They can push Par-shon out, much like Doma and Incendin push Par-shon out."

Roine crossed his arms over his chest and shook his head. "I wish I could believe that was all that we needed, Tannen, but we need to keep our people safe. The barrier will buy us time."

"Until when?" Tan asked, but he waved away Roine's attempt to answer. "What happens when Par-shon defeats our barrier? Incendin managed to overcome it, and they had nothing like the horrible strength that Par-shon has."

"Tannen—"

He shook his head and turned away, leaving Roine standing alone. He hurried down the street, making his way toward the archives. There might be something he could still do. He'd refused for so long, but if not now, when would he attempt to use the artifact?

"Where are you going?" Amia asked.

"It won't work if we don't all push Par-shon away, and if the kingdoms won't help, there's only one way that I can think of to stop Par-shon," Tan said.

She shook her head. "You're the one who told me that we couldn't use it, Tan. That it was damaged. You said it can't be repaired."

"Maybe I was wrong," Tan said. "If I can find a way to restore the artifact—"

Amia pulled on his arm. "Tan, think of what you're saying. Even if you repair it, do you think that *you* can control the artifact any better than Althem did? Do you think that you're going to use that power wisely? You're upset and you mourn the loss of Asboel, but this isn't the way to honor his memory."

Tan lifted them both on a shaping of wind, carrying them toward the university. As they landed in the circle, Tan realized that much of the construction on the building seemed to be complete. Stone walls rose several stories high. Windows set into the stone peeked out into the courtyard. No longer did Tan sense the effect of shaping all around him working on the building; what he sensed now was something different. This was shaping, but different, and with less control than any of the master shapers would manage, more like Tan's faltering shaping had been when he first came to the university.

Voices called out, and he realized that the university had reopened. Ferran's construction was finally complete after months of work. Now the students who had been housed in the palace, those who Roine had found, mostly the heirs of Althem, ran through the halls of the new university. Some played in the yard and watched him as he landed, eyes going wide as a shaper appeared. He heard them speaking in hushed tones about the Athan, and overheard whispers of some of the things that Tan had accomplished.

He paused, wishing that he would have the time to teach in the university, or at least that he would have had the opportunity to have known it as it was. When he'd come here, there had been no time for him to experience it; he'd needed to find a way to help Elle and then stop the archivists from attacking the city and destroying Amia. What must it be like to be so innocent but understanding that you would one day have the ability to shape?

"You never had that, did you?" Amia asked him.

Tan shook his head. "I knew I was a senser, but my ability to shape came to me later than most. I don't even know if my father ever knew that I'd be able to shape."

Many of them were the result of the king's spirit shaping that he'd used to take advantage of those who trusted him. None of these children would have parents who would be able to teach them the lessons that Tan had learned. They would need to rely on the masters, shapers like Ferran.

As Tan thought of him, the earth shaper appeared through one of the doors. He was simply dressed, in a dark brown shirt and pants, with a solid smile on his face. His eyes had changed to a flinty gray, different than they had been when Tan had first met him, but so, too, had his demeanor. Then, Ferran was more interested in learning where the students came from and less in teaching. It was that way with all of the instructors, from what Tan had seen. Now, Ferran looked at each of the children in the yard with a warm and welcoming expression. He shaped a steady shaping through the earth, sending a rumbling request to the children as he summoned them back inside. When Ferran saw Tan, he waved.

The children squealed and ran toward Ferran. He guided them through the door and into the university, waving one more time to Tan before disappearing behind a door.

"He is good with them," Amia noted.

"Golud has changed him."

"The elementals change everyone, you've said."

Tan sighed. Asboel had certainly changed him. The draasin had made him confident and taught him to respect the pull of fire, but he'd also taught him the value of the hunt and the need to keep the elementals safe. Honl had taught Tan that he needed to continue searching for answers, and that the bond was all about understanding. He suspected the nymid's greatest lesson was simply the ability to recognize other elementals. Through the connection to water, he recognized that there were other powers greater than him. It had been that way since Tan had first met the nymid. And now the hounds. What would Kota teach him?

"The bond changes everyone," Tan said.

"And our bond?" Amia asked.

"You don't think it has changed you?" he asked.

Amia smiled and stood on her toes to kiss him on the cheek. "The bond has changed me. I sometimes wonder what I would have been like had we not met, but then I remember that I would probably not have survived without meeting you. I think the Great Mother blessed me in many ways when we began our journey together. Think of how much we've learned since we first sought the artifact."

"You don't think I should try to fix it."

"I think that you should do what you think is right. I trust your judgment, Tan." She touched the ring on his finger and twisted it. "Roine trusts your judgment as well."

"We can't defeat Par-shon," Tan said. "And I can't defeat the Utu Tonah."

"Are you certain? He might have bonded the elementals, but you can use their strength. You are able to borrow from them. You are capable of so much more than the bond."

"Without Asboel, I'm not sure that I can."

She smiled at him and touched his face where she'd kissed him. "You are more than any single elemental. I think that even Asboel recognized that."

He sighed, listening through spirit and earth, enjoying the sounds of the children running through the university and the sense of the people in the city. There was life here, and power within that. If Par-shon attacked, how much of that would change? How would these people change?

Tan couldn't let something happen without trying to stop it. More than anything, that was the reason the Great Mother had called him to serve.

221

"All we need to do is keep him out," Tan started. "Return the elementals to Chenir, and they can shape as Doma does. If the kingdoms do the same—"

"And then what?" Amia asked. When Tan didn't answer, she pressed, "He grows stronger. I sense it somehow. As he does, everything changes. This cannot only be about keeping him from the kingdoms."

"And Chenir. And Doma. And Incendin."

"Sooner or later, he will have to be stopped."

Tan looked around, wishing he knew of some way that would work, but the only thing he could come up with led to him facing the Utu Tonah alone, and he wasn't certain that he could. "I don't think I can."

He took Amia's hand and started out of the university, making his way down streets that had been repaired since the lisincend and the draasin attack. The streets were noisy and filled with carts and people. He saw clothing of all kinds and was reminded of his first night in the city, when he'd seen people from Xsa Isles and Chenir. He remembered thinking how impossible it was that so many people were in the city, that so many from outside the kingdoms had come here. It had been months since he had noticed people of different nationalities here. Within the kingdoms, everyone came together to trade, but especially here in Ethea. Perhaps Roine was right that Chenir should be allowed in and that the barrier could hold out Par-shon. Maybe all they needed was a little longer to find some way to stop the Utu Tonah.

He entered the archives. As he made his way to the lower level, he took the time to light shaper lanterns, giving the walls a dark glow and casting back the shadows. The first time he'd been down here, he'd been chased by an Incendin shaper. Now, Incendin shapers were his allies, and he would even call one a friend.

222

At the bottom of the stairs, he entered the room where he'd stored the artifact. He pushed open the case. It was long and slender and made of the same deep gray metal that he'd seen in the pool of the Mother, almost as if the shapers from long ago had managed to coax the Mother into maintaining the shape. Runes were etched along its surface. Now that he'd learned to read them, he recognized how the runes marked each of the elementals. Tan wondered if they were the elementals that had been involved in the creation of the artifact.

There was fire. Not the draasin, though they had protected the artifact, drawing from their fire to create the pillar that had prevented others from reaching it. The runes were not for inferin, saa, or saldam. Tan recognized that it indicated fire, but not which elemental had gone into its making.

It was the same for earth. He could make out the rune and knew that it signified earth, but it was not the rune for golud, or nodn, or even for the hounds, though he would have been surprised had those ancient shapers used the hounds. Water and wind were much the same.

Only spirit was the same rune that he'd seen, though there was no elemental for spirit. The only elemental that Tan had ever come close to seeing was the pool of spirit. "I don't know what I was thinking," he said, tracing a finger over the runes.

Amia looked over his shoulder. Her shoulders were tense, as if she was afraid to touch the artifact, but she was willing to study it. She'd held it before, but that was before any of them knew how powerful a creation it was.

Tan thought of the book he'd taken from the hut. Part of the hope he'd felt had stemmed from the possibility that he might find the secret to repairing the artifact, but now he wasn't as certain that would even matter.

"It might not be any more useful than my sword," he said, tapping it. He was thankful that he hadn't lost it when battling the warrior in Chenir. He'd had it unsheathed when he'd fallen and hadn't bothered to ask his mother if she had grabbed it or if he'd simply been unwilling to let go of it. "It's the elementals," he said. "It's always been about the elementals. When I used it with Althem, I was bound to fire but borrowed from the nymid, golud, and ashi." He'd thought it was ara at the time, but he had learned that it was really Honl when he had first summoned. "Without fire and without spirit, I don't know that I can control it."

"You never controlled it."

Tan looked up and saw Roine standing in the doorway to the archives. His brow was creased and he looked at Tan with worry in his eyes.

"I don't think you did anything other than stop Althem."

"I healed the draasin," Tan said. He should have done the same again, only Asboel hadn't wanted him to attempt anything more than he had. The draasin understood that there were things that he couldn't change. Maybe he welcomed the return to the Mother.

"Was that you, or was that the elementals?" Roine asked.

Tan shook his head. The elementals hadn't been able to heal Asboel this time, but maybe it was different. That had been an attack by Althem. Asboel's injury now was from an elemental. "I thought it was me."

"I've been thinking about this as well." He reached for the artifact and took it from Tan, running a finger along the long crack that had formed in it when Tan tried to understand how it was made. His eyes narrowed slightly and he shook his head. "The artifact is powerful. We know that. But we also now know that the shapers of that time weren't the benevolent shapers that we thought them to be. They were willing to harness elementals, and they were willing to experiment on them as well."

Roine closed his eyes and took a few deep breaths. "I'd always thought that they were what I aspired to become. The stories of the ancient shapers were always impressive, the feats that they accomplished always more amazing than anything that we could accomplish, but they did it through ignorance that I would not have us repeat."

"Not all of them," Tan said, thinking of the hut in the middle of the swamp. It had given him hope that not all the ancient shapers had been the same. "I don't know how to stop them, but we can keep them out until we do."

Roine nodded. "Neither do I, but weren't you the one who tried to teach me that we can't repeat the mistakes of the past?" He smiled. "There is wisdom in that lesson, Tan, more than I was willing to see and understand at the time. I think that I understand it now."

"But you continue to want the barrier in place. Isn't that a mistake of the past?" Tan asked.

"I think the mistake there was in not understanding it. The barrier was a creation of Lacertin's. Most of us forgot that, myself included. Without him, I don't know that we are able to control what it filters through, but we *can* create safety around our borders. All of our borders, at least until we understand a way to stop Par-shon. If we're careful, we can lower sections if needed to allow access to Doma."

"What about Incendin?"

"Do you think that Incendin wants to reach us? Do you think that they will help?"

"Cora has helped several times already. When can we accept the fact that Incendin is different than what we knew?"

"Cora is not all of Incendin. Cora is not the lisincend."

"And the lisincend are not the lisincend that you knew," Tan said.

225

Roine clapped Tan on the shoulder. "This is my decision, Tannen. I need your support. I might even need your help to make sure it happens."

Tan glanced at Amia but couldn't answer.

CHAPTER 25

Request to Old Enemies

TAN SAT IN THE LOWER LEVEL of the archives, holding the broken artifact and trying to understand why it had been created, when the summons came. Amia had left him to return to the wagons outside the city. The Aeta needed their First Mother, though Tan sensed her reluctance in leaving him. He flipped through the book that he'd found in the hut in the middle of the swamp, trying to make sense of the *Ishthin* and understand what had motivated the shaper who had written it, hoping to ease the aching inside him. So far, he hadn't been able to make sense of it.

The rune coin pulsed in his pocket and he pulled it out, glancing long enough to realize that it was wind that summoned. Zephra. Tan thought it odd that his mother would summon him, especially after the way things had been left between them, but then, she never summoned him.

He made his way to the traveling circle in the university. Daylight was fading, leaving the sun sending shafts of light filtering around the city buildings, creating something of an orange glow around everything that reminded him of looking through Asboel's sight. There were no young shapers out, though a few candles flickered in windows.

Tan pulled a shaping toward him and exploded away from the city on a warrior shaping.

He followed the summoning coin, letting it guide him, and emerged on the edge of Nara.

Zephra waited for him there. She floated on a shaping, Aric holding her in place as she looked out past the border of Nara and into Incendin. Tan felt the building energy of the barrier, though he didn't see the shapers creating it. It had grown more powerful since the last time he'd sensed it. Soon, it would be as strong as it had been before it had fallen to Incendin.

"You summoned me, Mother?" Tan asked.

She waved a hand toward Incendin. "What do you see?"

Rather than arguing, Tan humored her and stared into Incendin. He stretched toward Incendin with spirit and earth, but found that the barrier blocked him. Tan frowned. If the barrier prevented him from even sensing beyond the border, would it prevent him from reaching Cora? Would it prevent him from knowing if the elementals on the other side of the barrier needed help?

He used a shaping of water that he'd seen Elle use and created a shaping that allowed him to look into Incendin. With the shaping, he saw the reason his mother had summoned him to Nara, and the reason that she hadn't called any others.

There were lisincend on the other side of the border.

Tan counted nearly a dozen, and one was larger than the rest. At first he thought that it was Fur, but he realized that it wouldn't be. Fur would be focused on remaining in the Fire Fortress, and would be focused on trying to maintain the shaping that prevented Par-shon from reaching their shores. But the lisincend that he saw resembled Fur.

"Issan," Tan said.

"You know them?"

"I healed all the lisincend, Mother."

"They do not seem pleased."

Tan noticed that there was a sense of agitation from them. Issan had been the most vocal about his irritation with Tan for bringing him back into the fire bond, but there had been others like him. What if Issan had found a way to return to the twisting of fire? What if he intended to oppose Fur?

"If I cross the barrier, what will happen?" he asked.

"Nothing will happen to you. You are of the kingdoms."

Tan didn't think that it worked quite like that. "Will it prevent me from returning?"

"Tannen, as I've said, you are of the kingdoms. The barrier is not meant to prevent shapers of the kingdoms from crossing her border."

"What if it decides that I'm not of the kingdoms?" Tan asked.

"The barrier isn't sentient," Zephra answered. "And you wear the ring of the Athan. I think that you'll be fine."

If he wasn't? If he was trapped and unable to return? He doubted his mother would lower the barrier to allow him to pass. But he needed to know why Issan had come.

Tan shaped himself across the barrier.

On the other side, the heat of Incendin changed. It was warmer than he remembered, warmer even than it had been in Nara, though they should be similar. Tan floated on a shaping of wind mixed with fire and reached the lisincend. He remained in the air, staying above Issan until he knew what the lisincend intended.

The lisincend noticed Tan immediately. Fire shot toward him, but when it struck Tan, it did nothing more than shift him in the air. Tan lowered himself to stand next to Issan, but remained far enough away that the creature couldn't reach him.

"The warrior returns to attack again?" Issan said.

"Not to attack. I wanted to know what brought you here."

"This is all part of the Sunlands. Have you got Fur so far under your thumb that we cannot be here, either?"

Tan frowned. "I don't have Fur under my thumb at all. Had he been, he would have helped when I faced Par-shon."

The lisincend hissed at the mention of Par-shon.

"Where did you face Par-shon?" Issan demanded.

"Chenir. They have settled in Chenir, much like they attempted in Doma."

Issan turned and looked toward the north. His nostrils flared, and Tan felt a surge of fire from him, as if he reached through the fire bond. Tan wasn't sure that the lisincend knew *how* to reach through the fire bond, but when Issan turned back to Tan, his thin lips were pulled into a sneer. "You leave Chenir to face them alone yet come to the Sunlands to taunt Issan? You are not as mighty as Fur believes, Warrior."

"I would have remained," Tan began, "but there were too many."

Issan laughed. Steam hissed from him as he did. "Too many for a warrior like yourself, but not too many for Issan."

"Chenir is dangerous. There are nearly a thousand from Par-shon within their borders."

Issan's demeanor changed. The steam eased and he leaned toward Tan. "Does Fur know this?"

"Fur didn't answer my summons. Only Corasha Saladan answered."

At the mention of her name, several of the lisincend made deep, hissing noises. Tan wondered what Cora had done to anger the lisincend. Whatever it was, he wasn't sure he wanted to know.

"The kingdoms place a barrier around themselves again. You think to prevent Par-shon from reaching you. What of the Sunlands?" Issan asked.

"I have asked Theondar to consider the need for the barrier—"

"Theondar," Issan said with a snarl, "thinks nothing of the Sun-lands."

"Why have you come here, Issan?" Tan asked.

The lisincend glanced behind him at the others. "Fur thinks that he can control us now that fire now longer sings within our veins. We are those who would still serve as fire requires."

"And you have come here to learn what fire wants of you?"

"We have come to learn."

"You would rather face Par-shon?" Tan asked.

Issan sneered at him again. "You choose not to face Par-shon but you ask if the lisincend will?"

"As I said, I can't do it alone. But with help," he began, "there might be more that we can do." Roine wanted to keep the borders safe, but doing so meant that places like Doma and Incendin were in danger. What if Tan went around what Roine wanted? What if he took it upon himself to complete what needed to be done?

Tan could get the elementals to help, but he would need shapers able to counter the sheer numbers that Par-shon possessed. There were dozens of lisincend, each powerful fire shapers. Doma had shapers, and more than he had expected. If Chenir would use their shapers, they had a unique strength, different than any other shaper in the way that they were able to connect to the elementals. All that left were the kingdoms' shapers.

Tan glanced over to Nara, toward his waiting mother. After what she'd been through, he doubted that she would help. Others might. Tan could call to Cianna through Sashari and the fire bond. He might be able to reach other shapers bonded to the elementals, but would there be enough to make a difference?

Maybe.

Knowing what Par-shon did to Chenir, how they poisoned the land, he knew what he had to do. It was what Asboel would have wanted him to do.

"If you would face Par-shon, convince Fur to help. Let us stop waiting for Par-shon to attack, and let us finally take the fight to them."

Issan flared with heat for a moment. "Why should I work with a kingdoms shaper? It is your fault that I no longer burn."

"You control it now. Is that not better?"

"No."

"Then do it for the Sunlands. Do it because if you do not, Par-shon will move through Doma next, leaving only the Sunlands remaining. Do it to show Fur that you deserve his respect." Tan added the last without knowing what effect it would have on him, and the response from Issan told him that he'd read it correctly.

"You have even stolen the hounds," Issan said.

"Not stolen. Did you even know they were elementals? Did you even know how powerful they could be?"

The other lisincend behind Issan began murmuring.

"Come. I will convince Chenir to fight. Doma already resists. You must convince Fur to answer if I summon."

Issan glared toward the kingdoms, and heat radiated from him. "You say this only to destroy the lisincend."

Tan created a shaping of each element that slammed into the ground next to Issan. "Had I wanted to destroy you, I never would have attempted the healing. Be thankful that you have a chance to serve, Issan. That is all that fire asks of you." Tan turned his attention to the other lisincend and spoke loud enough for them all to hear. "Par-shon is the enemy. Not the kingdoms, not Doma, and not Fur. We can work together and have a chance, or we can shut each other out, and we can all fall separately. They come in numbers and steal the elementals from our lands. If we do nothing, we all will fall. Perhaps not today, but it will happen. If we work together, we might do more than survive."

With that, Tan shaped himself back toward Nara where Zephra waited, leaving the lisincend to watch him depart.

The barrier tingled over his skin, and it felt something like sliding through thick mud as he passed through. His mother had thought that he shouldn't have trouble passing over the barrier, but Tan wondered how much longer that would be the case, especially if he made it clear that he would work against Roine's wishes. What would that make him? Something other than of the kingdoms, but what?

Zephra waited with her hands on her hips, one foot tapping impatiently. "Why have they gathered?"

"Not to attack, if that's the reason that you brought me here," he said.

"Are you so certain that they don't mean to attack?" she asked.

"They are healed. Brought back into the fire bond. There were lisincend who did not want to be healed, who preferred the mindless draw of fire. Issan—Fur's brother—was one of them. The rest felt much the same." Tan shaped water to study the lisincend again. They had begun to move away from the border, but Tan couldn't tell which direction they headed. "They don't know what their purpose is anymore. They resent Fur for what he's done, but they also miss the draw of fire."

Tan thought of when he'd been consumed by fire and the way that it had called to him. He understood how the lisincend felt, the way they desired the return to the connection. Tan had been able to reach the other elementals and had Amia to help him, but these lisincend would have been twisted by fire for a long time, some possibly longer

than Tan had been alive. That most had tolerated the healing was actually surprising.

"Your willingness to accept what they had been is troubling, Tannen."

"As is your inability to recognize that people change. You were not
always so stubborn."

"I've always been stubborn," Zephra snapped.

"Then it's not Aric's influence," Tan said. "Good. Now that you
know it's you, you can work on fixing it." He took his mother's hands
and squeezed. "I saved you so that you could help, but also because I
love you, Mother. In spite of your unwillingness to recognize that I've
become . . . " He trailed off, not certain what to call himself. Cloud
Warrior didn't quite fit, because Tan felt that he was something different than the Cloud Warriors. He was not like the Utu Tonah, the
Bonded One, though in some ways he *was* more like him than anything else. "Capable," he finished. "And in spite of your inability to forgive. Not only Incendin, but you've struggled with Amia and the Aeta.
They are not the reason that Father is gone. They are not the reason
that you lost your first bond."

Her eyes narrowed. "Incendin *is* the reason that Grethan and Alyia
are gone. Had Incendin not attacked, both would still be with me."

"And without all of this happening, you would never have re-
connected with Theondar. I've seen it, and I've seen the connection
between you both. I don't resent the fact that you can find comfort
in Theondar. He is a good man, even if he's nearly as stubborn as
you. But like you, he struggles to forgive. We've all made mistakes,
and we all have the potential to change. For us to survive, we all
must change."

His mother pulled her hands away from him and Tan dropped his,
letting her go.

234

"I'm not sure that I can ever move past what Incendin has done over the years. Theondar has the same struggles."

"Mother—" Tan started.

She shook her head. "Tannen, you will do what you must." She smiled, and her eyes softened, warmth coming to them. "You have always been something of a mixture of myself and Grethan in that way. And you share much of your stubbornness with me. I see that you have made up your mind. I suspect that it has something to do with what you said to the lisincend. I didn't hear all of it, but Aric brought enough snippets for me to know that you intend to return to Chenir. That way lies defeat and death. I would do anything to keep you from that fate, but you are a man." She crossed her arms and grabbed at each shoulder. "Seeing you these last few months, watching you become this shaper, and then this warrior, and then so much more . . . it has filled me with pride *and* sadness. I know there is only one way this can end."

"You don't know that, Mother."

"I know that you are determined to do what you must to protect the elementals from harm. Tell me that I'm wrong."

"You're not wrong in that. But you are wrong that there is only one way that this will end. I may not have the bonds that the Utu Tonah possesses, but I have something that he doesn't. I have the support of the Great Mother. Whatever else happens, I *feel* that much is true." And he'd heard the same from Asboel, and from Honl. "Promise me something," Tan said.

His mother tipped her head and waited.

"When you sense my call, promise that you will work the wind. Ara will guide you and will know what to do. Listen to Aric. And convince Alan and any other wind shaper to help. I don't know why I feel so strongly that it will work, but it has to. That has to be the answer to cleansing Par-shon from our lands."

His mother inhaled deeply and her arms relaxed, dropping to her sides. She tipped her head toward him, her lips pursed. "I will listen," she agreed.

Tan thought that was all that he could hope for at this point.

With a shaping binding each of the elements, he traveled away from Nara and into Chenir.

CHAPTER 26

An Elemental Plan

THE LANDSCAPE AROUND CHENIR had drastically changed. The grasses that grew across the rocky plains had a faded appearance, sagging into the earth. Not so much like grasses that had dried from the change in season, these looked as if they had somehow lessened, as if more than simply the life had been drawn from them. The tall oak tree Tan appeared next to was much the same, the branches sagging, making it droop, the leaves curled and faded, slowly dropping to the ground. Even the bark of the tree had a different appearance, as if the color had been blanched from it.

The steady, rhythmic sounds of the Chenir drumming rolled over him, a call from their distant shapers. With each beat, Tan felt the elementals recede further, and with each beat, he felt the life leave these lands even more quickly.

They had nearly reached the border with the kingdoms. Another day, and they would be there, and then what? Would Chenir stop withdrawing the elementals or would they continue, pulling them deeper into the kingdoms, leaving those lands altered as well?

In the east, he sensed the distant pull of Par-shon. Their shapers pushed against Chenir. Tan felt the force of their thousand bonded shapers, something like a weight upon him. In time, they would overwhelm Chenir. Then there would be nothing to oppose Par-shon. Chenir would be abandoned and lost.

Tan inhaled and lifted to the air on a shaping of fire and wind, inspired by how Asboel had flown. Tan wished he had the draasin's insight about what he needed to do, but then, didn't he carry much of it with him? Asboel had shared with him everything that Tan needed to be able to stop Par-shon. Now Tan had to do it.

The shaping carried him higher and higher. Tan soared above the earth, above the clouds, high enough that he felt as if he could see all the land spread out beneath him. From this vantage point, he saw the kingdoms, Incendin, Doma, and Chenir. Everything appeared so small. He saw beyond the sea, where islands dotted the blue expanse, places like the Xsa Isles and then Par-shon. From here, Par-shon was larger than he remembered. Perhaps that was what the Utu Tonah intended. Did he intend to do the same as the kingdoms' shapers long ago and draw land from the sea?

Shapers filled Chenir to the east. There were hundreds, so many that he couldn't count them all. His connection to the hounds, and through them, to earth, gave him insight. Chenir's remaining shapers seemed so few in comparison.

This high up, Tan felt only the sun as it burned on his face. Even the winds left him alone. He enjoyed the warmth of the sun and drew strength from it. In that way, he felt close to Asboel as well.

Waiting did nothing more than delay what he needed.

Pulling on the strength of the elementals, Tan streaked toward the ground. As he did, he called to Kota and to the other hounds, not certain if the pack would respond to him.

He landed in the midst of the Chenir camp with a thunderous explosion. For a moment, the rhythmic drumming stopped, the steady pull on water and wind eased, and even the call to fire lessened. Tan felt the return of elementals and called to them. *Assist me.*

The new Supreme Leader came to him, followed by shapers that Tan had seen before. The Supreme Leader wore the coat of office but did not have the same stature the last had possessed. He had a youthful face, and as Tan used a shaping of spirit to understand him, he recognized that he was only an earth shaper, not a warrior, as the last had been. The man was powerful—that much he could easily tell—but would he have the same concern for the elementals that Tolstan Vreth had possessed?

The water shaper was with him, her face neutral but her hands tightly clenched. A muscular earth shaper approached, carrying one of the long drumsticks their shapers used in the summoning of earth. His face was hard and pinched with an edge of anger. The fire shapers remained on the outside edge, as if unwilling to meet his eyes.

"Theondar granted us safe passage," the Supreme Leader said. He chose his words carefully and fixed his eyes straight ahead, as if forcing himself not to look at the shapers on either side of him. Tan wondered how tenuous a position he held. Could he fear losing his authority to the others? "That was the agreement. You would deny us that?"

"I won't deny your people safe passage, but you cannot remove the elementals. Your predecessor understood that."

The Supreme Leader took a step toward Tan. "He made the mistake of answering your call. With his passing, Chenir has lost the greatest weapon that we have. If we don't withdraw the elementals, they will be captured and used against us. This is the only way."

"Have you seen what you do to Chenir?" Tan asked. "Have you gone beyond the border of your camp? If you had, you would see that what you do is more than simply withdrawing the elementals. You withdraw life."

One of the earth shapers stepped forward. "If it will stop Par-shon, then so be it."

Around Tan, the drumming and the rhythmic calling to the elementals had resumed. It came steadily, with a drive that the elementals could not ignore. "How is what you are doing so different than what Par-shon does?"

The Supreme Leader's eyes narrowed. "Careful with your words. You are still within Chenir. These are our lands—"

"From what I can tell, I am not. This seems more like a part of Par-shon."

"You will watch your tone," rumbled the earth shaper. He tapped his drumstick on his leg as he approached. The ground beneath him quivered and shook.

Tan stepped toward the earth shaper, glancing from him to the Supreme Leader. He needed them to help, but more than that, he needed them to stop pulling on the elementals. Tan couldn't battle both Chenir *and* Par-shon. "You have abandoned Chenir, but I have not. I will not abandon any of these lands to Par-shon. Leave if you must, but the elementals will remain."

The earth shaper took a step toward Tan and leaned into him, his jaw clenched. Tan sensed the tension within him, and the shaping that he built.

The Supreme Leader studied Tan before nodding to the earth shaper. "Dolan," he said to the man, trying to ease him. "The previous

Supreme Leader might have had more authority, but this one was too new. He would need time to establish his rule. Still, the earth shaper stepped back but kept his gaze fixed on Tan. "Chenir is more than simply these lands. We are more than a place. When we depart, we do so to preserve Chenir, not abandon it. And we will not abandon the elementals."

"They will not be pulled beyond the barrier." The concern that Tan had been feeling solidified. He couldn't allow Chenir to bring their elementals past the barrier, much like he couldn't allow the kingdoms to ignore Par-shon. Were not all the elementals his responsibility? If they were, then he needed to ensure they were safe. Pulling them away from these lands was not the way to accomplish that. Tan wasn't sure that he knew *how* he was going to stop Par-shon, but he knew that he couldn't do it without the elementals.

"You intend to stop this?" the Supreme Leader asked.

Tan called to Kota. The massive hound was nearby, and with a few enormous leaps, she appeared at his side. Except for Dolan, the Chenir shapers all stepped away from her as one. The earth shaper tapped his drumstick along his leg in a steady fashion. The drumming was meant to call to earth, but Kota was a creature of earth and fire, and the drumming didn't call to them as it did to the other elementals.

She pawed at the ground, sending it trembling. The earth shaper stumbled and dropped his stick. He scrambled to grab it, but Kota was there, grabbing it in her long jaw and snapping it.

"She doesn't care for your drumming," Tan said. "None of them do."

The hounds began to appear around the camp. The drumming didn't call to them as it did to the other elementals. As one, they tipped their head toward the sky and howled, loosing a thunderous cry. The ground rumbled with it, and the elementals summoned away from Chenir were loosed.

When the last echoes of the call eased, Tan fixed his gaze on the Supreme Leader. "If you won't fight, all that I ask is that you allow the elementals to return."

"How can we fight?" the Supreme Leader asked. "You saw how many shapers they have. How can we hope to survive?"

"How can Doma? Yet they fight on, using the unique strength they possess. You may not have the same experience with Incendin that the kingdoms and Doma have, but they fight Par-shon as well, using a shaping of fire to keep them from their shores." Tan softened his tone. "Chenir is stronger than this. Tolstan Vreth saw this and came willingly to help. Use *your* shaping and push back. The elementals of these lands are strong, and your shapings are strong. If you do that, you can drive Par-shon away."

"We have tried." This came from the small water shaper. "When they first landed on our shores, we tried, but they use our elementals against us."

"Not all of them. And you won't be alone this time. You will have help. There are new elementals of earth, and a shaping you did not know before."

Dolan's face contorted. "We have asked the kingdoms for help, and there has been none. We are permitted to retreat, to cross your border, but are not offered any assistance."

"I have come. Zephra came."

"That is two shapers."

"It is two more than you had," Tan said. "And more than two answered my call. You had a shaper from Doma, and one from Incendin. You do not have to suppress Par-shon alone, but you must do what you can. If we do nothing, Par-shon wins. Chenir loses. The elementals lose." Tan turned and met the eyes of each shaper. "I can teach you a shaping that will push Par-shon away. It is a powerful shaping, and one that has worked for others. But you cannot continue to call the elementals in as you do."

Kota circled the shapers and then sat, fixing her eyes on the earth shaper first, and then turning her attention to the Supreme Leader. Neither looked her way.

Moments of silence passed, but then the water shaper stepped forward. "I will help," she said softly. As she did, the movements that she made, tapping on her leg and rubbing her fingers together, movements that Tan had barely been aware that she did, changed. Tan sensed the effect immediately. It was subtle, but focused as he was on these shapers, he sensed how the water elementals pushed out and away from her shaping.

One of the fire shapers stepped forward—a man with a bald head and a deep, sloping forehead—and nodded deeply to Tan. "I will help," he said.

Tan couldn't see what he did, or determine how he summoned fire, but something shifted. He felt it most strongly through the fire bond and the way that the elementals that had been pulling on him, retreating away from Chenir, began to push out.

Other shapers stepped forward, more than Tan had realized had circled him. One by one, they each offered to help, and one by one, the rhythmic pulling on the elementals changed, slowly pushing back out and into Chenir.

It left only the Supreme Leader and the earth shaper. The Supreme Leader made a point of turning to each of the shapers around him. Tan's connection to Kota told him that there were nearly fifty shapers. That would rival the shapers that the kingdoms possessed, though it was fewer than the number of lisincend. Finally, the Supreme Leader nodded. "Chenir will help."

A knot loosened in Tan's chest. "Combine your shapings. Work together like this." Tan demonstrated a shaping that combined each of the elements, pushing earth to the forefront of the shaping. For what he had planned to work, earth would need to be strongest.

Each shaper began to shift their shaping, water and fire combining first, then air, and finally earth. The Supreme Leader controlled the shaping, drumming softly on his thigh as he did.

The hounds howled.

As Tan turned to leave, Dolan stepped forward again, clutching the broken remains of his drumstick. "You will leave us? After all of that, all of your claims, now you leave? What if this doesn't work?"

Tan had no answer. If the shaping didn't work, there would be nothing else they could do that would stop Par-shon. "It will work," he said.

He wished he felt more confident.

* * * * *

Tan reached Doma on a bolt of lightning. Kota managed to arrive only moments after him. He appreciated her presence. For so long, he'd had an elemental with him. First Asboel, then Honl, but now they were both gone. Tan hadn't heard from Honl since he'd returned to the kingdoms, but he sensed him still floating in the back of his mind. Having Kota with him gave a reassuring sense that maybe he still did right by the elementals.

The intensity of Doma's shaping struck him as soon as he landed. There was immense power in the way that water swept out from Doma, the shaping even more powerful than what he'd sensed when he was here the last time. There was a complexity to it that he hadn't noted either. Now, the shaping wrapped around Doma in a powerful sweep, eventually reaching Incendin's shaping. Tan couldn't tell what happened when the shapings joined.

Elle. This close, he could reach her through the spirit connection. Tan hadn't worked out why he could reach Elle when he couldn't speak to anyone other than Amia, but there was value in being able to reach her this way.

I sense you, Tan.

He waited outside the walls of Falsheim, standing along the wide river that flowed beneath the city. The blackened walls still hadn't been scrubbed clean, but Tan wondered if they ever would be. Doma wore the markers as something akin to a badge of pride, a marker of their survival. The water shapers were more powerful than Tan had expected, and each time he visited, there was a new surprise.

Elle appeared, sliding on a rainbow of mist. She wore a damp, white dress and her brown hair was pulled into a braid behind her head. Her sagging shoulders pulled back as she saw him.

"The shaping has grown more powerful," Tan noted.

Elle glanced toward the sea. Water followed her and created a long lens in front of her eyes. "I don't understand it. Water claims another each day." She turned back to Tan, and the shaping of mist returned to form the platform she stood upon. "We now have five bonded shapers, Tan. There hasn't been more than one or two in generations."

"The same is happening in the kingdoms," Tan said. "We've had shapers bond to wind and water, and that's in addition to those that had already bonded."

"Why?"

Tan shrugged. "Maybe there's not a reason."

Elle glared at him. "There's always a reason. Why would the elementals suddenly begin bonding?"

"Perhaps it's fear of Par-shon. Maybe there's something else that we don't understand."

"Our shapers are stronger than they were, too. Ley was never much of a strong shaper, but he's managing to help control water in ways that I'd only seen those at the university do. He thinks to reach water as well."

"You don't think he will?"

"It's possible," Elle said.

Tan listened to the sea, focusing on the ways that the waves crashed along the shores. Water pulled on him, drawing him out, pulling him away. It was the effect of the shaping, he knew, but it was compelling and more powerful than he would have expected from Doma.

He shared the same questions as Elle. Why would the shapings have changed? And why would the elementals begin to bond? Could it really be simply about Par-shon, or was there another reason, something that he hadn't yet seen? Maybe the elementals granted their strength, knowing that without shapers, Par-shon would overpower places like Doma.

"You're preparing something different," Elle said.

"Is it so obvious?" Tan asked.

"I'm not sensing you, if that's what you're asking. But I see it in the way that you're watching the water. It's like you're calculating the cost."

"We need shapers, but we also need to maintain these shapings. They are important. If we can push Par-shon from our shores, I think we have a real chance at holding them away."

"And then what?" Elle looked to the north, toward Chenir and where Par-shon gathered. "*If* we can push them off the shores, then what? How long will it be before they attack again?"

"Elle—"

She shook her head. "No, Tan. Will we be like Incendin has been all these years? Will we have to maintain our own Fire Fortress, pushing against Par-shon, always afraid that they might attack again? We've seen what happens when you're constantly at war. Look at Incendin. How have their people been affected from their time facing Par-shon? Would you have the same for Doma? For the kingdoms?"

"I would rather have peace." Without any real peace, he would always have to remain vigilant. He would have to serve as Athan, wandering as Roine had once done, unable to settle and unable to find happiness of his own. That wasn't the life that Tan wanted, and that wasn't the life that he deserved. After everything they had been through, shouldn't he have an opportunity to have peace? "If we can push back Par-shon, I will eventually have to face the Utu Tonah. I don't think another can do it. But I need time to understand how."

"Tan," Elle began, "you sacrifice so much and you think you must do all of this alone, but you've *never* been alone. Don't you see what's happening here? Even if we do as you suggest, even if we manage to push Par-shon away, the shaping is no better than what Chenir does."

A thick cloud began to form overhead. Honl appeared, coalescing from the cloud of smoke into the form of a man. He stood before Elle and Tan and nodded to the mist.

"She is young, but she is wise," Honl said.

Elle gasped. "What is this?" she asked. She reached toward Honl and her hand passed through him. Her mouth remained open and her eyes were wide.

"This is my bonded elemental of wind," Tan said.

"How is it that I can see him? How is it that I can *hear* him?"

Tan studied Honl. He looked fully formed, as if whatever he had spent his time doing had given him a chance to take on all the elements of his new shape. "He is something more than ashi now," Tan said.

There was texture and layers of color to his face that hadn't been there the last time that Tan had seen him. "For you to have peace, you must bind it," Honl told him.

Tan shook his head. "I don't understand."

"Don't you? The Mother chose you for a reason."

Honl made a swirling motion in the air, pointing toward the sea and then south, toward Incendin. "I have been contemplating this," Honl said. "Incendin is most familiar to me. Their lands, a place of fire, have long pushed outward. Now these lands do the same. You would have earth and wind follow."

Tan nodded.

Honl seemed to smile. "The shaping is right, but also is not. You must take that shaping, you must bind it, and bring everything together."

"Honl," Tan started, revealing his name without meaning to. He winced, hating that he had. "I don't know what you're talking about."

Honl seemed unconcerned that his name had been shared and he smiled again. "The Mother will guide you, Maelen. You must trust. I know what I must do. Your kingdoms must be a part of this." He drifted through Tan, leaving him with a strange sensation where the elemental had touched. Tan sensed excitement from Honl, almost an eagerness. "He would have enjoyed this hunt, Maelen, but he is still with you. Never forget that." Honl started toward the sky and looked down to Tan. "I will reach ara. Zephra is needed. Theondar too."

"For what?" Tan asked.

But Honl had already disappeared.

Tan turned to Elle, but she stared after the wind elemental, her face wide with amazement. What had Honl meant that he would have to bind the lands together? What had he meant that the shaping was right, but also not? What had Honl detected that Tan had missed?

He studied the sea, listening again to the power of the shaping and how it pushed out and away from the lands. The shaping would keep Par-shon from the shores. It was powerful, the combined effort of all the Doman shapers. Much like the shaping in Incendin, it would hold Par-shon away. Chenir could do the same, as could the kingdoms, but Elle was right. Shapings like that would not bring them lasting peace.

For that, they would have to stop Par-shon. They would have to stop the Utu Tonah.

Could the shaping change?

Tan considered what Honl suggested. *Bind it.*

Binding each of the massive shapings would be powerful, but changing the shaping was risky—and something that he wasn't sure would even work. Worse, if it failed, they would be exposed.

But if it worked, they might do more than simply keep Par-shon away. They might have a way to finally defeat Par-shon.

CHAPTER 27

Border Meeting

THE EDGE OF INCENDIN was a barren place, radiating the heat of the land but with less intensity as was found in other parts of the country. The plants were different along the border as well, the deadly and dangerous poisonous-barbed plants thinning to nothing more than thorny bushes. Tan stood on a rock ledge, looking down at a narrow strip of water, a river whose name he didn't know. All along the river, life flourished. Bright greens and splashes of color from blooming flowers contrasted with the emptiness of Incendin, as if the plants wanted to bring more life to the land.

Standing where he was, Tan could sense the distant drumming of Chenir. There was the tingle of the barrier, nearly complete and creating a real impediment to crossing into the kingdoms. Doma was there, connected through the water.

Tan found it strange that he'd never stood in this spot, a point where each of the nations came together. There was power here in a way that surprised him. If only the others would recognize it.

He waited. It was all that he could do. Elle knew of his plan and worked to try to convince the others of Doma of its merit. Through Kota, Tan hoped to reach the Supreme Leader, but he wasn't certain that it would work. Honl had claimed to call to Zephra, but Tan had used the summoning coin just the same. And he had called through the fire bond, requesting both Cora and Fur to come to him. Tan wasn't sure that they would answer, but he had to try.

Zephra reached him first. She landed with a shaping of wind that barely disturbed the ground, fixing him with a curious expression. "I received your summons," she said.

Roine followed almost immediately after.

"Thank you for coming," he said to them both.

"I told you that I would listen."

"I didn't expect your elemental to take the form that he did," Roine said.

Tan suppressed a smile. He wondered what Honl had done to convince both of them to come. "You were able to hear him?"

"Hear him?" Roine said. "Tannen, I could see him. What did you do to him?"

"I kept him from kaas," he answered.

Roine breathed out. "We are finishing preparations with the barrier. We don't have time to be answering summons like this. Tell me, why did you summon me? The elemental would not answer, but said that you would explain. I didn't know where to find you until your summons."

"We will wait," Tan said.

"For what?" Zephra asked. Roine looked annoyed, but Tan's mother seemed more curious than anything.

He felt the hound coming before he saw him. Sitting atop the hound, riding with a terrified expression on his face, was the Supreme Leader. When the hound stopped, the Supreme Leader climbed off. He glanced from Tan to Zephra and Theondar.

"This was you?"

Tan nodded.

"Why? You have already convinced me of the need to press out with our shaping. We are doing as you asked. Why send your hound to abduct me?"

"This is yours?" Zephra asked.

"He is not mine," Tan said, "but he is a part of the pack." He sent a deep thanks to the hound for bringing the Supreme Leader. He wasn't sure if it was able to hear him. The connection was there at the back of his mind, but not as solid as it was with Kota.

A shaping of fire crackled with energy, and Cora arrived with Fur.

When the others saw Fur, they immediately formed shapings.

Tan leapt in front of him, placing his hands out in front of them. "He is here at my request."

The others slowly released their shapings. Tan noted that Roine was the last to release his shaping. When they did, Tan stepped away from Fur and turned to the lisincend. "Thank you for coming," he said.

Fur snorted, and heat radiated from him. "Did you give me a choice?"

"Didn't I?"

Fur laughed. "Between Issan coming to me, and then Corasha, that would have been enough. But then kaas demanded my presence here as well. Tell me, Warrior, what is it that you need? The Sunlands stand before Par-shon. You do not need to fear."

"The Sunlands is but a part of what is happening," Tan said. "Doma shapes as well, and they are able to keep Par-shon away from their borders. But Chenir has fallen."

"Not completely," the Supreme Leader said.

"What is it that you want?" Fur asked, sniffing at the Supreme Leader. "Why have you brought us all here, at the corner of the Sunlands?"

"Not only the Sunlands," Tan said. "Each of you stands on your border. This is where all the nations come together, so this is where I would bring you to meet."

"Doma isn't here," Roine said.

"Aren't they?" Tan asked. "Do you see the water flowing down below? That river flows into Falsheim, reaching into the city. That is Doma."

Fur laughed. "You make bold claims, Warrior. Now, what is it that you demand now?" Fur looked over at the hound and studied it for a moment. He seemed to recognize that Kota prowled behind him and turned to her, his eyes narrowing when he faced her.

"We need to fight Par-shon together. We have tried it separately, and each works to keep them from our shores, but now is the time to bring the fight here."

"Tannen—" Roine started.

Tan waved him off. "The Sunlands shape fire, pushing away Par-shon. Doma does the same with water. Chenir has begun using earth, as have the kingdoms with wind. I thought that would be the key, that we could defeat Par-shon by keeping them from our shores, but that will only delay the fight that must happen. For us to find a lasting peace, we need to change our focus."

It was Fur who understood what Tan intended first. "You would risk all of us."

"There is a risk," Tan agreed. "But if we don't, then what will happen? Even if we manage to push Par-shon away from Chenir, what next? How long will it be before the Utu Tonah finds a new way to attack? How long before he finds a way past your shaping?" he asked

Fur. "We need to draw them here, force them to face us, and use the advantage of our shaping."

"Tan, they outnumber us. Even you must have seen that," Cora said.

"They outnumber our shapers, but not the elementals. Why do you think that your shaping is working? Do you think that you exclude Par-shon simply by the strength of your fire shapers? Did that work, or didn't it require the bonding of elementals? How much stronger are you now, Fur, now that you have bonded to kaas?"

The lisincend was silent as Tan spoke.

Tan turned to Roine. "You would close your borders, but what will happen when Par-shon comes from the sea? How will the kingdoms keep safe then? We've seen how they can reach beyond the borders, how they can trap our elementals."

"That was before the barrier," Roine said.

"And what will happen when they find a way past the barrier?" Tan asked. "The lisincend found ways beyond the barrier; what makes you think that Par-shon will not as well?"

He turned to the Chenir Supreme Leader. "And you have lost much already. Your people were willing to withdraw beyond your borders in the hope that there might be safety in the kingdoms." Fur snorted and Tan shot him a hard glare. "You have agreed to fight. All that I ask is that we change our focus."

"To where?" Zephra asked.

Tan tapped his foot. "Here. We will bring Par-shon here. Use the shapings to drive them, and then," he took a deep breath, "then I will bind them."

"You do not have the capacity to understand the shaping of fire," Fur said with a sneer.

"I can join the fire bond and can hear the guidance of the elementals. Tell me, Fur, how could I not understand your shaping?" He turned to Zephra. "You have seen my connection to wind. Know that I can handle that shaping." And then to Chenir. "The hounds may be new to earth, but they are strong. I trust that you sensed that as you traveled here?" The Supreme Leader nodded slowly. "Then know that I can work with earth."

It had not taken much to convince Elle that he could work with water. After speaking to masyn as he rescued Zephra, she believed that he could.

"What will happen when you bind the shapings?" Roine asked.

"Then we will draw on the one thing that the Utu Tonah cannot reach: spirit."

* * * * *

The shapings washed toward him. Tan hadn't been sure that it would work, but once Fur agreed, so too had the Supreme Leader. Only Roine remained skeptical. Tan had to suppress his surprise that it was Fur who agreed to his suggestion first, but in some ways, that made sense. Incendin had faced Par-shon the longest. They knew the limitations of the shaping that they used, and Fur knew the extent that Incendin shapers had gone to prevent Par-shon from reaching their shores. Incendin had been willing to sacrifice their best shapers to keep their people safe. Why not take a chance at finally stopping them completely?

Tan stood at the intersection of the four nations, feeling first fire and then water as the powerful shapings washed over him. Earth came as a distant rumble of thunder. It would reach him in time. Only wind hadn't joined. Tan worried that Zephra or Roine resisted, though they had agreed to discuss it.

Tan waited for the other summons he'd made, the other request to Honl. He wasn't sure that the wind elemental would respond anymore, not as he once did, but he needed help with what he planned, and there was only one way that he suspected that he would reach it.

As the cloud of smoke appeared, Tan tensed. Would Honl have done as asked? Would he bring Amia to him?

She stepped free from a thick cloud, and then Honl appeared in his human form. Amia nodded to him. "Thank you," she said.

"No thanks are needed, Daughter," Honl answered. The wind elemental looked at Tan. "You have convinced the others?"

"All except wind."

A troubled look crossed Honl's face, making it even darker than it had appeared since he'd begun taking on his form. "Zephra knows what I have told her."

"But Theondar rules in the kingdoms," Tan answered. "He needs to lower the barrier, and doing so risks exposing the kingdoms. He still thinks that he can keep everyone safe by staying behind the barrier."

"You could remove it," Honl suggested.

Tan had considered that, but doing so would force Roine, and Tan suspected that it needed to be a choice freely made. Without that, it would feel no different than the coercion used by Par-shon.

"Theondar will understand. You will need to see to that," Tan said.

Honl tipped his head, looking very human as he did so, and then disappeared in a cloud of smoke.

"Only you?" Amia asked.

"Not only me. The others have different roles to play. This is ours."

She touched his hand. "What do we need to do?"

Tan took a deep breath, drawing elemental power into him. Kota remained nearby, mostly to watch over him, much as Asboel once had. The connection to Honl was intact, more prominent in his mind than it had been in weeks. The sense of water surged through him, filling him with awareness brought to him by the nymid. Only fire was absent.

Tan missed the connection to Asboel. Could he even form the shaping that he needed without the draasin? Should he have attempted to bond another before now? Asgar might have been ready for the bond. If not Asgar, then possibly another of fire. Saa had always answered him; perhaps he could bond to saa?

But there wasn't the time to reach for another elemental. Tan would use what strength that he could summon. The Great Mother would have to ensure that it would be enough.

"I will bind the shapings," he said. "Fire, water, earth, and wind. Binding them together—"

Amia nodded slowly. "Spirit. You intend a massive shaping of spirit."

"It's what the artifact did," Tan said. "I'm not sure how, but it gathered the elementals together and bound them with spirit. I think if we can do something similar, we might be able to create enough spirit to stop Par-shon, but strength that can be controlled. With it, we might have enough to stop the Utu Tonah."

"And if it doesn't work?" Amia asked, squeezing his hand.

Tan glanced at the sky, wishing that he was able to reach the Great Mother, wishing that he could find some way of knowing whether the shaping would work, but he couldn't reach her, not without summoning the pool of spirit, and not without the artifact.

"If it doesn't work, then we will have tried," Tan said. "We will have worked together and attempted something that has never been done, not even when the ancient shapers created the first archive." He smiled. "There is value in that, I think."

"I will be here with you, regardless of what else happens," Amia said.

"My shaping started with you. My first bond was to you. It is only fitting that we should be together to attempt the most important shaping I've ever considered."

CHAPTER 28

The Lost Bond

T HE AIR THRUMMED with power. Tan pulled on the shaping of fire and water, mixing within it the shaping of earth that thundered toward him. He added a shaping of wind, using all the strength that he could summon, calling upon Honl, on ara, and all of ashi that blew through Incendin. They added to the shaping but were overpowered by the strength of the others, leaving the shaping with an unbalanced sense. Without the addition of the kingdoms' shaping, Tan wasn't sure that it would work.

He drew the strands of the shaping toward him, using his sword as a focus, and twisted them together, forging it into something of spirit. Amia reached through their connection and helped, pulling on the connection to fuse true spirit to the bond. For the moment, the shaping held, but it was precarious. Tan could sense how it might fail.

Wrapped as he was in the shaping, he had a sense of everything around him. It was a sense that reminded him of the times he'd known true spirit directly. He'd experienced something similar when standing in the pool of liquid spirit, and even more so when shaping through the artifact. An understanding of everything flooded through him. He used this and pushed beyond the barrier to send a call for help from the kingdoms.

After everything that he'd done to protect the kingdoms, everything that he'd done in service to the kingdoms, why should they be the last to come?

A sense of other shapers pressed upon him. Par-shon recognized the change in the shaping but didn't understand the purpose. For now, Tan hoped that was enough.

He shaped for hours, the power of the different shapings enormous and more than anything that he'd ever experienced, but Tan was connected to the elementals, and they granted him strength and the ability to maintain control. Without that, he would have been overwhelmed, possibly destroyed.

As he shaped, he became aware of a steady sense that became more and more prominent the longer he worked. Tan focused on what he sensed, not certain what it was. Amia tensed, squeezing his hand more tightly than before.

"Tan," she said. It was the first word that either of them had spoken since starting the shaping. "Par-shon."

It had been inevitable that Par-shon would reach him. The shapings coming from Incendin, Doma, and Chenir pushed Par-shon in this direction. If the kingdoms ever joined, they would have a similar push.

Kota, Tan started, focusing his attention on the hound, *will you keep her safe?*

The hound rumbled in response.

Tan took to the air, streaking high into the sky. He'd been shaping the combination for so long that he no longer knew how much of what he'd done was from him, how much was from the elementals, and how much was from the shaping sent toward him.

Shapers approached. Tan sensed them coming in a flood. Hundreds of Par-shon shapers, more than he could handle without help. Tan pressed with the shaping of spirit, through the bonds linking the shapers to the elementals. There was resistance, much like what he'd encountered when he found his mother in Chenir. Tan pushed, drawing on more strength, and the bonds failed. Dozens of shapers fell.

More followed.

They swarmed, too many for Tan to keep track of.

He had expected this as well. Hopefully, his friends would answer the summons one more time. If this worked, it would be the last time that he would call for help when facing Par-shon. If it worked, they might finally be rid of Par-shon. All he knew was that the call would come, and the timing depended upon Tan's need.

Using his connection to spirit, Tan made his plea.

The connection touched on Elle and Vel in Doma. He reached for Cora in Incendin, and skimmed past Fur, not wanting to distract the lisincend from his steady shaping. He reached for the water shaper and the Supreme Leader in Chenir. And then in the kingdoms, Tan reached for all the shapers he knew. The kingdoms had so many more that he could call upon. Cianna and Wallyn, Ferran and Roine. He left the wind shapers, praying that they would take the time to shape wind.

Then he released the spirit shaping that connected him to them and focused on the Par-shon shapers around him. Shaping through his sword, Tan pushed spirit at one bonded shaper after another. They fell, but not quickly enough. Too many remained. Their numbers began to force Tan to the ground. If only he had the extra assistance from the kingdoms. He fought as well as he could, only needing to hold out a little while longer . . .

Lightning exploded. Tan expected it to be Cora, but Theondar appeared.

As he did, the barrier dropped.

Wind surged toward Tan, and he grabbed at the shaping, pulling it into the others, binding it into the spirit bond.

Theondar attacked with a fury that Tan hadn't seen from him before. He held his warrior sword, pulling on shapings of each of the elements, drawing them together and binding them, before sending a combined shaping through his sword. The shapers were forced to focus on Roine as well, and they gave Tan space.

Cora appeared as well, coming on lightning, but Enya attacked, swooping through the Par-shon shapers, tearing at them with her massive jaws and sharp talons. Cora held a warrior sword with a long, curved blade and used it as both a weapon and a way to focus her shapings, drawing spirit through the sword with as much fury as Tan saw from Roine.

Then Cianna appeared. Sashari came with her, streaking through the sky, moving in coordinated strikes to attack at the Par-shon shapers. Another winged shape appeared, and Tan realized that it was Asgar, flying with a certain reckless abandon, tearing and biting at Par-shon shapers. Through the fire bond, Tan sensed the excited way that he attacked.

Other shapers appeared. Ferran with earth. The Supreme Leader and a dozen of his shapers. Vel and Elle answered the summons. Dozens of lisincend, winged and not, appeared. All of them working together.

Still, it would not be enough. There were simply too many Par-shon shapers. For every one that fell, two more followed, and more appeared every moment. They could cause damage to Par-shon, but would they be able to stop them?

Tan strained for more strength, drawing on the shapings coming toward him from each direction. They had power, and he could be the focus. He reached through the connection with Amia, borrowing her ability with spirit. Together, they bonded the elements together, turning the combined shaping into spirit that Tan turned against Par-shon.

Still, it wouldn't be enough.

Assist me.

Tan sent the request to all the elementals and to everything that he sensed all around him. He drew on their strength, but he needed to do more than that. He needed the elementals to fight.

For a moment, nothing changed.

Then Tan felt everything shift.

Wind whipped out of the south, the hot gusts of ashi joining in. Thunder rumbled from the north as the hounds raced to help. Water surged from the river, joining the attack, either nymid, masyn, or udilm. The draasin already fought, but saa and saldam joined.

Par-shon pressed with a fury. They had the numbers, and Tan could tell that they knew it. He used shapings of spirit against all of Par-shon, but he didn't have the strength needed to stop them all.

He pulled on more spirit, binding the elementals that he sensed around him, pulling them together as he surged spirit. This was what he'd wanted: the chance to stop Par-shon. Now that they were here, the end was close.

For a moment, Tan thought that he might have the strength needed to make it work. For that moment, the shapings all around him seemed to slow. Everything seemed to slow.

Then the air exploded with white light.

The attack changed in a heartbeat as the Utu Tonah appeared.

With him came Par-shon shapers bonded to elementals that Tan had no name for. They were the crossings, creatures like kaas or the hounds before he had healed them. They had power, but they were unstable. If freed from their bonds, they would be like kaas, and they would not stop fighting for Par-shon.

The others seemed to notice the change. The attack shifted. Shapers were pressed back. Tan saw one of the Chenir shapers had fallen, their back twisted in an impossible direction, and realized that it was the water shaper, the first shaper who had agreed to help. Another shaper, this one Jisan, an earth shaper of the kingdoms, fell. The others were pushed back.

The Utu Tonah streaked toward Tan on his shaping. Tan had thought the other Par-shon bonded shaper had glowed, but it was nothing like the Utu Tonah. His bonds consumed him, and still he somehow controlled them. He drifted with unnatural grace, practically an elemental himself with the way that he was bonded.

"You think that drawing me here would frighten me?" he asked.

Tan pulled on the shapings, wrapping himself with spirit. "I think to stop you from stealing elementals. They are not to be forced to bond."

He smiled, and it was almost sad. "You think that I am some kind of monster, but how am I any different than you? I have seen the way that you call to them. They listen. Imagine how powerful that you could be if you bonded."

"I have bonded," Tan said. "The bonds were chosen by both, not forced upon them."

"You are foolish to think that it's any different." The Utu Tonah swept his hand around, motioning toward the Par-shon shapers.

All around him, shapers were pressed back toward Tan. Even the elementals struggled. Tan saw twisted elementals, creatures that should not exist, combinations that were not meant to exist. There was a feral quality to them and an anger, much like what he'd sensed when chasing kaas. It had been the same with the hounds.

"You cannot hope to win. My shapers will destroy your people. These lands will then be mine. I will reclaim the homeland of my ancestors."

Tan almost lost control of his shaping at the comment.

"You didn't know?" the Utu Tonah asked. "We are the same, Warrior. Only my people have not forgotten the lessons of the past. Soon I will have the last bond."

With that, the Utu Tonah jumped.

Tan tensed, thinking that he readied to attack, but he didn't. Instead, he streaked into the sky, moving faster than Tan could follow. When he stopped, he landed atop a great winged shape.

Asgar.

With a sharp motion, the Utu Tonah jabbed toward Asgar. There was a surge of light that mixed with a strange shaping of fire.

Asgar had bonded.

Tan felt the bond through the fire bond. The draasin attempted to rebel, but the Utu Tonah had known too many bonds, and he knew how to control them. Within moments, Asgar was controlled, tamed as if he were nothing more than a horse.

Sashari and Enya roared.

Fire burned through Tan. Anger and rage at what the Utu Tonah had done to Asgar. Were Asboel alive, he would have hunted the Utu Tonah until he was destroyed. Tan owed it to his memory to do the same.

The Utu Tonah turned Asgar toward him. A triumphant smile twisted his face. The runes marking the bonds glowed across his skin so brightly that he lit the waning day like water reflecting sunlight. Tan refused to look away. He refused to turn away.

This was his fight, and this had been his plan. No one else could stop the Utu Tonah, so if he did nothing, they would fail. Everyone would fall. For Asboel, and for all the elementals, he could not fail.

Asgar shot flames at him. Tan faced the draasin, unafraid. He had a combination of the nymid armor and his connection to fire to keep him safe. The flames parted around him.

The Utu Tonah roared. Asgar echoed the sound.

The draasin snapped his jaws toward Tan, who raised his hands to defend himself. He would not harm the draasin, but he would not turn away in fear, either. Asgar was not his enemy.

No, Asgar.

Tan sent the words through the fire bond. Names were powerful to the elementals, especially those that were freely given. Asgar's name had been given to him by Tan, and had even more power when Tan used it.

The draasin shook, slowly at first, but then with more and more force. The Utu Tonah went flying off, but he quickly regained his composure. Asgar tumbled toward the ground, convulsing as he did.

Honl!

He didn't have the chance to see if the wind elemental could help. The Utu Tonah raged at him, his fist raised as a shaping built all around Tan with more strength than anything Tan could counter. The Utu Tonah pulled through all of his elementals, drawing strength from dozens of elementals, most of which Tan had no name for. He wondered how many were the result of crossing, and how many were naturally occurring.

The shaping pressed down on him.

The Utu Tonah smiled. "You will not surprise me again. I will reclaim that bond when you are gone." The shaping squeezed. "That will not be long now."

His connection to the shapings coming from each nation began to fade. The Utu Tonah was separating him more completely than even the room of separation had managed. He could not fight, not like this.

In that moment, Tan relaxed.

He was separated from shaping, but he was never separated from his bonds, not truly. And Tan had bonded in ways that the Utu Tonah could never understand.

Tan understood now what he had to do. Not simply to gather all of the elementals. That was part of it, but he needed the connection to them, the freely given bond, that which made him unique and the reason the Great Mother had chosen him for this task.

He reached for wind and found Honl. He reached toward earth, and Kota granted him strength. The nymid were there, wrapped around him in their armor. He thought he had lost his connection to fire with Asboel's passing, but as he connected to his elementals, he realized that he hadn't. Fire was different to him now. Even without his bond to Asboel, he could reach the fire bond, reach into Fire. He didn't need an elemental for that.

Tan bound each of the elementals, and added to the strength they lent him that which he could pull from the shapings all around him.

Amia pressed through him, granting her ability with spirit. In that way, she was something like an elemental as well.

Power flooded him. He was joined to the elementals, joined to *all* of them, not only his bonded. The connection was deeper than anything he had ever experienced.

Light exploded and time seemed to stop.

Understanding washed through him, much as it had when he had held the shaping through the artifact. For a moment, Tan held strength enough to do anything. Stabilized by his connection to Amia, the temptation was not there as it had been before. The only thing that he would change would be to return Asboel.

He considered bringing his friend back.

But Asboel would not have wanted that. He had returned to the Mother.

With the thought, he sensed warmth and closeness to the Great Mother, and he sensed Asboel still present in the fire bond.

Tan smiled. He *hadn't* lost his friend. As Asboel had often said, the draasin were fire, and he had simply returned to it.

I miss you, friend.

You will never hunt alone, Maelen.

Tears came to his eyes and Tan blinked them away.

He stopped in front of the Utu Tonah, who was caught in Tan's shaping, no differently than all the other Par-shon shapers. With a swipe of his hand, all the bonds upon the Utu Tonah were gone. He was not harmless even then. Tan had learned that he was a warrior shaper, even without his bonds. This was a man who could not live.

Using spirit, he shaped the Utu Tonah until his heart stopped beating.

Tan turned to the other shapers of Par-shon. Connected as he was to the source of all things, all it took was a thought and their bonds failed. He reached across the sea, recognizing the remaining Par-shon bonded, and severed those connections as well. There would be no further attacks.

Then he turned his attention to the elementals that Par-shon had brought with them. He had thought that the dangerous crossings would be the hardest to repair, but as he used his understanding of fire, earth, wind, and water to bring those elementals back into line with where they should be, he felt guidance from beyond him, as if the Great Mother herself sought to ensure they were saved.

With another surge of light, Tan knew that it had worked.

His strength began to fade, and the shaping that he held together began to sag. Tan focused on the fire bond, clinging to the sense that was Asboel within it.

Is the Mother pleased?

There was a moment of silence, a moment where Tan wasn't sure if the memory of Asboel would answer. And then, distantly, he heard him.

You have done well, Maelen.

EPILOGUE

Fur's words had stuck with Tan.

Tan sat atop Asgar, not bonded to the draasin, but enjoying flying with him. Since stopping the Utu Tonah, he no longer had to reach for the fire bond; it simply burned through him. Within it, he sensed Asboel, even if he could not speak to him as he had. Knowing that he was not gone completely gave Tan a sense of peace.

Sitting behind him, Amia squeezed him.

Riding Asgar was different than riding atop Asboel, but the draasin shared many of his father's traits. He had a steady and powerful sweep with his wings. The heat rising from his back reminded Tan of when he'd first ridden Asboel, as did the careful way that Tan needed to keep his attention focused on what the draasin was doing. Over time, he'd grown comfortable with Asboel and had barely had to pay attention while riding.

Sashari soared next to him, with Cianna riding atop her. On the other side, Enya flew, with Cora on her back. The other hatchling trailed them. She had gotten larger and was nearly the size of Enya now.

They flew over white-capped swells of water, racing toward Par-shon. Asgar clutched the body of the Utu Tonah in his talons. Tan would show Par-shon what would happen if they forced another bond. There would be no replacing the power void that now existed in Par-shon, at least not with another like the Utu Tonah.

"Are you sure this is safe?" Amia asked.

The moment that he'd sensed Par-shon shapers, when he'd freed the bonds from the Utu Tonah, had told him what needed to be done. There could be no further attacks. The trapping of elementals would stop. The forced binding of elementals would stop.

"You don't have to come," he said.

She laughed. "The People are safe. Soon Lyssa will be able to replace me."

"Are you sure that's what you want?"

Amia squeezed him again. "There might have been a time when I wanted to be the First Mother, but that is gone. I would have a different role."

Tan glanced over his shoulder at her and smiled. She leaned forward and kissed him.

They reached the edge of Par-shon and moved quickly through. The last time he'd been here, the land had been barren as it led up to the city. Now Tan understood why that was the case, that the trapping of the elementals had caused the land to change. In the time since he'd severed the bonds, the land had already begun to change. Color and a sense of life had returned. In time, even Par-shon could be restored.

"What do you intend?" Cora asked, using a shaping of wind to augment her words.

"I intend to show Par-shon that they will not attack again."

Cora grunted. "Fur won't know what to do if he doesn't need to maintain the shaping."

"He can focus on serving the people of the Sunlands."

"Do you think that he ever stopped?" she asked.

Tan shook his head. Perhaps Cora was right. Fur had done everything that he could to keep his people safe. Through it, he had risked everything, including himself, but it had given Incendin a chance for safety. Now, Tan would see that it was no longer necessary.

The draasin continued inland. As they did, Tan began to feel the draw of the palace at the heart of Par-shon. Darkness radiated from it.

As they neared the city, Tan glanced at Cianna and Cora. "Are you ready?"

They both nodded.

With a powerful shaping, he leapt from Asgar's back, carrying Amia with him, and traveled into the heart of Par-shon. Tan landed in the courtyard outside the palace. It was a place he had only seen but never visited before.

The draasin circled above, ensuring that he would be safe.

Runes were set into the walls of the palace, working all the way up the sides. The pressure they exuded attempted to prevent him from shaping, but he had held onto his shapings, and he was connected to the elementals. There was nothing that Par-shon would do to prevent him from shaping.

Using spirit, he destroyed the runes set into the walls. They exploded with a thunderous crack. Tan made his way into the palace, ignoring the surprised stares of the people he passed. Most were servants, dressed simply in white gowns. At each rune, Tan paused, destroying it as he made his way through the palace. He reached the stairs that led up and paused at the second level.

"This is where they *tested* me," he said.

"Do what you need," Amia said.

Tan hurried down the hall and threw open the door. Inside, the runes were as he remembered, set throughout in some unrecognizable pattern. With a shaping that required him to pull on each of his connections, he shattered these runes as well, leaving the testing room no more.

Then Tan made his way back into the hall and up the stairs. At the top, a heavy woman wearing a floral dress skidded to a stop in front of him. Her eyes widened, and she looked away from him, bending her neck in a bow.

Tan recognized her. "Garza."

Tan sensed her and felt no bonds remaining. He would leave her unharmed.

He continued onward, finally reaching the room where he had first met the Utu Tonah. Inside, more runes were set into the walls, each one intended to separate shapers from their abilities. Tan shattered them all. The last was atop the throne near the back of the room. The people standing around it all stared at him. None made any attempt to attack. Tan had expected some sort of resistance, but there had been none. It was as if Par-shon had expected him.

"The Utu Tonah is dead," Tan said. "No more elementals will be forcibly bonded. If any bonds are formed, I will see that they are shattered."

The faces of those gathered in the room stared at him. Tan made a point of meeting each person's eyes. No one spoke.

Finally, a man stepped forward. He had dark hair and a narrow face. His eyes were heavy and sunken, with dark rings around them. His shoulders sagged, as if carrying weight that he was unaccustomed to supporting. He bowed to Tan.

"You have returned," he said.

Tan recognized the man. He had met him when he had first come to Par-shon. An earth shaper, but one who had been almost fair with him. "Tolman," Tan said. "Your Utu Tonah is gone."

"When the bonds faded, we knew that he was," Tolman said.

"The draasin have returned his body. You may do with it as you like. As I have said, whoever takes his place will not force bonds."

"As you wish," Tolman said.

Tan glanced at Amia. He had expected more resistance. Roine had warned him against coming, suggested that he bring more with him, support in case Par-shon was not as weakened as Tan suspected, but Tan wasn't willing to bring any more than he had to into Par-shon. Allowing Cianna and Cora to come with him was his concession to Roine's suggestion.

"Do any shapers remain?" Tan asked. "Trust that I will find out if they do."

Tolman nodded to a younger boy standing near the back, and then motioned to an older man who was probably a few years older than Tan. Both stepped forward with heads bowed. "These, and then Garza."

Tan reached out with a sensing of earth and detected Garza watching from the door. She didn't come any closer, as if afraid to do so. "Would they learn to control their shapings without the bonds?" Tan asked.

Tolman tipped his head. "It will be as you wish."

Tan frowned, trying to understand if they were stalling, but he found nothing that would make him think that there was anything more than what he saw. He started to turn, letting Amia know through the bond that they would leave.

He hadn't known what to expect, but certainly not this. Had the Utu Tonah controlled them so completely that they didn't know what to do now that he was gone? If so, he felt sorry for these people, sorry for what they had experienced.

Forgiveness is your greatest gift, Amia sent to him.

"What will you have us do?" Tolman asked as Tan turned away to leave.

Tan paused. "Do?" he repeated. "I would have Par-shon find peace. I would have you understand that your elementals should be respected. I would have you not live in fear."

Tolman tipped his head. "It will be as you wish."

Tan spun back to face him and crossed the distance between them. "What are you getting at, Tolman? Why do you keep saying that it will be as I wish?"

Tolman frowned. "You don't know?"

Tan shook his head.

"Then why did you return?"

"To give warning. To ensure that no others are treated as I was treated. Why do you think that I returned?"

"Because you defeated him. You are now the Utu Tonah."

DK HOLMBERG is a full time writer living in rural Minnesota with his wife, two kids, two dogs, two cats, and thankfully no other animals. Somehow he manages to find time for writing.

To see other books and read more, please go to www.dkholmberg.com

Follow me on twitter: @dkholmberg

Word-of-mouth is crucial for any author to succeed and how books are discovered. If you enjoyed the book, please consider leaving a review online at your favorite bookseller or Goodreads, even if it's only a line or two; it would make all the difference and would be very much appreciated.

OTHERS AVAILABLE BY DK HOLMBERG

The Cloud Warrior Saga

Chased by Fire
Bound by Fire
Changed by Fire
Fortress of Fire
Forged in Fire
Serpent of Fire
Servant of Fire

The Dark Ability

The Dark Ability
The Heartstone Blade
The Tower of Venass

The Painter Mage

Shifted Agony
Arcane Mark
Painter for Hire
Stolen Compass

The Lost Garden

Keeper of the Forest
The Desolate Bond
Keeper of Light

Made in the USA
Coppell, TX
12 May 2023

16756699R00173